KERRY CRISLEY

When the Rose Briar Blooms

First edition

ISBN: 979-8-9852499-4-1

This book was professionally typeset on Reedsy.
Find out more at reedsy.com

For Sara and Lisa,
with gratitude for your lifetime of friendship

Love is like the wild rose-briar,
Friendship like the holly-tree—
The holly is dark when the rose-briar
blooms
But which will bloom most con-
stantly?

Emily Brontë, "Love and
Friendship"

Acknowledgments

It's a thrill to be back here, writing an acknowledgments section for my second book. While my first novel contained many elements of my real life, *When the Rose Briar Blooms* was invented from whole cloth. Creating it was equal parts exhilarating and exasperating; the plot veered away from me on its own accord more than once, until finally revealing the story it wanted me to tell. I didn't get there alone, however. I'm deeply grateful to the friends and family who helped me reach my goal of typing "The End" for a second time.

Enormous thanks to my writers group — Henry Dane, Maribeth Darwin, Gregory DeLaurier, Tim O'Leary, and Lisa Viliott — for their invaluable feedback, encouragement, and consistent willingness to show up and write. The simple fact that I owed you all my pages on a regular basis was a stronger incentive than you know.

To my *amazing* cousins and beta readers, Deirdre, Joanna, Julie, and Kelly. Thank you for your insight, your humor, and your continued enthusiasm to read my nearly 300-page drafts. I f**king love you!

Finally, thank you to my parents — Patricia and Tim O'Leary — and to John, Ben and Erin, who collectively cheered me on (and supplied me with coffee, seltzer, and takeout) while I waded back into these literary waters. I love you all.

Chapter 1

It was raining the day my life fell apart. I used to *love* the rain. If it rained on a weekend, I'd park myself on the sofa with baskets of not-yet-folded laundry and a movie and call it time well spent. If it was a weekday, I'd open my office window a few inches – even if it was chilly – so the sound and the smell of it would fill the space. Forget lemon and eucalyptus oils. Rain, to me, was always the scent of productivity.

They even took the rain from me.

"Where's Holly? Is she ready?" I asked Matthew, shaking the droplets from my bright yellow umbrella before stashing it in the stand in our mudroom. "I'm starving. Just let me change." I slipped out of my waterproof clogs and stepped into the kitchen, where Matthew was sitting at the island, a half-full bottle of Dos Equis in front of him.

It was a Friday, the night dubbed by Holly to be family-dinner-but-no-one-cooks night. When she was four, no less. Even then, she was using clever strategies to avoid eating her peas. But it was still my favorite night of the week, despite the recent undercurrent of tension between Matthew and me. Or maybe it was my favorite night *because* of it. Because in public with Holly, I could still pretend there was nothing wrong.

Matthew took a swig from his beer. "Holly's sleeping over Monica's house tonight," he said. "It's just us."

I paused, surprised. "Really? Isn't six a little young for wanting to ditch your parents on a Friday?" I rested my forearms on the island and pushed back on my heels, enjoying the feel of stretching in sock feet.

Matthew didn't smile. "I set it up with Monica's mom after school," he said. "We have to talk, Kay."

The familiar weight I'd been carrying around in my stomach grew denser. This was it. After three months of replying "it's nothing, Kay, just work," when I asked what was wrong, Matthew was finally going to tell me. My mind doomscrolled through the possibilities: health, money, another woman. I sent up a silent prayer to whomever would listen for it not to be Door Number One.

"Matt, are you sick?" I blurted.

He started, seeming surprised. "What? No."

I looked at him, suddenly unsure if I should feel relieved at the answer.

"OK," I said cautiously. I reached one hand across the island and squeezed his wrist. "Then what's going on? Tell me, Matt. You're not *you*, and I miss you."

He covered my hand with his free one, and gently freed his wrist. Door Number Three creaked open.

"I'm leaving," he said. "Tonight."

I held his gaze, waiting for him to say more. He broke eye contact, looking down to examine the white marble of the island.

"You're leaving," I said. He nodded slowly – once up, once down – not looking at me.

"Just like that?"

Matthew looked up, a hint of defiance in his face. "No. Not 'just like that.' Things haven't been good for a while. You know that."

I reached over, grabbed the Dos Equis by its sleek green neck, and drained it in a series of gulps as I turned away from my husband. I walked the three steps from the island to the sink, tapping the bottle's base lightly against the matching marble countertop encasing the stainless steel. We'd picked out the marble four years ago, together.

I thought of the date nights he missed while our daughter took tap and ballet.

It's nothing Kay. It's just work.

The distance when we were alone.

It's nothing Kay. It's just work.

The recent lack of intimacy.

It's nothing Kay. It's just work.

"You know it, Kay."

Matthew's voice shook me to the present. Months of pent-up anxiety swelled inside me, turning to rage. I whirled around, inverting the bottle with my fingers, and hurled it at the wall behind him. The green glass shattered against the kitchen's whiteboard and rained onto the floor, a few chips catching in the tray housing the dry erase markers. The residual beer ran through the October calendar I had made up the weekend before, causing streaks of blue ink – or whatever it was inside dry erase markers – to run through our family schedule.

Matthew ducked, covering his head. He turned to the whiteboard and then back to me, eyes wide.

"Things haven't been good?" I yelled. "And why is that,

Matt? Could it be that every time I tried to talk to you, you insisted it was work? Could that be it, huh?"

Matthew stared at me, open-mouthed, brushing at his t-shirt to remove nonexistent Dos Equis shrapnel.

"I guess now we both know it wasn't work," I added. "Who is she, Matt?"

His mouth snapped shut. He turned away again, looking guilty for the first time. "It doesn't matter."

I must know her, I thought. A mom at Holly's school.

Holly.

The image of our daughter's sweet face shook me out of my fury. Everything we had made in this house since our wedding nearly eight years ago – the traditions, the silly jokes, the quietly comforting habits – was for her, for *us*. What was I going to tell her? What was I going to *do*?

"Look," Matthew ran his fingers through his blond hair quickly, twice. He always did it twice when he was stressed. "We need to figure out what we're going to tell Holly, and how we're going to handle the next few weeks, or months or whatever, until this is all settled."

I swayed slightly, the kitchen walls shifting in my vision. Every ounce of me screamed *run!* I shook my head, drew in a quick breath and looked at my future ex-husband.

"No," I said. "*You* can figure out how to tell our daughter why you're walking out on us." I pointed to the mess behind him. "Clean that shit up and get out. Be gone when I get back."

I headed for the mudroom, pausing to yank my purse from its hook, and ran through the ongoing downpour to my car. I reversed, screeching the tires, and slammed the brakes once in the road. The pedals didn't feel right.

Did he do something to my car? I thought, irrationally. No.

I'd left without my shoes.

I extracted my phone from my purse. "Call Anna!" I shrieked.

"Calling Anna," my phone chirped dutifully. I swerved to avoid a water-filled pothole and clutched the phone to my ear. Voicemail. I hung up and threw it into the passenger seat footwell.

When I finally pulled up to Anna's duplex, I was crying. Enormous, shuddering sobs wracked me. Tears made wide, messy rivers on my face. I swiped my cheeks and staggered out of my car to her door, giving it a cursory pound before using my key to get inside.

Anna was standing in her living room, frozen. An open copy of *Real Simple* hung from one hand, her favorite blue blanket pooled on the floor at her feet. I'd frightened her.

"Kay," she stuttered.

I drew in a deep, watery breath. "Matthew's leaving me," I told her. "He's been cheating on me, and now he's leaving me." I crumpled to my knees, cradling my head in my hands.

Anna stayed standing, dropping her magazine onto the plum chaise where she'd been reading. "He's cheating? That's what he said?"

I lifted my head to face her and nodded. "I asked who it was. He said it didn't matter."

Anna grimaced and looked away. "Coward," she muttered.

I resumed crying, distantly aware that I should ask my best friend for a tissue, if only to protect her expensive carpet.

Coward?

I lifted my face again, a silent roar in my head. My body felt like parchment, the moisture baked out of it.

Coward?

Anna stood, looking at nothing.

The realization that the last eight years of my life had been obliterated by a nameless, faceless woman had sent me running, sock footed, through sheets of rain to this house, this haven. Were the last *20 years* of my life gone as well?

"Anna?"

She raised her eyes to her ceiling, shaking her head slightly. It was several moments before she could bring herself to face me.

"I'm sorry, Kay. He was supposed to tell you."

The last thing I remember before fainting was vomiting a few mouthfuls of beer onto her gray oriental rug.

* * *

Then (Portsmouth, New Hampshire — 1997)

"Have a good day?" Mom said, as if it was a suggestion I might consider.

I rolled my eyes as I unbuckled my seat. "M'kay," I said, yanking my backpack out of the footwell. I shut the door and trudged toward school, fixing the strap on my denim overalls.

Middle School. The fifth-grade classes of Portsmouth's three elementary schools were now flung together as sixth graders. Already we were the lowest in the pecking order; the eighth graders were firmly in charge, and the seventh graders – relishing their elevation to the middle ranks – would be flexing their muscles, seeing how much power they really had.

And us at the bottom? We'd be figuring out our own social caste system, jockeying for position – whether we wanted to or not – to see who emerged as The Smart Ones, The Funny Ones, The Athletic Ones, The Artsy Ones, The Weird Ones, or The Hopeless.

At least, the others would be doing the jockeying, each relying on support and reinforcement from their cadre of elementary school pals. I was on my own, stripped of the safety net of my three best friends, who'd decamped to the Catholic school one town over. Without them to vouch for me, it was up to the masses to decide where I'd land.

I took out the slip of paper with my locker number and combination and found my way to the right hallway. About ten feet in front of me was the thick neck and comically round head of Billy Arthur.

Perfect.

I stepped in line behind a gangly and as-yet-unknown fellow bottom-runger to avoid being seen. Billy and I had been classmates since kindergarten at Little Harbor Elementary. Six out of those seven years had been unremarkable, then Billy developed the unnerving habit of monitoring which of his female classmates were now wearing bras. He gained playground notoriety for predicting exact cup sizes, and then recruiting accomplices to cajole the answers out of the targeted girls.

"Ignore him," my mom told my friend Bethany, unhelpfully, one day after school at my house. "He probably just likes you."

Having developed myself over the summer, I was in no rush now to discover if Billy and I would share a homeroom.

Locker 024. My home for the next three years.

I reached for the combination dial, when my hand was

knocked out of the way by a flash of red plaid canvas.

"Oh, hey! Sorry. You OK?" The girl asked, regaining control of her backpack.

She was tall, with dark brown hair pulled back in a high ponytail and a smattering of light freckles across her cheeks and nose. She was wearing high waisted black pants and a black crop top, *Girl Power* emblazoned across it in pink.

"Fine. S'OK," I replied nonchalantly. Inwardly, I was full of questions. *Who is she? Is she important? Was that on purpose? Did I piss her off? Crap.* I took a half step to my right, giving her more room to open her locker, which was right to mine. She gestured back, *after you.*

I sensed her taking me in as I twisted the dial. What was she seeing? My First Day Outfit, carefully curated to make it look like I didn't curate it at all. Two blonde ponytails, denim overalls covering up a white Union Jack t-shirt, and Doc Martens. I kept the books and folders I'd need for my first two periods, shoved everything else inside, and slammed the door shut. Finally, I met her gaze. She was smiling. Just barely, but it was there.

"Baby Spice?" She ventured.

A grin flashed across my face before I could stuff it down again. I shrugged, then took in her First Day Outfit with fresh eyes.

"Sporty?"

She executed a shallow mock curtsy, then pointed at me.

"I know you," she said. "Were you at that art camp in July?"

I nodded, recognizing her. We had been in the girls' bathroom, and I happened to have an extra maxi pad just when she'd needed one.

"You saved me that day. Me *and* my white shorts. I, like,

really owe you."

I laughed and shook my head, *no big deal*. Who was this girl? Could she send some of that twelve-going-on-twenty-one confidence my way?

"You in Room 111 for Homeroom?" she asked.

I nodded. "Yeah."

"Same here," she said. "Bell's gonna ring. Let's go. I'm Anna, by the way."

"Kay."

"I can't wait for *Spiceworld*. My cousin was in England last year for college, and she…"

We fell into music shop talk while choosing seats for homeroom. Room 111, I now discovered, was the art studio. Instead of desks, four tables had been pushed together to create a single large square in the center of the room, with chairs spanning its perimeter.

"Hey, Barrett," Billy Arthur's smug greeting reached me, coming from behind Anna.

Oh, no.

He glanced over his shoulder, making sure the teacher hadn't entered the room yet, and grinned at me, looking pointedly at the bib of my overalls. A second chin peeked out as he nodded at me.

"Wow, you graduated to an A-cup over the summer I see." He glanced around, seeking approval from the other boys, before finally noticing Anna. She was studying him, her face neutral.

"What?" Billy asked.

Anna shifted in her seat so she was fully facing him. She peered closely at his New England Patriots t-shirt, and then looked up at him, smiling.

"And you've graduated to a B-cup," she said. "How's the underwire? I've heard it pinches."

Snorts from around the room. Billy's face hardened, turning crimson. "Who are you?" He challenged.

Anna didn't blink. "Anna Becker."

"Pecker?" Billy said, smugness creeping back into his voice. "Your name's Pecker?"

Anna rolled her eyes and shook her head, as if she'd hear this a hundred times. Which I figured she probably had. Unfortunately for Billy, she was ready for it.

"No. *Becker*. It means 'user of axes.'" She leaned in again. "Want me to prove it? Keep talking, dipshit."

Billy glanced around again – more desperately this time, I thought – for support. No one volunteered. He focused on the paper schedule on top of his notebook, muttering into his second chin.

Anna turned back to me, grinning. "I overheard my mom say that once," she whispered. "I've always wanted to use it."

I smiled, awestruck. *Who* was *this girl?* I thought again. "I don't think any girl has ever talked to him like that," I whispered back. "Thank you…Sporty."

Anna grinned wider. "Girl Power, Baby."

Chapter 2

Zzzzzzzzt. Zzzzt-zzzzzzzzt!

My phone was a hornet's nest of notifications. Pawpermint Patty (Minty for short), my sister Joy's orange tabby cat, leaped from my lap in protest, throwing a final you're-dead-to-me-for-the-next-half-hour scowl before stalking into the bedroom.

I was sitting cross-legged on Joy's chocolate suede sofa, cried out (for now), showered, and dressed in her flannel pajama bottoms and Salem State sweatshirt. Upon arriving – dripping in rain and snot – at her apartment just under an hour ago, I managed a garbled synopsis of my short conversation with Matthew and even shorter non-conversation with Anna. Then I sank to my knees.

Just as I had done at Anna's.

Joy held me, still on the floor, as I cried. My initial release at Anna's had been choked off by her revelation. This time I gave into it fully. We huddled on the unforgiving tile of her foyer, my head buried in her thick cotton tunic, until I was spent. She calmly talked me out of showing up at Monica's house to collect Holly, reasoning that my daughter would have a far better time at the sleepover while I rode out the initial shock. Then she gently steered me to her bathroom and ordered me to take a long, steaming shower while she brewed us both tea.

"I might need something stronger," I said, the heel of my hand pressed against my left eye where a post-crying headache was forming.

"Tea first," Joy said firmly. "And maybe a glass of water. We'll open the wine after that, if you still want it."

I obeyed – the good little sister – and emerged later, clean of both rain and snot, to accept a mug of chamomile from Joy and a snuggle from Minty.

Joy sat on the opposite end of the sofa, facing me, her legs stretched out nearly to my lap. "Matthew called while you were in the shower," she said, between quick shallow sips of the hot tea. "'Good Day Sunshine' was coming out of your bag." She gestured to the end table next to me, where my handbag sat.

My eyes filled again. "Guess I'll have to change the ringtone for his number," I said. I turned to my sister. "Any suggestions?"

"I dunno. Lily Allen's 'Fuck You'?"

I chuckled and swiped at my eyes with the sleeve of Joy's sweatshirt, then pulled my phone out of my bag's side pocket. Three missed calls. All from Matthew.

"Well, he can wait," I muttered, more to myself than to Joy.

That was when the buzzing started, sparking Minty's outrage. Texts from Matthew.

Buzz. *We need to talk.*

Buzz. *We need to be on the same page with how we talk to Holly about this.*

Buzz. *Where are you?*

Buzz. *Kay, WE HAVE TO TALK ABOUT THIS.*

I flicked over to my phone's settings and selected "Do

Not Disturb," then dropped my phone onto the end table, marveling at the time. It wasn't even eight o'clock. Two hours ago I was pleasantly tired from work and about to go out to dinner with my husband and daughter. Two hours ago I was happily married. At least *I* was happy. Apparently, Matthew was not.

"I know I need to deal with him, with all of this. And soon. Like, tomorrow soon," I began. "But I can't do it tonight." I turned to Joy, seeking her approval. "I can't."

She nodded. "You can stay here. Are you hungry?"

I tilted my head back and forth. *Meh.* "Sort of?"

"You want our favorite comfort food?" Joy asked. She shifted deeper into her end of the sofa, bringing her fleece-socked feet into my lap. Her warmth and closeness was reassuring. "I have a big fat order of dumplings arriving at eight."

I shrugged. "I guess."

We sat in silence for a moment.

"Kay."

Joy sat up and leaned forward, a lock of her shaggy blonde-and-silver hair falling from behind her right ear.

"Did you know? Did you suspect?"

"I knew there was *something* going on," I said, my eyes focused on the framed map of Acadia National Park on the opposite wall. "It started over the summer. He started working so much more." I grimaced. "*Working*. A new client. A big new client and suddenly he doesn't want to have sex. A big new client and he can't make our Wednesday happy hours when Holly has back-to-back dance classes. But there's time for CrossFit!" I drained my tea and showed Joy the empty mug. "You said there was wine if I wanted it. I want it. And if you have vodka, I want that more."

Joy remained on the couch. "Did you suspect Anna?"

I stopped, my next *big new client* rant evaporating. "Anna? No. Why would I? I mean," I paused, rewinding the last few months of lunches, drinks, and texts. "She's just been…I don't know…*Anna*. Nothing's changed."

"*Everything* changed," Joy corrected. She stood up and collected our mugs into one hand. In the foyer, the doorbell rang. I flinched. Was Matthew here?

Joy held up her hand. Calm down. "It's the food. I'll fix our plates and get the wine." She looked at me pointedly. "*Wine*, not vodka. One glass. You have a big talk tomorrow. You need to be focused."

Joy left to answer the door. Minty decided that I had been punished enough – if she only knew – and returned to my lap.

Everything changed.

I scratched Minty's neck. "So, either Anna's an amazing actress, a clinical sociopath, or I'm not a very observant friend."

Minty butted my hand. *Pet me, human.* I obliged.

"What did I miss, Minty?" I asked.

Scratching the tabby with one hand, I picked up my phone in the other. One more text from Matthew.

Please call me.

Instead, I opened Facebook and scrolled to Anna's name.

It wasn't there.

I sat up taller and checked again. Not there. Did she delete her account? No, she posted something this morning. A photo of the foam heart in her cappuccino. I commented on it.

Yum! Enjoy!

"She blocked me," I whispered to the cat. "*She* blocked *me.*"

I exited Facebook and found Anna's number in my Contacts folder. I pressed the *Call* icon. It rang once, then went straight to voicemail. Instead of her recorded greeting, I was met with a robotic *please leave a message.*

I laughed, my voice still hoarse from crying. "She screws my husband, and *she* blocks *me?*"

"What?"

Joy is standing in the doorway to the kitchen holding a serving platter piled with pan-fried dumplings, two forks tucked into one side.

"Nothing," I said. "I'm going to send exactly one text to Matthew, and then I'm turning off my phone."

I DON'T want to talk tonight. Leave the house. I'll get Holly tomorrow. Do NOT pick her up. I'll tell her that you're away for work. We'll talk Sunday after she's gone to bed.

I paused, then sent a follow-up.

If you don't like that, tough. You *did this to us.*

As I put the phone away, a wave of exhaustion hit me.

I looked at my sister. "Will you come get Holly from Monica's house with me tomorrow?"

She nodded.

"Then let's eat," I said. "This looks really, really good."

We dug in, studiously avoiding any talk of marriage, infidelity, and my future.

It didn't occur to me until later – much later – to wonder why Joy had already ordered enough dumplings for two or three people before I showed up at her door.

A lot of things didn't occur to me before my life fell apart.

* * *

Then (Portsmouth, New Hampshire — 1999)

"I'm hungry," Anna declared. "Are there any more dumplings?"

I kept my eyes on the screen, where Norm MacDonald – convincing as Burt Reynolds – insisted to Will Ferrell's Alex Trebek that his new name was Turd Ferguson.

"Hello?" Anna nudged my shin with her bare foot.

We were sitting on my family room's sofa, propped up on each end. Our feet tangled together on the center seat cushion and we shared a faded blue fleece blanket.

"Gimme a minute and I'll check," I said. "I want to see this."

Anna turned back to the TV. "My mom loves Burt Reynolds."

"I know," I said. "I remember the day she found out I hadn't seen *Smokey and the Bandit.*"

Anna giggled. "She said she was gonna 'barbecue your ass in molasses.'"

The sketch ended, and I felt another soft kick under the blanket.

"Feed me, Seymour," she said.

I got up, nodding to the DVD clock under the TV. 12:04 am. "Isn't it dangerous to feed you after midnight?"

"Nah," Anna said. "That's gremlins." She sank deeper into the sofa and pulled the blanket up to her chin.

"Are you coming?"

She looked at me, eyes wide in the flicker of the TV. "I'm keeping the couch warm for you."

I stuck my tongue out and padded to the kitchen.

There were, in fact, some dumplings left. I emptied the

contents of the takeout carton into a shallow bowl and stuck them inside the microwave. I leaned against the counter, lulled into a daze by the low drone of the oven.

12:04 am. It was officially my 15th birthday, celebrated a few hours early with Chinese takeout, my mom's Boston Cream Pie, and a sleepover with Anna.

"I'm 15," I whispered to the still-dark kitchen, trying the words out to see if they made me feel different.

Did I feel different?

Fifteen had seemed so old, so *mature*, when I was a kid. When I turned 12, the prospect of imminent teenhood fascinated me. I drew vivid images of my first year of high school. *Surely I'll have a boyfriend,* I thought back then. *Maybe I'll even be a* cheerleader.

What I'd really been thinking – hoping – was *I'll know what I'm doing by then.*

Ha.

In reality, my freshman year had been underwhelming, my status defined in terms of other people. I was Joy Barrett's sister and Anna Becker's best friend. That counted for something, shielding me from the bitchiest of sophomores and putting me in immediate good standing with teachers. And for those not-so-small mercies I was grateful. But I'd yet to make my own mark. Or even come up with a sketch of an idea of one.

Did I feel different?

Not yet, I decided. *But there's always next year.*

I clicked open the door of the microwave with one second to go, in an attempt to avoid waking my parents with its unnecessarily long your-food-is-ready digital symphony. As I did, headlights swept into the kitchen from the driveway. Joy was home.

She ran lightly up the three steps to our back deck and slipped inside the door to the kitchen. She met my eyes and smiled.

"Happy birthday," Joy whispered, and opened her arms for a hug.

I grinned back, placed the bowl of dumplings on the countertop, and folded into her, breathing in the familiar scent of her leather jacket and cucumber melon body wash. There was a hint of Polo there, too. Her boyfriend's cologne.

She released me and glanced at the clock. 12:08.

"Was I the first to say it?"

I nodded, still smiling. She won every year.

"Is Anna asleep?"

I shook my head. "Family room. We're raiding the leftovers."

"Well, I'm glad I beat her to it."

I moved to collect the bowl when Joy stopped me.

"Wait…do I look different?"

I stared at her, surprised by her question coming so soon after my own thoughts on the matter.

"Umm," I stumbled. "I don't think so. Why?"

She smiled and looked down.

I gasped and grabbed her hand. "Did you and Brian…*have sex?*" The last two words barely audible. She nodded.

I started to pull Joy to the table, then caught movement in my peripheral vision.

Anna was standing in the doorway.

"Hey," she said. "I thought you were growing wheat for the dumpling dough, you've been in here so long. Hi, Joy."

"Sorry. We were just…umm, talking," I handed her the bowl. "I'll be right there, OK? Sorry."

Anna raised her eyebrows and glanced from me to my sister.

"Okaaaay," she said, drawing the word out in that universal code for *I know something's going on that you don't want to tell me and even though I'm kinda pissed I'm going to pretend that I'm not*, and returned to the family room. A second later, the volume on *Weekend Update* went up a notch.

I turned back to Joy, a million questions swirling in my head. What was it like? Was it romantic? Where were you? Are you glad?

"Tell me," I pleaded.

She did. She told me about his empty house. The three-hour window they had before his parents came back from the theater. The way his hands trembled as he fumbled with the condom. The quiet creak of his wooden bedframe. She told me that it hurt, and that Brian felt bad that it hurt. Which, oddly, made it seem to hurt less. She told me she was happy. So, so happy.

"You do look different," I said. "But I think it's because I know."

"You're the only one I'm telling right now," Joy said.

Joy went upstairs to her room, and I returned to Anna, glowing with my sister's secret and her trust. Anna was sitting cross-legged on the sofa, chewing and watching Eminem perform. I joined her, snagging a dumpling and pulling the blanket over my legs.

"You're lucky you have a sister," Anna said. "Especially an older one. Sometimes being an only child sucks."

I glanced at her. "You're like her sister, too," I said.

She tilted her head in a *meh* gesture. "Not really. Maybe for the little stuff."

I flipped over to face her, leaning back against the armrest and poking her leg with my foot. "Your mom is practically a sister. She's the coolest, funniest mom I've ever met."

"Yeah, but she's still my *mom*," Anna reasoned. "She's awesome, yes, but it's not the same."

She looked at me. *Tell me*, the look said. *Include me*.

I couldn't. Not right away. Tonight, it was mine. It was Joy's birthday present to me. I pretended not to see it.

"Well, Joy won't be here next year, at school *or* home," I said, shifting the subject. "Looks like I'll have an opening. Since you need a sister and *I'll* need a sister…"

I sat up and plucked the last dumpling from the bowl.

"Anna, darling," I said, presenting the dumpling to her. "Will you be my honorary sister?"

Anna leaned toward me, her face filled with mock seriousness. "'You'll give me everything'?"

I sang back to her. "'All that joy can bring, this I swe-ear…'"

She nestled back into her original position on the couch, smiling again. "Happy birthday, weirdo."

"Thanks, sister-I-chose."

"Am I the first to say it?" Anna asked me.

I beamed at her. "You are."

Chapter 3

T he soft thud overhead was my nightly cue. I flipped shut the *Architectural Digest* on my lap – *Real Simple* was ruined for me now – and stood up, my near-empty glass of water in hand. I slipped into the kitchen, pausing to place my glass in the sink, and crept up the backstairs to Holly's room.

She was on her side, facing away from me. Her copy of *The Wild Robot* – the source of the thud – lay face down on the jewel-toned carpet. I picked it up and placed it softly on her nightstand, then switched off her pointe shoe reading lamp.

"That lamp is giving me *A Christmas Story* vibes," Matthew had said last December, when Holly lifted it out of the gift box, squealing. Later that Christmas evening, when our parents, Joy, Anna, and Mr. Becker had left – laden with gifts and full bellies – the three of us curled up on the den's olive green sofa and watched it, giggling and eating too many Holiday M&Ms.

I pushed the memory away and returned to the first floor, pulling out my phone to text Matthew.

She's asleep. The side door is unlocked. I'll be in the den.

His reply was quick.

OK. Be there in five. I've been waiting down the street.

I grabbed a lowball glass from the cabinet and mixed a rum-and-pineapple-juice on the rocks before returning to the den, avoiding the green sofa in favor of the vintage leather armchair given to me – to us – by my grandparents. Before I sat, I glanced at myself in the small wall mirror. My blonde hair was neat and my makeup understated. The pale pink cashmere sweater I'd chosen added color to my cheeks. Around my neck was the gold locket Matthew had given me after I gave birth to Holly.

Would he notice? If he did, would he care?

A minute later he was there, standing in the wide doorway between the kitchen and den.

"Hey," Matthew said.

I tucked my legs – clad in charcoal yoga pants – underneath me and sipped my drink.

"Hey."

Matthew half-turned to the kitchen, then stopped and looked at me, a slight flush coming to his face.

"Uh, is it OK if I get myself a drink?"

I gestured to the kitchen. "Make yourself at home, Matthew."

He returned with another green bottle of Dos Equis – risky, considering I'd hurled the last one at the kitchen wall just two days earlier – and sat on the sofa. As he reached for one of the cork coasters on the coffee table, I noticed the book tucked under his arm.

"What's that?" I asked.

He pulled it out. "It's for Holly," he said. "For when we talk to her this week. Tomorrow, I'm thinking."

On the cover was an androgynous-looking toddler holding up two crayon drawings of different houses. He – or she –

was smiling, as was his/her dog.

"*Two Homes*?" I said, incredulous. "Is this really where we are, Matt?"

He dropped the book onto the table and took a pull from his beer. "Yes, Kay. It really is."

"And what are you planning to tell her?" I pressed. "Because it sounds to me like you've already figured it out. Which is rich, really, because you haven't even explained any of it to *me*."

Matthew flipped up his palms in a *hey, I'm trying to be the good guy here* gesture, the neck of the beer clenched between two fingers. "I tried, Kay. You took off, remember? And then avoided me all weekend."

I sat up, planting my heels back on the patterned carpet, my palms on my thighs.

"Seriously?" I said. "I find out you're screwing Anna, and I'm supposed to sit down and divvy up our wedding china with you an hour later? And the first thing you bring to this conversation is that you're ready to talk to our daughter *tomorrow*? Who are you right now?"

Matthew took an even longer pull from his bottle, then set his drink down and leaned forward, his elbows on his knees. "Fine. Let's talk. What do you want to know?"

I want to know how you can be so blasé about the end of our marriage, I thought. *I want to know when – and why – you stopped loving me. But most of all, I want to know what I did to make my best friend turn against me so completely and irreparably.*

I couldn't. Something – pride, rage or both – stopped me. Instead, I grasped for the lowest-hanging fruit.

"When did it start?"

Matt looked down at his hands, rubbing a thumb over the

opposite palm. "Sebago Lake."

June, then. Four months ago. The week after school ended. Anna came up for two nights at the midpoint of our stay. They stayed up late by the fire pit while I crawled into bed at eleven, happily exhausted by lake life.

"You left early. Three days early. The same day Anna did," I reminded him. "A new client, you said."

Matthew nodded. "A lie. I'm sorry."

"A lot of lies," I said. "From both of you."

My husband stayed silent.

"Why Anna, Matthew?"

He looked at me. "Why does anyone fall for anyone? It just happened, Kay. We didn't plan it."

I shook my head at him. "That's not good enough. She was my best friend. Why would you both choose to do this to me?"

"For Christ sakes, Kay, we didn't choose it," Matthew whisper-hissed. "And anyway, she's my friend, too. I've known her longer than I've known you. Sebago wasn't the first time the thought had occurred to me. It was just the first time I acted on it."

He drained his beer and placed it firmly on the coaster. "Look, we're telling Holly this week. Sooner rather than later. I thought tomorrow would be best because she doesn't have dance on Mondays."

He picked up the book and shook it at me. "We need to tell her that it isn't her fault and we both love her."

"And you're going to tell her that it's your fault, are you?"

He sighed. "I'm not telling her about Anna. Not yet."

"No?" I asked, skeptical. "Where are you staying, Matthew?"

He looked grim. "At Anna's."

I leaned forward, my palms still on my thighs. "She has a

one-bedroom condo," I pointed out. "And if you think for *one second* that Holly will be spending nights on her pull-out couch, you're out of your mind."

Matthew squeezed his hands together. "No, Holly's not going to sleep on a *pull-out*," he said, exasperated. "She'll sell her condo, and we'll get something bigger."

"'We'?" I asked. "You're prepared for a second mortgage?"

He stared at me, defiant. "No. We'll sell this place, or you'll buy me out."

I hardened, turning cold. I couldn't afford that on my associate's salary, and Matthew knew that.

"Get the hell out of my house," I said, my body still.

Matthew blinked, momentarily silenced. "Well, we–"

"Don't say another word." I told him, my voice low. "Get out."

I turned away from him as he left, my gaze focused on the mantel over the small fireplace. It was chock-a-block with pictures. Holly, Joy, my parents and grandparents. A black and white candid of our wedding. A Holyoke college reunion weekend with my friend Jenna.

And throughout, Anna and Matthew.

The side door clicked, shutting Matthew out of the house. I gazed at the faces in the pictures.

Who else couldn't I trust?

* * *

Then (Portsmouth, New Hampshire — 2000)

"I can't believe you got us here in one piece," Anna said, sliding into the booth next to me.

Dad made tiny adjustments to his silverware, lining them up neatly on the diner's ad-covered paper placement. "Honey, I never doubted you for a minute," he said.

"You didn't reach for the *Oh Jesus* handle once," I said to him, feigning admiration.

"I couldn't find it with my eyes squeezed shut," he said.

I tore off the top of the wrapper from my straw and blew it at him, pegging his forehead with the remaining sleeve. He winked back.

Next to Dad, my mom pulled her reading glasses from the case in her purse and put them on. "OK, now I can have a proper look," she said, holding a hand out to me. "Let's see the official documentation."

Reaching into my Coach wristlet bag, I pulled my brand new driver's license out and presented it to her. She studied it for a long moment, then looked up at me, smiling.

"I'm glad you wore the fuchsia for the photo," she said. "It brings out the color in your cheeks."

Anna sniffed. "*I* wanted her to wear baby blue so it would blend with the background and look like a floating head, like mine."

"Yeah, but yours was by accident," I pointed out.

"So?" Anna said. "Show a little solidarity."

I took my license back and returned it to my Coach. "Blue, hot pink, whatever. I'm just glad I passed," I said. "I was too nervous to eat breakfast, and I'm starving. I want my celebratory Reuben and fries."

The four of us fell into an easy conversation over lunch. We discussed Joy's recent shift in college major from Early Childhood Education to Nursing, a move that my parents approved of but that Anna and I dismissed as having too high a gross factor. Anna filled us in on her mom's latest consulting work with a software development firm in San Jose, which would include the perk of accompanying her to California over April vacation.

"Aw, you're going away?" I asked, crestfallen. "I thought we were gonna road trip to Boston one of the days." Anna shrugged.

"You did?" Dad said, raising his eyebrows.

"Just for the day," I said, defensive. "For more highway practice."

"You'll get plenty of practice driving to and from the Schmitt's house."

I wrinkled my nose.

"What?" Mom asked. "You don't like sitting for them anymore?"

"No…well, not exactly," I began.

"What, then? Is something making you uncomfortable?" she asked, suddenly alert.

"Relax, Mom, it's nothing bad," I reassured her. "It's just that the last couple of times I've sat for them, they've had the two little boys who live next door over, too. So now I'm watching three kids instead of one for the same pay, and…I guess I just don't think that's fair."

I glanced from my parents to Anna, unsure.

"That's because it isn't fair. It's B.S." Anna said, pointing a ketchup-topped fry at me for emphasis. "Total B.S."

Anna shifted her eyes to my mom for approval. Mom

nodded.

My relief was instant. "Right? I've been wondering if I should say something. I feel, I don't know, like they're taking advantage of me."

"Umm, *yeah*," Anna said. "They're probably splitting the cost, and now the Schmitt's are saving money on the deal."

"I can call Mrs. Schmitt for you, if you want," Mom offered.

I hesitated. A part of me really, *really* wanted a grownup to handle the whole thing for me. One sternly-worded message from Mom, and either the two extra boys would go away, or I'd get a raise.

Then I thought about the next time. Or the time after that. At some point, I was going to have to fight my own battles. I pictured the shiny new driver's license in my bag, just hours old. Now was as good a day as any to start. I just didn't know how.

"No," I told my mom. "Thanks. I should talk to her myself, I think. What do you think I should say?"

Mom pursed her lips, her *let me think* look, the one Dad said she always made when she was bluffing at cards.

"Well, first I think you should figure out what you think your hourly rate for three kids should be," she began. "Then you tell Mrs. Schmitt that when you first agreed to your current rate, you were only watching her son. Now that you're taking care of three kids—"

"Say 'three times as many,'" Anna interjected. "It sounds like more."

"It also sounds flippant," Mom chided gently. "And this is a business negotiation. Let's leave the sass out of it. Tell her now that you're caring for three instead of one, either she pays you *X*, or she sends the other boys home."

I nodded slowly, my stomach clenching. Anna, I knew, could sense my discomfort. She'd seen it often enough in school, even if others didn't.

"Here, let's practice," she said, shifting in her seat to face me. "I'm Mrs. Schmitt."

She folded her arms and sighed dramatically. "Yes, Katherine? You had something to say?"

I rolled my eyes, but played along. "I think that, if Joey and Robby are going to be here when I'm here, I should be getting more per hour."

Anna shook her head. "Too wishy-washy. The boys aren't just there when you're there. You're legit watching them."

She tapped my right leg, which I'd hitched onto the bench seat to better face her.

"Both feet flat on the ground. Shoulders back. Palms on your legs," she said. "Do it again, but to your Dad. Start by addressing her by name."

I did as I was told. "Mrs Schmitt," I began, a new confidence stirring inside me. "When we agreed on my current rate, I was only watching Jack. Now that I'm taking care of Joey and Robby as well, we need to discuss an increase, or agree that their parents find their own sitter."

"Boom!" Anna exclaimed. My mom clapped quietly in approval.

My dad patted his pockets. "I feel like I should be writing you a check."

I turned to Anna. "How did you do that?"

She grinned. "It's like, a power pose thing. My mom knows all about that kind of stuff," she gestured to my mom. "As soon as you said 'business negotiation,' I thought of it."

"Nicely done, Anna," Mom said. "It worked like a charm."

"Do you have any tricks from your dad?" I asked. "In case she says no?"

"Oh, definitely," she said. "Imagine someone just threw a bucket of ice water all over you. Get real still, real fast. Lean in, like this, and make your voice real low," she said. She narrowed her eyes at me, her voice turning to a growl. "You send those little brats back home. Right now."

"Oooh," I said, impressed. "Bad. Ass."

Dad chuckled. "Is that his 'mad dad' voice or his firefighter voice?"

She grinned. "Both."

"I'll file that one away for when this one comes home late with the car," he said, pointing at me.

"So will I," I said. "I just don't know what for yet."

Chapter 4

"That *bastard*."

My dad gripped his beer bottle, his knuckles whitening underneath the spiky black hairs of his fingers. He looked around my kitchen as if seeking a target for his anger.

"Don't throw your beer, Dad," I told him wearily. "You'll wake Holly. Besides, I already threw mine when I found out."

His eyes lit on me. "Did you hit him?"

I shook my head. "I was aiming for the whiteboard."

Dad released his hold on the bottle and walked around the marble top island. He enveloped me in a hug and I pressed my face to his chest.

"I'm sorry to bring you both out so late," I murmured into the soft cotton of his watch plaid shirt.

"Shhh. I'm so glad you did," Dad said.

For the last two days, I'd told no one about Matthew and Anna except Joy. I hadn't known what to expect from my husband's visit earlier this evening. I *did* know that I wanted him to walk into the home we made together and realize what he stood to lose.

Let's sell the house was not the reaction I was hoping for, and it had unnerved me to the point of panic. Less than an hour after his abrupt departure my parents rushed in, summoned by my three-word call of "Matthew's leaving me." I relayed the details – from Matthew's Friday night bombshell to this evening's *Two Homes* – haltingly, shaking from the finality of it all.

"Bastard," my dad said again, releasing me and planting a kiss on my temple.

My mother was uncharacteristically quiet, fixated on a point over my shoulder. The painted wooden signs on my kitchen wall. One of which read *Friends gather here*.

Not anymore, I thought.

"Mom?" I prompted. "Are you OK?"

Mom shook her head, her shoulder-length silver hair swinging. She leaned forward and placed her elbows on the countertop, squeezing her hands together.

"I don't understand this. At all," she said.

"What *I* understand is that our son-in-law is a–"

"No, not Matthew. Forget Matthew," Mom cut Dad off with a smooth toss of her wrist. "Matthew's dead to me. I'm talking about *Anna*."

Mom looked at me. "How could she, Kay? How could she?" Her hazel eyes filled with tears. "She was *family*."

Family.

Are you family?

My throat constricted at my mother's words. Snatches of scenes flitted through my memory, just out of reach. A buzzing fluorescent light. A clatter of metal.

My stomach hollowed, then filled with a sensation I couldn't place. Until I did.

Shame.

My mind – perhaps saving me from myself – shut down

the unwelcome, vaguely sinister images, and I snapped my attention back to my mom. She was looking at me through her tears, expectant.

"I–" I swallowed, forcing moisture back into my throat. "I don't know, Mom. I've been asking myself that all weekend."

Had I, though?

My mother's shoulders slumped. She wiped her eyes and took a small sip from the glass of neat rum she poured herself upon arrival and tried again.

"Did you have a fight?"

I stared at her, incredulous. "Did we *have a fight?* Mom, we're not thirteen. She didn't steal my boyfriend. She had an affair with my husband," I said. My voice rose, cracking. "Are you saying that *I* caused this? That somehow I drove my best friend to sleep with my husband?"

Mom put her palms up, as if to say *OK, OK, I see your point.* Or maybe it was *Calm down, you'll wake Holly.* Perhaps a little of both. Dad inched closer to me, rubbing my back with his warm, comforting hand.

"Of course not," said Mom. "I'm sorry if that's what you thought I was saying. I'm not. It's just…the two of you are like sisters. She's–"

"I don't want to talk about Anna," I said, cutting Mom off. I couldn't bear to hear her say *family* again. Every nerve in my body screamed CHANGE THE SUBJECT!, but I wasn't wholly sure why. The memory was *just* around the corner, but like Danny Torrance on his Big Wheel inside the Overlook Hotel, I wasn't ready to pedal around that particular corridor. The one with the yellow floral wallpaper.

Mom nodded, and reached across the marble top to clasp my hand. "How can we support you?"

I relaxed, sinking a little more into Dad. "I…I just need you to be on my side, whatever happens."

"You got us," Dad said, squeezing my shoulder. "And we've got you."

"That includes if Matthew and I decide to stay together," I said. "I mean, it's not impossible, right?"

My mom swallowed, and shook her head. "No, it's not impossible," she said. "Is that what you want?"

"I don't know *what* I want," I cried. "This whole thing was thrown at me two days ago! One minute I want to chuck all his clothes onto a giant bonfire, and the next I want him to come bursting through that door–" I gestured to the door to the mudroom, the one I had run out of in sock feet Friday night. "And beg me to forgive him."

I massaged my temples with my fingers, feeling a headache coming on. "One minute I was married and happy, and now we're selling the house? I feel…well, *everything*. Blindsided. Betrayed. And helpless. Mostly helpless. Don't I have a say in what happens here?" I looked to my mom for reassurance.

She squeezed my hand again. "Yes, you do. You have a say in what happens with Holly, and you have a say in what happens with this house. And if Matthew decides that he *does* want you to forgive him, you have a say in that, too."

She gave my hand a small shake, refocusing my attention. "And if I were you, I'd focus on Holly and house. That's where you have the most control."

I nodded and wiped my nose. It felt raw.

"And to exercise that control, you need time," Mom added. "Time to decide what you want. Tell that to Matthew. Tell him that you won't – not 'can't,' *won't* – decide anything for at least two weeks. Maybe more."

"You think?" I asked.

She nodded firmly. "Yes. He sprung this on you. He can wait."

I drew in a deep breath and held it, considering Mom's advice. Then I exhaled and slapped the counter lightly with my open hand.

"That makes sense," I said. "I have to tell Holly *something*, though. I can't pretend he's on a work trip indefinitely, and I can't not let her see him. I just…I'm not ready for it all to be so…final."

"Well, I'm afraid that's the conversation that can't wait," said Mom. "And it needs to come from both of you, with no mixed messages."

A wry laugh escaped me. "I kicked him out, like, an hour ago. And now I have to bring him back in? Terrific."

Mom frowned. "He deserved to be kicked out, with that ridiculousness about the house," she said. "Let him stew in it for another day."

"Oh, I will," I assured her, then softened. "Thank you. Both of you."

"And call us. Any time. No matter what time it is," Mom added.

My dad pointed his beer bottle at me. "I second that. Especially if you decide to have that bonfire."

* * *

Then (Portsmouth, New Hampshire — Fall 2003)

The early October sun was warm, though the light breeze held the first hint of real fall. A few maple leaves – some still tinged with green – whirled in my wake as I jogged up the front steps, holding the short poster tube in one hand. Mr. Becker's navy blue Bronco was in the driveway, its engine still ticking from the journey back from the airport. I knocked twice on the front door of Anna's house and then opened the door a few inches. Anna's pale pink London Fog rolling suitcase sat just inside the door, Mrs. Becker's matching black one beside it.

"...definitely going to need a cell phone now, dad," Anna said gaily.

"Tell you what, I'll cover the cell phone if you cover tuition," was his reply.

"Hello!" I called into the foyer.

"We're in here, Kay," Anna's mother called from the living room.

I stepped inside the house and closed the door behind me. Mr. Becker was in his recliner, as usual, the Sunday *Globe* in a pile on the floor to his left. Anna and her mom sat together on the faded jade sofa. They were facing each other and smiling, their sitting positions perfectly mirrored. Anna had her right leg tucked underneath her and right elbow propped on the back of the couch, her head leaning on her hand. Mrs. Becker was sitting the same way, but with her left arm slung over the sofa and left leg curled underneath her.

I stood in the doorway to the living room, taking in Anna's shining face.

"Well?" I asked, already knowing the answer. "How was it?"

Mr. Becker leaned forward, kicking in the footrest of the

recliner, and stood.

"I'll let them tell you all about it," he said, then turned to his wife. "I'll bring your bags upstairs." She smiled softly in response.

I perched on the edge of Mr. Becker's chair, expectant, the cardboard tube resting on my knees.

"It was *great*," Anna sighed. "I loved it. Loved it, loved it, loved it."

She filled me in on her tour of the University of Chicago, going into detail about the campus, the handful of students she met, and the one math professor she managed to talk to. She spoke quickly – giddily – interrupting her own train of thought to tell a new anecdote about the tour.

When she finally paused to take a breath, Mrs. Becker turned to me, still beaming. "In case you can't tell, she loved it," she said. "My baby's going to Chicago."

"*If* I get in," Anna said, leaning forward to knock on the teak coffee table. "My guidance counselor says I should look for safety schools."

"Your guidance counselor is a misogynistic pig who wouldn't know the meaning of 'women in STEM' if it was tattooed on his forehead," Mrs. Becker said. "He told Billy Arthur he could be a CEO or senator? Then said your organizational skills would make for a good secretary?"

"To be fair, he said 'executive assistant,' and *you* were a secretary once," Anna pointed out.

"Yeah, and it *does* take good organizational skills, especially with a numb-nuts like Billy as CEO," Mrs. Becker. "But why is Dobson telling *him* to be the leader and *you* to be the assistant?"

"Senator Arthur? Ew," I said, shuddering. "God help us all. When'd you hear this?"

"Just before I got dismissed for my flight on Thursday," Anna said, rolling her eyes. "I went to tell Mr. Dobson about the visit and he was meeting with Billy with the door open."

"My point is," Mrs. Becker interjected. "I think you're better off if that man isn't involved in your application process any more than he has to be. But you can do it in a smart way."

She grinned. "A way that makes him think *he* came up with the idea."

I watched, fascinated, as Mrs. Becker coached Anna on how to pretend to ask Dobson his advice on which teachers to ask for recommendations, and quietly guiding him to all the right ones.

"And you're *not* going to doubt yourself," Mrs. Becker said, wrapping up. "You're a leader, Anna Banana. You'll get in. I can feel it."

"Just don't ever say 'Anna Banana' in front of Dobson," Anna said. "He'll put it on my transcript." She smiled at her mother.

I cleared my throat. "Well, if that's where you're heading, then you'll need this."

I tossed the tube lightly, like I was launching a paper airplane, and Anna snatched it from the air with both hands. She pried open the cap and spilled the poster onto her lap. Smiling quizzically at me, Anna slid the rubber band off and unfurled the paper.

"What is it?" Mrs. Becker asked.

Anna laughed and turned it around to show her. "It's a promo poster for the *Spice World* tour."

"Not just *any* poster," I added. "It's for their show at Tinley Park in Chicago. I found it online."

"Omigod, really?" Anna peered at the print.

"Yeah," I said. "So, you know, while you're here, it'll keep you thinking of Chicago, and when you're there it'll keep you thinking of me."

"Oh, Kay," Mrs. Becker said. "That's so sweet."

"I love it," Anna said, rolling it up carefully so the edges didn't catch. "Thank you. And hey, I almost forgot. How was Mount Holyoke?"

I nodded, a little put out by *I almost forgot*. Anna had originally signed up to tour the school with me, but canceled when her mom snagged a last-minute spot in Chicago. But this was typical of Anna when she glommed onto something new. In eighth grade, she'd landed a last-minute spot on the middle school field hockey team. I didn't hear from her for almost two months. The sport didn't stick, thankfully. We jokingly referred to it as the Field Hockey Experiment of 1998.

"Good. I really liked it. The campus is *so* pretty."

They looked at me, clearly expecting more.

"The tour was nice. Um, I didn't really get to meet students or professors, but yeah. I really liked it," I said again, trying to drum up the same enthusiasm she'd shown for Chicago.

And I *had* liked it. Just not in that giddy, stomach-flipping way that Anna had liked Chicago. Anna was running headlong toward graduation, the Midwest, and a mathematics program I could barely grasp the concept of, let alone *do*. And me? The only stomach-flipping I experienced was when I thought of leaving home next year. Alone. My actual sister had left for her junior year of college a month ago, and my honorary sister was, mentally, already boarding the plane for Illinois. It was all happening too fast.

"Anyway," Anna continued. "I suppose Dobsie has a point about applying to a few places where I have a good chance of getting in."

"You'd get into Loyola," Mrs Becker suggested.

Anna wrinkled her nose. "I couldn't be in Chicago and not be *at* Chicago, though, you know?"

"You'd get in Mount Holyoke," I said.

Anna looked at me. "Isn't that, like, pretty rural?"

"Not really," I said, finally feeling a stirring of excitement.. "There are a lot of cute towns out there, and it's only, like, two hours from New York. It's so pretty there, Anna. And I *know* you'd get in, with your grades and SATs. You should think about it."

Anna flicked her hand in a *why not* gesture. "Well, I guess if I can't have Chicago, then you'll be stuck with me," she said.

I was a joke, I knew. But I clung to it, grateful for this buoy in a roiling sea of uncertainty.

Chapter 5

I t was raining again. Stupid rain.

I closed the oven door and strode to the sink to snap my kitchen window shut, muffling the nerve-jangling sound of water pelting concrete. On the counter, my phone stared at me, a silent reminder of the call I still had to make to Matthew.

He sprung this on you. He can wait.

I'd turned my mother's words over in my mind all day. And it had been a *long* day. I'd lain awake most of the night after my parents left, snatching bits of fitful sleep here and there. When a low rumble of thunder woke me at five, I felt sunken and hollow. I could neither face my office nor a day by myself.

Thank goodness for Holly.

She'd cried out in her sleep just before six a.m. When I reached her, she was sobbing into her caramel-colored teddy bear. I felt her forehead; it was warm from sleep, but not feverish.

"What is it, Holls?" I asked.

"There was a fire," she hiccupped. "There was a fire in the hospital and I couldn't find you."

I gathered her in my arms as she wept.

"It was just a dream. I'm here," I whispered. "I'm here."

When she was spent, she asked for a glass of water. "My throat hurts," she added. "Monica's sick and so are Jasper and Zach. Everyone in my class is sick."

She sniffed dramatically.

I didn't fully buy that part, but I didn't care, either.

"You want to sleep some more and then I'll make pancakes?"

She nodded, eyes still closed.

"Want to come into my bed?" I asked her.

She peeked at me. "Can I?"

I smiled and nodded. "Come on, Holly Jolly."

Back in my bed, I sent a quick email to my office claiming a sick day and then fell into a deep and grateful sleep. When we both woke, hours later, it was after nine.

I sat up and looked at my daughter. Outside, another growl of thunder rattled the window pane.

"Boy, are we *lazy*," I said. "Could we get any lazier?"

Holly nodded. "I think we could."

"Prove it," I said, sliding my feet into my tartan slippers. "I bet you can't stay in your pajamas all day."

She grinned. "I bet I can."

"And I bet you can't read books and watch movies all day on the couch with a fuzzy blanket," I added, raising an eyebrow.

She giggled. "Can too."

I shrugged. "Well, I guess we're just gonna have to do that. But first, pancakes."

"With chocolate chips?" Holly asked.

I pointed at her, feigning seriousness. "Try and stop me from putting them in the batter."

A half hour later, we were perched on stools at the breakfast bar, munching our respective short stacks.

"Holls," I said, after taking a careful sip of my tea. "You dreamed about a hospital last night. Do you remember?"

She swallowed and nodded.

"A little. I mostly remember the fire."

"Was it the hospital you stayed at last spring?" I ventured.

Holly had had a minor meningitis scare last April, which resulted in spending a few days under observation. She'd fully bounced back, but I'd always wondered if there would be any lingering emotional wounds. Was this one of them?

Or was she sensing another kind of turmoil at home?

She shook her head. "Nah. That was fun. There was TV and pudding in bed. Can we put on a movie now?"

OK, then.

Between books, movies and more cups of tea, I wrestled with the advice my mother had given me last night. Now, with Holly occupied with a paint-by-number canvas and a chicken and broccoli casserole bubbling in the oven, I couldn't put it off any longer. I dialed, only a little surprised when he picked up on the second ring.

"Hey," he said. Not *Hey, babe* or *Hi, honey* or, if he was feeling especially light, *How's my little Kay of sunshine?* He had me on speaker phone, I could tell.

"Hi," I said. "Are you alone?"

Or are you with my best friend? I thought. *Is her hand resting on your right leg, like mine used to do during long car rides?*

"Yes."

"We need to meet again."

"Yes, we do," Matthew said. "I was hoping I'd be there tonight so the both of us could talk to Holly."

I glanced toward the den and lowered my voice. "Well, that's not happening yet," I said.

"You need to talk to me first."

"I tried last night, Kay. You threw me out."

"No, not about *Two Homes* or *our* home," I said. "We need to talk about *us*. You, me, and our marriage. I can't – I *won't* – have any other kind of conversation with you before this one."

On the other end of the phone, Matthew was silent. Sounds of the road – rain, windshield wipers, the drone of a heavy truck – filtered through in the absence of words. Based on the time, I estimated he was in that snarling half-mile of stop-and-go traffic on Route 95 just before his exit. It was his least-favorite part of the ride, and I'd just made it worse.

Good.

I waited, fighting the urge to fill the silence with justifications I didn't need to make.

I pictured him, instantly and clearly. Jacket off and tie loosened. His left wrist resting on the top of the steering wheel, hand bent downward. The fingers of his right hand would be tapping the outside of his thigh in sync with whatever 90s Alt Rock band was streaming on his go-to satellite radio station.

Except he wouldn't be tapping right now. His right hand was likely clenched into a fist.

"Delaying this isn't going to change anything, Kay," Matthew said finally.

My stomach twisted. *Stay strong*, I told myself.

"It's less about changing anything and more about wrapping my head around it," I said. "Unlike you, I haven't had six months to get used to the idea."

"Four," he muttered, an aside most likely not meant for me to hear.

"How's Wednesday?" I asked.

More silence, then a sigh.

"Fine. Where?"

"It's Wednesday, isn't it? So let's do our Wednesday."

"What? Oh. Yeah."

My eyes misted at Matthew's lukewarm acknowledgment that Wednesdays used to be our weekday happy hour dates while Holly took tap and ballet.

"So, you want me to meet you at Water View after you drop Holly at dance?"

It was my turn to sigh.

"No, Matthew. I don't want to *meet you* at Water View," I said. "Come home after work, and we'll take Holly to dance together. Because it's Wednesday and that's what we do."

Used *to do*, I thought. *Until Sebago.*

"But…," Matthew began, frustration creeping into his voice. "Aren't we confusing her?"

"How so?" I asked. "She thinks you're away for work. Now I can tell her that you're getting home tomorrow."

"And when I leave after dinner?"

"*Don't* leave after dinner," I reasoned. "You can tuck her in, and in the morning, I'll tell her you've already left for the office."

Still more silence. *Too far?* I wondered.

"Fine," he said. "I'll come home after work on Wednesday."

Home! My heart leaped, whether my brain wanted it to or not. *He said* home*!*

"Great," I said, letting my voice thaw a little. "Would you like to talk to Holly? I know she'd love to talk to you."

He cleared his throat and raised his voice an octave. "Yes, please. Thanks."

"Holl-lly!" I called, keeping the phone close enough for Matthew to hear. "Daddy's on the phone!"

"Daddy!" Holly jumped up from the old flannel sheet I had draped over the den carpet and raced into the kitchen, grabbing the phone from my hand.

"When are you coming home?" she asked, pausing while Matthew said something I couldn't hear. "Really? Good!"

I smiled, and turned to the stove to check on dinner, listening to Holly chatter happily with her father. As if he was really on a work trip and was really coming home in two days.

It's not impossible, right? I had asked my parents last night.

No, I decided. *No it wasn't.*

***

Then (Portsmouth, New Hampshire — Winter 2004)

Anna's room was freezing, and I was starving.

The last of the late winter sunlight strained through the open window before giving up, leaving the two of us in purple gloom.

I shivered and nestled closer to Anna in the double bed. Her new black wool dress was itchy against my forehead, and smelled vaguely of perfume and body odor. She'd been wearing it since the funeral three days ago, leaving her bed only to pee. And those trips stretched further apart the less she drank.

She hadn't eaten at all.

"Anna?" I whispered into her back. "I'm going to close the window, OK?"

"No."

"It might snow tonight," I lied. I got up and tiptoed across her bubble gum pink carpet.

"Good. Maybe I'll freeze."

I eased the sash down and returned to the bed, sitting at its foot. "And that would prove what, exactly?"

Anna's gaze was fixed on her closed bedroom door. "Nothing. But it's a fitting end for a daughter who killed her mom by begging for a new winter coat."

She rolled over onto her back and looked at me. "Did I tell you that? I saw the coat and simply *had to have it* for Chicago. Had to! And then I found that stupid coupon in the stupid paper and gave it to her. 'Please, mom? Pleeeeease?' And boom!" Anna drove her left fist into her right palm. "Enter truck. Hello, truck. Please smash into my mom's car."

She flopped back onto her side, kicking the blanket I had thrown over us to the floor.

"OK, freezing-slash-starving to death in your own bed is one way to go," I said. "Or, and hear me out, you could get up, shower, eat something, and keep doing that for a few more months until it's time to go to Chicago and do all those nerdy math things you're so good at and win, like, twelve Nobel Prizes and make your mom really, really proud. As proud as she was the day you got accepted. Remember when she–"

"I'm not going to Chicago," Anna said into the crook of her arm.

"What?" I asked. "Why not?"

"I'm just not," she replied. "I don't want to be that far away from my dad."

This surprised me. Anna wasn't particularly close to her dad. In the five and a half years I'd been coming here I'd probably spent only a handful of hours with him. When he wasn't working at the fire station, he was playing cards with other firefighters or reading the *Globe* in his La-Z-Boy. He'd returned to his shifts right away. Whether it was for his own comfort or to avoid seeing Anna's devastation, I didn't know. Probably both.

We have to step up and really be there for her, I'd heard my mom whisper to my dad over the post-funeral buffet. *Craig is going to be lost without Elizabeth when it comes to Anna.*

"I don't want to be that far away from you, either," she added, as if she'd known what I was thinking, which she probably did.

For the first time since the church soloist belted out "Be Not Afraid" to the hundreds of mourners gathered at St. Mary's three days ago, my eyes filled. As happy as I was to be going to my top choice for college, there was a sliver of anxiety persistently rising to the surface. What was I going to do without Anna? With her, I was confident. Bold, even. I'd navigated the mean girls and clueless boys relatively unscathed with Anna having my back. Messing with me meant messing with her, and no one wanted to be on Anna's bad side.

Would there be an Anna waiting for me at Mount Holyoke?

I blinked back my tears and refocused on my friend.

"So what are you going to do?" I asked. I tried to remember where else she had applied, but the University of Chicago had been front and center for so long that the only college I could come up with was Mount Holyoke, where she'd applied as her safety, just to appease me.

I grabbed Anna's foot and squeezed. "Are you thinking about Mount Holyoke?"

She shrugged, still staring at her bedroom door. "Maybe. I mean, I got in."

I bounced up and down on the bed, still squeezing her foot. "But that would be amazing! We could room together, and come home together. You could keep coming to my house for Thanksgiving if your dad's on duty. And you won't be alone, Anna. You'll be with *me*."

I was giddy. Mount Holyoke *and* my best friend! *This was the dream*, I thought.

Unbidden, a memory pushed in. Anna's mother, spraying two full cans of Silly String over her daughter the day she was accepted into the University of Chicago's mathematics program. *This is the dream!* She screamed, spraying the string – white and maroon, of course – into Anna's hair. *This is the dream, Anna Banana!*

I shoved the image aside and threw myself next to my friend, tossing an arm over her body. "As soon as you accept, we'll tell them we want to be roommates, OK?"

Anna was silent. I leaned closer and started whisper-singing into her ear.

"'It's a brand new day…'" I sang.

Anna groaned. "Oh my God, Kay."

"'I got a feeling things are going my way, 'cause…'" I stopped, waiting for her response.

Nothing.

I shook her. "'Cause…'"

Anna sighed. "'Cause the girls are back in town,'" she sang, her mouth finally curling into a smile.

I crawled over her and got up from the bed. "Get up, Sporty

Spice. We got plans to make. And I'm *starving*. There are, like, a kajillion lasagnas downstairs. And I think someone left homemade pizza. I call dibs. What time is your dad back?"

"He's doing the overnight shift," Anna said. "Again."

"More pizza for me, then. Let's go." I pulled open her dresser drawer and extracted her favorite red sweatpants. I spotted her white cable knit sweater on the floor and grabbed that, too.

"Here," I said, tossing the clothes onto the bed. "You don't have to shower tonight, but definitely tomorrow. I'll hold you under the water myself if I have to. See you downstairs."

I pulled open her bedroom door and headed for the stairs, singing the chorus to "Right Back At Ya" and eager for the comfort of hot pizza in Anna's mom's kitchen. I glanced over my shoulder to see Anna step out of her dress and stuff it into her tiny plastic trash can.

I continued down the stairs. Anna was going to be OK.

She was going to stay with me.

Chapter 6

On the other end of the phone call, there was silence, save for the dull buzz of clacking keyboards.

"Hello?" I asked. "Jenna?"

"I'm here," my friend said. "I'm….processing."

"Yeah," I replied. "Good luck with that."

"Anna and *Matthew*?" Jenna said. "Damn."

I stood at the drafting table in my office, staring down at my initial drawings for a pitch my boss, Tom Dawson, was giving to restore a 19th-century mill building in Massachusetts.

"…sense at all."

"I'm sorry, what?" I asked Jenna.

"I said this makes no sense at all," she repeated. "For either of them. God, Kay. How are you doing? How can I help?"

"I don't know, Jen," I said. "I just wanted you to know in case Anna reached out."

"I can't imagine she would," Jenna said. "I mean, she and I haven't been that close for a while. Hey, want me to do a hit piece on her?"

I laughed. "Is that what *New England Magazine* is up to these days? Take downs?"

"It's the natural progression of reality TV culture, Kay," she said. "I don't make the rules; I just know which ones to live by."

"I'm good for now, but I'll text you something cryptic like 'the lights of Mandelle are green' if I change my mind," I said, summoning the name of our old dorm at Holyoke.

Jenna chuckled, then her tone grew somber. "Have you thought about counseling?"

"For me?" I asked. "I feel like I haven't had much time to think about it. I was going to hear what Matthew had to say when we have dinner tomorrow and go from there."

"I meant for the two of you. Together," she said. "It's just too out of left field, Kay. I – oh, hey, I gotta run. I'm late for a meeting. I'll call you later, OK?"

We said our goodbyes and hung up. I rolled up my drawings and inserted them into a tube, thinking.

Counseling.

It's too out of left field, Kay.

I didn't hate the idea. And it would give me something to bring to the table – literally and figuratively – when we met. Why should he get to dictate the discussion?

"I don't make the rules, but I know which ones to live by," I muttered.

A minute later, a light knock interrupted my toxic fantasy involving Anna, Matthew, and a spilled vial of flesh-eating bacteria.

I turned from the window to see Tom in my office doorway, smiling, a postcard in one hand. The smile shifted to a look of concern. "Is everything OK?"

I forced my shoulders to relax and returned his smile. "Of course," I lied. "Ever have one of those moments where you're sure you forgot to do something at home and can't think of it? I was just having one of those, but it's fine. False alarm."

Tom's eyes crinkled in understanding as he walked toward my drafting desk. "Those are the worst. For me, it's always 'did I turn off the coffeemaker?'"

I chuckled, relieved – and a tiny bit impressed – by my convincing lie. If he only knew what I had *really* been thinking.

Tom laid the postcard on my desk. "Can you go to this? It's tonight. It's pretty much now, actually. I'm sorry for the short notice; I let it kick around in my inbox for too long before opening it. I'm kicking *myself* now."

I picked it up. Not a postcard, an invitation. A heavy cardstock of glossy black, gold, and cream, cordially inviting me – or someone at Dawson & Tilman Restoration Architects LLC – to a cocktail reception sponsored by a national real estate firm and hosted by the regional chapter of the League of Historic American Theatres.

"A fundraiser for restoration work," I said. It wasn't a question. Tom nodded.

"The CEO of the sponsoring firm is apparently gung-ho for restoring our fine country's historic independent theatres."

"And Dawson and Tilman are certainly gung-ho about doing the restoring," I added.

"Absolutely. So, can you go?" Tom pressed. "I'm going, but I'd like you there with me."

I paused. It was Tuesday. My mom picked Holly up from school on Tuesdays and usually brought her home in time for dinner with Matthew and me. When there was a *Matthew and me.*

It's nothing, Kay. Just work. A big new client. I won't be home for dinner.

Now *I* might have the big new client. A *real* one, at that.

I don't make the rules, but I know which ones to live by.

I smiled at Tom. "I would love to come. I'm glad you asked me. Just a sec, Tom."

I drained the last swallow of my now-cold lemon ginger tea and glanced at my watch. Right. Holly first. I tapped my parents' number into the phone on my desk, fingers flying from sheer muscle memory, and confirmed that Holly could have dinner with them.

I promised to be there by eight and hung up, then strode over to the floating shelves behind my desk moving with the practiced efficiency that six years of working motherhood had created. As Tom watched, a look of curious bemusement on his face, I lifted a makeup bag from one of the black canvas storage cubes lining the lowest shelf. Reaching into my office's closet, I pulled out a crisp white blouse on a hanger, still shrouded in dry cleaner's plastic. I kicked my pointed toe flats into the closet and stepped into a pair of red patent leather heels.

I grabbed my suit jacket from the back of my chair and marched past Tom, heels clacking on the polished concrete. "I'll meet you downstairs in 10 minutes. Don't be late."

"Wow. Is there a red 'S' under that shirt?" Tom called.

"No," I replied. "And if you mistake me for Superman one more time I won't let you ride in my invisible jet."

* * *

Then (Holyoke, Massachusetts – September 2004)

"Should I use two Command Strips or one?" Anna asked me, frowning at the frame protecting the Spice Girls tour poster I'd given her the year before.

I studied the package. "It says one can hold up to five pounds," I said, tossing the strips onto her dorm bed. "You're the math major; do your thing, Sporty."

We were putting the finishing touches on our room on the second floor of Mandelle North. My parents and Mr. Becker had moved us into our Mount Holyoke dorm the day before, and there were still three days to fill before Convocation. We were pacing ourselves.

I set a mini succulent on the narrow windowsill and looked beyond the glass to Lower Pond.

"When you're done with that, let's go outside," I said. "We can hang out by the pond or walk the trail."

Anna nodded and pressed both hands on the strip, securing it to the wall. She'd been quiet since we arrived, and I knew she was feeling the loss of her mom all over again. I'd seen the same hollow look in her eyes on the morning of our graduation. And Mother's Day. With every new milestone, her grief returned.

She hung the framed poster and stood back to study its placement. I stepped beside her and slung my arm around her back.

"Nothing short of perfect," I remarked. "And can I say – again – how happy I am that we're roommates?" I lowered my voice. "I'm so glad we're doing this together."

She turned to me and smiled, a real one, and we hugged. "Me too," she said into my shoulder. "Now let's get out of here and be social like your mom instructed."

I rolled my eyes at the memory and opened the door to the hallway, nearly knocking down a girl exiting the room across the hall.

"Sorry!" I exclaimed, as she closed her door, cutting off what sounded like a French ballad. "You OK?"

The girl was my height, with long black hair tied up in a high neat ponytail. Her dark brown eyes widened with low-level panic as she took both of us in. The names on the two squares of bright yellow construction paper on the door behind her read "Jenna" and "Sylvie"

"Save me from my roommate," she whispered. "Where are you going, and can I come with you?"

Anna shut our door. "We're heading to the pond trails," she said in a faux serious whisper. "Blink once if you need us to smuggle you out of here."

She exhaled with palpable relief and we headed to the stairs. "Thank you, I'm Jenna."

We pushed open the door to the sunny, hot afternoon and walked over the grass to the pond three astride, Jenna in the middle.

"What's up with Sylvie?" Anna asked, her eyes sparkling with curiosity. *That's a good sign*, I thought.

Jenna glanced over her shoulder, as if expecting Sylvie to be sneaking up behind her. "She's an unbearable Francophile," she began. "And don't get me wrong, I love me a good croissant, but she's played nothing but French pop for two straight days. She has this crazy Parisian accent and pretends to 'accidentally slip into' French when we're talking."

"Where's she from?" I asked.

Jenna looked at me. "Buffalo."

Anna and I stopped and stared at her, waiting for a punch-line. Jenna held up one hand and placed the other on her heart.

"I swear to God."

Anna threw her head back and laughed. It had been so long since I'd heard it that I had a rush of gratitude for both Jenna and the odd Buffalo native who was reinventing herself as Juliette Binoche. We gasped and giggled as we walked further into the forested campus trail.

Jenna was a journalism major from Marblehead, Massachusetts, and I liked her immediately. Not just because she'd given Anna a desperately-needed belly laugh; she was cheerful and open, with just enough first-week-of-college nervousness and insecurity to make me feel like I wasn't nuts for feeling the same.

When we'd circled the pond and returned to Mandelle, the late afternoon sun was sinking behind the trees. There was an hour to go until dinner, and then our first official floor meeting. I grinned at my two friends, one old and one new.

"What?" Anna asked me.

"You guys wanna do…happy hour before dinner and the floor meeting?"

"How?" they said together.

"There's lemonade n' stuff in our fridge, right?"

"Yeah," Anna said. "Your mom brought it."

I grinned wider and turned to Jenna.

"I have a sister," I explained. "An *older* sister. She bought something for me, too."

Anna nudged me. "You've been holding out on me!" she said.

I laughed. "I was waiting for the right moment," I said. "This feels like it."

I refocused on Jenna. "You don't have to drink, obviously, but come and hang out in our room if you want."

"I can't pass up my first college happy hour," Jenna insisted, pulling open the door. "I don't make the rules; I just know which ones to live by."

Once in our room, I hefted the glass handled bottle of Tito's out of my backpack with a flourish. We experimented with varying blends of lemonade, cranberry juice and vodka until we arrived at a pleasing mixture we dubbed the not-French Martini.

Buzzing contentedly, I asked out loud the question that had been drifting in the back of mind for the last few days.

"So where do we meet boys? And when do we meet them?"

Jenna upended her Solo cup and moved to mix herself another. "All in good time, young grasshopper," she said. "If there's a decent party happening on one of the other campuses, word inevitably will arrive here."

I sighed happily. "Oh, good. Boys, Sporty! *College* boys." I drained my cup and shook it at Jenna, the ice rattling flatly against the plastic. "And there'll be tons of them. No more wading through a shallow puddle of Billy f'ing Arthurs. Ugh."

Anna giggled and hiccupped.

"I told him he was a B-cup in sixth grade," she said. "Remember?"

"Remember?" I yanked a decorative sunflower pillow from behind my back and threw it at my best friend. "It was the day I pledged my undying loyalty to you."

"I don't know who Billy is," Jenna said, kneeling carefully onto my bed with our now-full cups. "But I don't like him. Here's to moving beyond the shallow puddle and into deeper waters."

I tapped my cup to hers, and gestured to Anna, including her in the toast.

"And here's to friends, old and new," I said, wagging a finger importantly, if a little tipsily. "Friends first, and guys second. Can we agree on that? Right here?"

"Yeeesssss," Anna cheered. "What'd you say, Jen? I don't make the rules; I just know which ones to live by. Well, I'm livin' by that one."

"Girl Power, Sporty," I said. And we hiccuped in harmony.

Chapter 7

My plastic smile was hurting my face. I felt like Looming Divorce Barbie. A knockoff one at that. I turned from the doorway of the family room, where Holly was busily showing her father the painting she had made during yesterday's "sick day." Ducking into the tiny powder room off the kitchen, I allowed the facade to fall and stared into the mirror to give myself a silent pep talk.

It's going to be OK, I said to my nervous reflection. *It's just dinner. With your* husband.

I smoothed on a coat of clear gloss and gave myself a final once-over. My forest green silk shirt – with a wide and almost-but-not-quite-too-deep neckline – was one of Matthew's favorites, and once again I'd secured his gold locket around my neck, because why not? I'd taken extra care with my hair, too, leaving it in soft waves around my shoulders.

Remembering that smell was the sense most closely linked to memory, I'd dug out my old perfume from a box in my closet. Hints of it filled the small bathroom as I stood, exhaling out the worst of my nerves.

Matthew came into the kitchen, holding Holly's hand, as I was switching off the bathroom light. His smile looked as fake as mine. Adulterer Ken.

"Ready?" he asked, too brightly. "I'm hungry."

I nodded and looked down at Holly. "Got everything?"

"Yup."

"Tap shoes? Ballet shoes? Dance booties?"

"Yup, yup, yup," she chirped.

"Dance booties?" Matthew asked, looking at me quizzically.

"For in between classes, or in between numbers on recital day," I clarified. "They're new."

An expression – Pain? Guilt? – flashed across his face.

See? I thought. *You miss things when you leave your wife and daughter.*

We left the house together, stepping gingerly over the puddle of yesterday's rainwater that still lingered at the base of the brick steps. *I gotta call that masonry guy,* Matthew had said after every storm in the last year. *The step swamp is back.* This time, he skirted the pooling water and said nothing.

Holly, however, descended behind me with a joyful splash in her waterproof boots, sending a sprinkle of drops onto my bare shins.

"Hols!" I exclaimed. "That's freezing."

I climbed into the passenger seat of Matthew's red Audi and opened the glove compartment, where I knew there'd be a supply of Dunkin Donuts napkins. Inside, on top of the latest napkin stash, was a piece of cardstock-weight paper with the logo of Hudson Hotels, a local hotel chain. The kind of paper they tell you to place on your dashboard overnight. I grabbed a napkin and snapped the compartment shut, dabbing at the droplets on my ankles and reeling.

Was Matthew staying in a hotel?

Throughout the short ride to the studio, my husband

peppered Holly with questions. *How was your weekend? What did you do? Did you miss me? Because I missed you!* I stared out the passenger side window, occasionally turning to add my own details to Holly's running commentary.

We pulled into the public parking lot on the corner of Penhallow and Bow, Matthew nosing his Audi into his preferred end space. He always told Holly it was to leave the closer spaces to people who had trouble walking. It was true-ish, but I knew it was also because the end spaces were less likely to get dinged by other passenger doors.

He turned off the engine, but didn't unbuckle his seatbelt. "I'll wait here," he said, as Holly and I climbed out of the car.

I stooped down to meet his eyes. "We're going across the street for dinner, aren't we?" I said, jerking my head in the direction of Water View "So come in with us. Say hi."

I held his gaze for a beat longer. *Like you used to do*, I added silently.

A minute later, we pulled open the dance studio's sun-bleached wooden door, nestled between a consignment boutique and the Portsmouth Fabric Company. Holly bounded up the stairs to the building's second floor, hung up her jacket and plunked down on the bench next to her friend and classmate, Monica. The girls traded their street shoes for booties, Holly proudly showing off her sparkly neon green pair.

I greeted Monica's heavily-pregnant mother, Cindy, offering the standard *how much longer* and *how are you feeling* small talk, and thanked her again for the Friday sleepover.

"Anytime. They had a blast," she said. "You look so pretty, Kay. Are you two heading out somewhere special?"

"Thanks. Just across the street," I said, feeling my fake Barbie-smile spread across my face. I half-turned to Matthew and placed my hand lightly on his back. "It's our little Wednesday night ritual."

Cindy tilted her head at us. "Aw, you guys are so cute," she said, rubbing her belly absently. "I can't remember the last time Greg and I went out alone. I'm a little jealous."

I smiled back and waved goodbye, swallowing a surge of my own jealousy at her growing – and seemingly stable – family. Outside, navigating the uneven brick sidewalk, I braced for a quiet admonishment from Matthew over the "Wednesday night ritual" comment, but none came.

"You do look nice," he offered instead as we crossed the street to the restaurant. "Oh, hey. It looks busy for midweek. That's nice to see."

The emotional whiplash was making me dizzy. My mind ticked over Matthews's behavior in the last twenty-four hours, searching his gestures for hidden meaning. I weighed *you do look nice* against his stoic ignoring of the step swamp. His "I'll come home" on the phone yesterday with his new reluctance to come into the studio with me.

But he'd left. He'd been gone for four nights. I had nothing to weigh against that.

Except the hotel parking permit. *Which*, the half-empty side of me thought, *could have been a memento from a month-old tryst.*

No, the half-full side chimed. *Matthew's not that sloppy.*

True, half-empty agreed. *The last four months proves that!*

So what was going on?

I thought of my conservation with my parents Sunday night. My tearful confession that despite everything, I did, in fact, want my husband back.

Maybe he wanted me back as well.

We reached the entrance to the bar, and Matthew held the door for me. We opted for a corner table near the windows and ordered our traditional Tuesday night drinks. A lemon drop martini for me, an old fashioned for him. As the waiter left with our order, I was suddenly very aware of being alone with Matthew for the first time since I threw him out of our house on Sunday night. I looked out at the row of tugboats in the old harbor with growing unease.

"Oh my God," I blurted. "I'm terrified right now."

My eyes misted over. Matthew deftly swiped the clean napkin from under his water glass and pressed it into my hand.

"It's OK," he said. "It's going to be OK."

I held the napkin to my eyes, willing – pleading with, actually – the lump in my throat to recede. When I was able to look at my husband again, our server was approaching with drinks in hand.

"Here you are," he announced. "Will you be ordering some dinner as well?"

"Yes," Matthew said. "But give us a few minutes."

I glanced down at my lemon drop. It was translucent. I sipped it and winced.

"Ugh, it's pure vodka," I said, craning my neck to spot the bartender. "Alan's not here tonight, I guess."

Matthew plucked the orange wedge from his old fashioned and squeezed it over my glass. He dropped the fruit into my drink and then lifted his water glass, pouring a tablespoon into my cocktail.

I sipped again, and smiled weakly.

"You fixed it."

He smiled back. "I always do."

* * *

Then (Holyoke, Massachusetts – March 2006)

Anna's red Ford Focus whined at the start of the hill on Route 116 in Hadley, Massachusetts. She patted the dashboard gently.

"Come on, baby," she cooed. "You got this."

"What's under the hood, a blender?" I asked.

"Shhh," Anna chided. "You'll hurt her self-esteem."

I sipped Zima from my water bottle and watched the trees flash past, bobbing my head to Corinne Bailey Rae in the car's CD player. "This is my first 'ZooMass' party," I told her. "What should I expect? Keg stands at the door? Togas?"

She laughed, glancing at me before turning her attention back to the road. "No. Well, maybe if we were going to one of the towers in Southwest, which we're not. And it's only your first party because *Reginald* wouldn't deign to imbibe with the commoners." This last bit was said in Anna's version of a snooty British accent.

My shoulders tightened at my ex-boyfriend's name. Anna never warmed to Reg, dismissing him as "Mr. Darcy's more pompous, less likable cousin" when he showed up at an off-campus Holyoke party this past September, the start of our sophomore year. A study-abroad student from the University of Kent in Canterbury, Reg had me – and several of my friends – at "'Ello."

For the next five months, I regularly took the free campus shuttle north to Amherst College. Those trips came to an abrupt halt in early February, when I floated the idea of spending my junior year abroad in Canterbury with him.

"But you've just declared for Architecture, 'aven't you?" Reg said. "A year abroad would set you back, wouldinnit?"

"Not really," I reasoned, trying not to see the panic in his eyes. "And I could use the year to finish up the requirements for my Art History minor."

Less than an hour later, I was waiting for a return bus to Mount Holyoke, tears streaming down my face. Not only had Reg's response to my year abroad been a resolute *no,* he also decided that we needed "some time apart."

"Kay?" Anna's voice shook me into the present. "You OK?"

"Yeah, fine," I lied, sipping more Zima. "Well, I'm a little nervous, I guess."

"It'll be fun, you'll see," Anna said. "And you've been in your Reggie-induced isolation for a month. That shit is *over.*"

I shrugged.

Anna sighed. "OK, I promised myself I wouldn't do this, but you leave me no choice."

Ejecting Corinne, Anna pulled her battered *Spiceworld* CD from the driver's side pocket, popped it in, and queued up "Spice Up Your Life." The quick drumbeat was infectious, and it shook me out of my wallowing. I grinned and shimmied my shoulders.

"When you're feeling sad and 'lone, we will take you where you gotta go," we sang. "Smiling, dancing, everything is free. All you need is positivity." At this line, Anna pointedly sang at me, rather than with me.

"OK, OK, I got it," I told her, laughing.

As we drove through downtown Amherst, I avoided looking out my window. The last thing I wanted to do was see Reg, or something that reminded me of him. Instead, I shifted in my seat to face her. "So, what's this thing called again?"

"A Round Robin. It's like a whole-floor party. Each room is mixing up a different drink."

"And who invited you? Or us?"

Anna rolled her eyes. "Have you heard one thing I've said this semester? Some friends I made in the Econ class I'm taking at UMass."

We reached the dorms on the eastern edge of campus. Anna maneuvered her car into a space in a lot overlooking a long, seven-story building and turned off the engine.

I peered out the window. "Is that the dorm?"

She nodded. "It's two dorms, actually. We want the left side. Field."

I drained my Zima. Dutch courage. "Lead the way, Sporty."

We crunched down the short hill – still crusted in week-old snow – and followed a group of students into Field through one of the back doors. When the elevator opened onto the fifth floor, a wall of sound enveloped us. Music punctured by short, loud eruptions of cheers. We stepped onto the floor and glanced around. Two hallways extended from the landing, one on each end. The first room off each hallway was a smallish common area. One was dark, save for the fairy lights strung along its walls. Inside, about a dozen girls danced to the All-American Rejects, who were singing about keeping someone their dirty little secret.

I swiveled around to peer into the other lounge. It was bright, and packed with boys all crowding around something. Beer pong, maybe. Or quarters.

"Anna!"

A model-tall, model-thin redhead in a black babydoll dress – hair swept back in a long French braid – skipped out of the darkened lounge. She gave Anna a quick hug then pointed at us both, a red SOLO cup clasped in one hand.

"OK, a quick tour," she gestured at the Beer Pong hallway. "That's Five South. About ten rooms are part of the Round Robin, and our lounge has games."

She turned back to the dancing lounge.

"This is Five North. There's dancing in that lounge, and five rooms are part of the Robin, 'cause Five South is cooler."

Redhead took the last swig of her cup, and marched us toward Five South.

"Drinks. You *have* to try the bocce balls in 517."

Anna craned her neck, scanning the games lounge. "I'll grab something in a bit, Shell. Are the other Econ guys here?"

Shelley nodded. "Yeah, some're playing Beer Pong."

Anna turned and slipped into the Five South lounge. Unsure, and a little annoyed with Anna for ditching me so soon, I followed Shelley into the bocce ball room. Six students were sitting three-across on the dorm room's two beds. A seventh was mixing drinks on the white built-in desk spanning the far wall.

"Tam! Hit us up!" Shelley called out to the drink-maker.

Tammy pointed to a series of cups lined up to her right. "These are good to go, Shell."

"What's a bocce ball?" I asked, accepting a cup from Shelley.

"Amaretto and OJ, cheers," Shelley tapped her cup against mine. "I'm gonna go dance more. See ya!"

I took that to mean *I'm not going to babysit you, New Girl, so don't follow me* and stayed where I was. I sipped my drink. It was sweet. Too sweet. I turned slightly away from Tammy so she wouldn't see the grimace that flashed across my face. Someone else did, though. A sandy-haired boy in a red crewneck sweatshirt.

He chuckled and got up from the bed. "Follow me," he said, his voice low. "I'll fix it."

"I heard that, you uncultured hick," Tammy said, smiling. "My bocce balls don't need fixing."

He laughed and turned left out of the door. I followed him down the hall, farther away from the lounge, to a different room. As the sandy-haired boy crossed the threshold, I paused and looked back, just in time to see Anna being pulled into another room by Shelley, both shrieking with laughter. I followed the boy inside.

The Who played from a wireless speaker. Two boys and two girls occupied the beds. One held a beer, the other three had various soft drinks.

"Are you 'fixing' another bocce ball, Matt?" One of the girls asked him.

Matt grinned and took my cup. He uncapped a bottle of seltzer and added a glug, followed by a half shot of vodka. He stirred it with a plastic knife, handed it back, and gestured to one of the two desk chairs. He sat in the other. I sipped.

"Ooo, this is much better," I said, sitting down. "Thanks. I'm, uh, I'm Kay, by the way."

"I'm Matt," Matt pointed at our companions. "This is Tim, Mikaylah, Heather, and Sam. This is my room. Mine and Sam's."

A new Who song began.

"Oh, I love 'Teenage Wasteland,'" Heather said.

"It's called 'Baba O'Riley,'" Matt and I said in unison. We grinned at each other.

The six of us chatted about music, concerts, and last week's Oscars. Matt brought me another bocce ball from Tammy, and then "fixed" it for me. Tim and Mikaylah left, and Matt and I moved to the bed, backs against the wall and facing Heather and Sam. Our shoulders were touching slightly. It felt nice.

"We still seeing *V for Vendetta* tomorrow?" Sam asked Matt. Matt nodded.

"Did you read the graphic novel?" I said, more to Matt than Sam.

Matt nodded, more enthusiastically this time. "It blew my mind. I'm dying to see the movie. Want to come with us?"

The four of us were debating the pros and cons of various movie adaptations when Anna walked in.

"There you are," she said. Her eyes skipped over to me, then back to Matt.

"Oh, hey, Anna," Matt said. "Guys, this is Anna from Holyoke. She's in my Econ class. I didn't know you were here."

"I've been here awhile," Anna said, studying the space where my shoulder touched Matt's.

"Did you find who you were looking for?" I asked.

She paused, then shook her head. "No. I thought I did, but no."

I turned back to Matt. "What time's the movie?"

As we made our plans, Anna retreated from the room. I didn't stop her.

Or even notice.

Chapter 8

Matthew and I sipped our drinks, unsure of where to begin. Around us, the buzz of the Tuesday evening dinner crowd mixed with the sounds of the harbor outside. I studied the painting – a swirl of bright reds, greens and oranges – on the brick wall over Matthew's shoulder, sensing that, since I insisted on this meeting, I was expected to take the lead. Instead, Matthew surprised me. Again.

"Look, I'm really sorry about Sunday night," he said, staring into his drink. "I was such a dick to you. I don't blame you for kicking me out."

I softened, but stayed silent. *Look at me*, I begged. *Look at your wife.*

His gaze finally lifted to meet mine. "I'm sorry, Kay."

Tears pricked at my eyes again. I swiped at them with the napkin Matthew had given me and then nodded. "Thank you for that."

Matthew leaned back in his seat and ran his hand through his hair. His French blue dress shirt complemented his eyes. It was something I always pointed out when he wore it. Had he chosen it for tonight? I had to know, but couldn't ask.

"You had asked me to explain the…to explain it," he said. "And I did a sucky job. Let's start that conversation over."

He drew in a breath, about to speak, but I was ready. The seed of an idea that I'd been incubating since we spoke yesterday afternoon cracked open.

"Matthew, I really don't think this is the time or place to go into detail about…*that*," I said, glancing around the restaurant. "That's not what I wanted us to talk about tonight. I mean, not exactly."

He took a sip of his cocktail, waiting for me to continue.

"This has come out of left field for me," I began. "You were the two people in the world that I thought I could count on the most, no matter what."

Matthew winced and looked down.

"I'm your *wife*, Matthew. We have a daughter. A home," I said, the last word catching in my throat. I swallowed the lump back down. "That still means something to me. Does it mean anything to you?"

He looked up again and leaned forward. "Of course it does, Kay."

I studied him, thinking of the hotel parking pass in his glove compartment. Questions flitted through my head.

Are you telling me what I want to hear?

Do you love me?

Do you even know what you want?

Are you staying in a hotel?

I couldn't ask them. Not here, not yet. I couldn't risk getting the wrong answers. Instead of a question, I made a statement.

"If it really means something to you, then we need to go to counseling," I said. "You owe it to me, and we both owe it to Holly."

Surprise flashed across his face.

"A counselor," he said, as if trying the word out. "You and I together?"

He was stalling, thinking. Again, I was ready. And this time, my voice was steadier.

"I made a few calls and found one in Foye's Corner. She can see us on Thursday at six. Thurs*days* at six, that is. Starting this week. Joy can babysit."

My hand shook slightly as I lifted my glass and took another sip of my martini. This was it. If he refused, I'd know we were well and truly over.

Matthew hunched his shoulders slightly and rolled his neck. It was his frustration tell. I sensed he felt set up with my *does it mean anything to you*, and now he was irritated he'd taken the bait. He couldn't refuse my request – reasonable as it was – without reverting back into a dick.

His word, not mine.

But was he resisting counseling because he was ashamed of his behavior, or because in his mind he was already gone? I was about to find out.

A part of me hated myself for guilting him into therapy, but what choice did I have? My marriage was like Wile E. Coyote careening toward a cliff on a road slicked with Acme grease. If I had to drop an anvil on it to slow things down, so be it.

Besides, a counselor was a good idea. Couples went to counseling *all the time*. When we sat down and talked properly again, he would see. He would see the mistake he was so close to making.

Matthew drained his glass with a final gulp and gestured to our waiter for a refill. He leaned back in his chair again, his jaw set.

"You're right. I *do* owe it to you. I'll go."

Relief flooded through me. The breath I hadn't realized I'd been holding whooshed out, and all of my bravado went with it. The tears returned, and a few disloyal ones broke free, slipping down my cheeks.

"Really?" I sniffed, swiping furtively at my face with the heel of my hand.

"I'll go," he said again softly, almost to himself. He met my eyes and managed a weak smile.

"Are you staying in a hotel, Matthew?" I blurted.

Shit, I silently cursed my impulsivity.

Matthew looked at me, wary.

"The parking thing in your glove compartment," I explained. "When I grabbed the napkins. I'm not, you know, *stalking* you."

He looked down again and nodded. "For a few days."

My stomach flipped. *He's in a hotel! Not Anna's condo, a hotel!*

He didn't offer more details, and I wasn't going to ask.

"You know you can come home," I ventured. "You can stay in the guest room if you want."

His shoulders tightened again.

"But you don't have to," I said, quickly backing down. "I mean, you can think about it."

He nodded, grateful for the reprieve.

The waiter arrived with his second cocktail and then pointed to my glass, his eyebrows raised. I shook my head.

"What'll you have for dinner, folks?"

I relaxed into my chair for the first time as we ordered. A haddock sandwich for him, lobster ravioli for me, and a farmer's salad to share. He was staying in a hotel, and I had him on Thursdays. On those days, at least, he wouldn't be with Anna.

I had slowed down the trajectory that led straight to the cliff, and I was going to fight and scratch and claw until we were safely back from the edge.

* * *

Then (Holyoke, Massachusetts – April 2006)

Alone in my and Anna's dorm room, I pulled on my new jeans – low-rise, boot cut – and studied myself in the mirror. Something was off. My favorite copper v-neck t-shirt. It didn't work with the jeans. Too baggy. I yanked it off and rummaged through my drawers. Everything suddenly looked Amish.

I couldn't look Amish today. I was meeting Matt, though he didn't know it yet.

Exasperated, I was about to trade my jeans and potential new boyfriend for sweat-pants and a family-size bag of Smartfood when I eyed Anna's dresser. I slid open her middle drawer and pulled out a small dusty rose top she purchased over spring break but never wore. The tag was still on.

I tried it on. It was snug, but in a good way. I sized up the new me. Two inches of midriff showed below the cropped hem of the shirt. Was it too much?

For Matt? Nah, I thought, and snipped off the tag.

Anna wouldn't mind.

"He's not into me," I'd complained to her a month after our *V for Vendetta* date, if you could call it that. He'd invited me, one point in favor of "date." But joining us were his roommate

Sam and a gaggle of Alan Moore fans from Sam's art class. Negative ten points.

Since then, we'd hung out three other times. The invitation always came from Matt through Anna. He'd tell her about one party or other, and we would both go.

"Maybe he's shy," I'd suggested to Anna one night as we were crawling into our beds after one of these non-dates. "Do you think he's shy?"

She shrugged. "I don't think so."

"Well, you know him better than I do," I said. "What do you think I should do? I mean, I have to think he's interested, because he keeps inviting us to stuff, right?"

Anna turned over onto her side to face me. "What about that guy you met at the Ale House," she asked. "He keeps texting you, doesn't he?"

I wrinkled my nose. "Josh? No. He likes opera. I mean, seriously. Who likes opera?"

Matt certainly didn't like opera. Admittedly, I didn't know that much about him from our limited group-hangs, but I knew enough. I knew he grew up in New Hampshire, like me. I knew he was in the School of Management and wanted to work in finance. I knew we had the same taste in movies and music. I knew that on paper, we were perfect.

So why weren't we officially dating?

I took a final glance at my reflection and smiled.

By the end of today we will be, I decided.

During the shuttle ride, I re-read Anna's text message from an hour ago.

Staying here after Econ exam. We're getting an early dinner at Blue Wall and hanging out.

We, I knew, meant Anna's Econ group. Shelley from the

Round Robin. One or two others I had met in passing. And Matt.

Once inside the UMass campus center, I ducked into the restrooms to reapply my pink gloss and make sure my hair – cut into long layers like Reese Witherspoon's – hadn't frizzed in the light spring mist. I gave myself a silent pep talk – *Be confident! Be flirty! Go grab what's yours!* – and headed for the Blue Wall before I could talk myself out of it.

I scanned the large, open food court and spotted Anna's dark brown ponytail. She was sitting at a small square table with Matt, grinning and nodding at something he was saying. He leaned in, gesturing, and she laughed. I could tell that his sandy hair had been recently cut. He was wearing a deep blue t-shirt, the short sleeves snug over his arms.

Here goes nothing, I thought, and sauntered over to the table.

"Hey," I said. "How was the exam?"

Anna and Matt looked up in unison. Anna's brow furrowed in surprise. Matt's eyes flitted to the deep V of my shirt. Anna's shirt. My stomach flipped in pleasure.

"Uh-oh," said Matt. "Here comes trouble. Is there a bocce ball that needs fixing?"

I laughed. Anna smiled.

"Hey. What's up?" Anna asked. "Nice shirt, by the way."

I posed, one hand on my hip, and smiled back at her. "Nothing. I got your text about the hangout. Where's everyone else?"

Anna rose from her seat, an empty cup in hand, and gestured behind her, where Shelley and other Econ students were seated a few tables away.

"I'm getting a refill," Anna said. "Come with me, Kay."

Matt shook his cup at her, the ice rattling inside. "Coke,

please. Since you're up."

"Lazy," she said, taking the cup.

"I believe the term is 'uncultured hick,'" I said, giving him a knowing grin.

Matt looked at me quizzically. "Wow. Coming in hot there, huh?"

"No, no," I stammered, my cheeks warming. "I mean, the bocce ball girl, Tammy. At the party."

"Ah, right. Yeah," Matt said.

I walked with Anna to the soda fountain, cringing.

"What's going on? You OK?" Anna asked, filling her cup with Diet Coke.

"Sure. Why wouldn't I be?"

She passed her full cup to me to hold as she filled Matt's.

"I was just surprised to see you here, that's all," she said. "I thought something might be wrong."

"Nope," I said. "Like I said, I got your text and decided to join you."

I took a half step towards the table, then turned back to Anna.

"That's cool, right?" I asked, handing her back her cup.

She paused to take a sip of her fresh drink.

"Oh. Yeah. Totally. I mean, *duh*."

I gestured to my – her – shirt. "And this is cool, too?"

"'Course. You look hot in it, Baby Spice."

"Good," I said, taking Matt's now full cup from Anna and using my free hand to link arms with her. "Because to paraphrase the real Baby Spice, I'm gonna 'trust it, use it, prove it, groove it, show him how good I am.' I am *going for it*, Sporty."

I shook my hips a little. From the corner of my eye, I could see Matt watching.

Good.

We walked, arm in arm, back to the table. I presented Matt with his new Coke.

"For you, Good Sir," I said.

"Ah, an upgrade from uncultured hick," he said, toasting me.

I sat in the seat next to Matt. Anna walked around to her chair, then picked her backpack from the seat next to hers.

"Where're you going?" he asked. "I haven't finished my story."

I leaned back, outside of Matt's peripheral vision and jerked my head towards Shelley's table. *Go.*

"I'm not leaving," she said. "I'm just sayin' hi to Shelley for a bit."

Matt watched her maneuver through the chairs and backpacks to the rest of the Econ group. I picked up his cup and took a small sip.

"What story?" I asked him. "I *love* a good story."

Chapter 9

"I'd like to begin by hearing from each of you on why you're here, and what you're hoping to get out of this. Who would like to start?"

Elena Garciá sat back in her cream-colored Queen Anne chair and smiled at us. Her long black hair – streaked a little with gray – was loosely gathered in a low bun, and her hands were folded equally loosely in her lap, with one elbow resting on an arm of the chair. She held no notebook. Her legs, clad in sage green linen slacks, were crossed. Behind her hung an abstract artwork depicting balancing stones in soothing shades of gold, blue and pink. I was oddly comforted by the idea that, no matter how heated these sessions might get, those stones wouldn't fall.

I glanced at Matthew, seated at the other end of Elena's taupe suede sofa. I was glad he'd elected to sit with me, as opposed to the matching accent chair catty-corner from the sofa.

He hadn't ended up staying the night after our dinner on Tuesday. We'd driven home after Holly's dance classes and Matthew had taken the lead on our daughter's bedtime routine. An episode of *Phineas and Ferb* after her shower, double-checking her backpack was packed and ready for school, and reading aloud from *Harry Potter and the Chamber of Secrets* in her bedroom.

"I'll be here when she wakes up," Matthew said to me after she'd drifted to sleep. "I'd like to take her to school."

I put away the red lasagna pan I'd washed and dried, mentally clocking *Williams-Sonoma, bridal shower gift from Jenna,* and faced him.

"OK," I said. As much as I wanted to repeat the offer of the guest room, I held back.

"Thanks, uh, for not reading ahead in *Chamber of Secrets* this week," Matthew said. "I really like reading it with her."

I folded the tea towel over the oven door handle. "I know you do."

He opened his mouth to speak, then closed it again and nodded once.

"'Night."

"'Night, Matthew."

Now we were here, in Elena's office. It was time to stop acting.

"I'll start," I volunteered. "So, um, last Friday night I came home from work and Matthew told me that he was having an affair, and that he was…leaving."

My voice was steady. I noted the box of tissues resting on the distressed wood coffee table, and hoped I wouldn't need it.

"I'm here because I'm trying to understand how and why this happened," I said carefully. "And my hope is to figure out what we both want. Whether it's to stay together or split up. Right now, I'm not sure what I want."

I knew this was a gamble. I had opened a door. All Matthew had to do was say *I want a divorce, but let's co-parent for our daughter* in front of Elena and that was it.

I also knew that Matthew loved a challenge. *I'm not sure what I want* might throw him a little. I could sense him looking at me, so I finally turned and took him in. He was looking at me appraisingly.

What do you mean, you're not sure?

I gave him an almost imperceptible eyebrow shrug in return. *You want me? Fight for me.*

"Matthew?" Elena prompted.

Matthew leaned back into the taupe cushion and clasped his hands awkwardly in his lap.

"I'm the bad guy, I guess."

Elena studied him, her expression neutral.

"You're not the bad guy, and you're not the good guy," she said. "You're Matthew, so let's start there. Just tell me why you're here and what, if any, goals you might have for this counseling session."

"I'm here because Kay asked me to come," he said, looking at his hands, which were now in loose fists in his lap. "And I agreed because I owe her the truth. An explanation."

Elena leaned forward, her gaze sharp and intelligent.

"The truth about what?"

I held my breath.

Matthew inhaled as if to answer. Once. Twice. Finally, he spoke.

"The truth about why I cheated on her. With Anna."

"And who's Anna?" Elena asked him.

"Her best friend," he said.

Elena glanced at me, as if to gauge whether I knew this

particular detail. I gave a curt nod. *Yeah, I know this part already.* She turned back to Matthew.

"Before we get to this truth, Matthew," Elena said. "Did you come here today already knowing what you want out of counseling?"

I stared at the abstract painting of perfectly balanced rocks. *Don't fall.*

"No."

Matthew's voice was new to me. It was strange, strained.

He was crying.

I turned to my husband, startled. Matthew didn't cry. He *never* cried.

Yet there he was, half turned from me and Elena, sobbing into the crook of his arm.

I glanced at Elena, stunned. She was quiet and still. Clearly, this was not her first breakdown.

I leaned forward and neatly yanked two tissues from the seashell-themed cardboard box on the coffee table. I laid one hand gently on Matthew's back and pressed the tissues into the hand still curled in his lap.

He dropped his arm from his face and turned to me, pulling me to him. We clutched at each other fiercely. I was stoic as he continued to sob, rubbing his back with one hand and gripping the back of his neck with the other.

"Shhh, it's OK," I murmured. "It's OK."

After a minute or so, his sobs reduced to hitches. Eventually, he untangled himself from our embrace and accepted the tissues, mopping his cheeks. He didn't look at either of us as he did so.

Elena rose and glided to a mini fridge tucked subtly into a corner, hidden by a tapestry and a jade plant. She pulled a small bottle of Poland Spring and placed it on a cork coaster in front of my husband. He still didn't look up. By now he was leaning forward, elbows on his knees, his hands clasped.

"Take your time, Matthew," Elena offered.

He exhaled loudly.

"I need to talk about it," he said.

"That's why we're here," Elena said, soothingly. "To discuss the affair."

"Not *that*," Matthew said, frustrated, flicking his hand. He turned to me, eyes pleading. "I need to talk about it. *It*. You know."

I stared at him, open-mouthed. What was he talking about if not his infidelity?

Elena leaned forward, watching my husband intently.

"What do you need to talk about, Matthew?"

Matthew swiped at the bottle of Poland Spring and cracked it open. He drank most of the eight ounces down in three swallows, then straightened up.

"I need to talk about when we almost lost Holly."

* * *

Then (Holyoke, Massachusetts – April, 2006)

"It's giving me Overlook Hotel vibes," Matt said.

I nodded. "Minus the menacing hedge animals."

Matt glanced at me, his eyebrows raised. "You read the book," he said, clearly pleased. "The hedge animals weren't in the movie." He offered me his fist, and I bumped it.

We were standing at the side of the Seven Sisters Trail, out of breath, looking at the Summit House, perched on Mount Holyoke. The peak, not the college. It was, rather grandly, referred to as "the westernmost peak in the Holyoke range." Given that said range encompassed all of nine miles and 1,000 feet, Matt and I had come here prepared to thumb our New Hampshire noses at the hike. *A hike?* We'd joked. *More like a dawdle.*

Instead, we'd found ourselves ascending, descending, and re-ascending over nearly six hard-fought miles and a cumulative total of 4,000 feet. I guessed hailing from the Granite State didn't count if you've never actually hiked up its mountains.

I didn't mind. On the contrary, I was delighted. I had Matt to myself, having hinted to him that the hike on the Seven Sisters trail would be too much for him. If it took a little challenge to inspire him to come out for our first kinda-sorta date, who was I to complain?

"It's giving me convalescence vibes," I said, studying the seventeenth century hotel. "Like what's-his-name from *Wuthering Heights.*"

"Heathcliff?"

I shook my head. "No, the guy who was being told the story of Heathcliff," I said. "The one who, like, went for a walk on the moor and then had to lie in bed for a month to recover. This is probably where old-timey doctors sent people from Hartford to recover from colds. Fresh 'mountain' air."

Matt laughed at my air quotes of "mountain."

I dug my new digital camera out of my backpack and stuffed my now empty water bottle inside. "Ready?" I asked as I started toward the house.

Matt fell into step beside me. "So what's this assignment

again?"

"My architectural history class," I explained. "The assignment is kind of open-ended. I'm going to do a photo essay of this place."

We climbed the porch steps to the entrance, where we were greeted by a park ranger offering to book us into the guided tour. We declined in favor of ambling the old hotel on our own.

Matt followed me as I took my pictures, zooming in on period light fixtures and crown molding.

"So why this place?" Matt asked. "Why the Overlook? Or, Heathcliff's Hotel?"

I tossed him a wry grin over my shoulder. "I dunno. I've always just really liked older buildings. Have you ever been to Strawberry Banke in Portsmouth?"

Matt nodded. "Once. Field trip in elementary school."

I widened my eyes in mock disbelief. "That's it? Philistine. I love that place. This one–" I gestured around the dining room we were currently in. "It's not even that old, comparatively speaking. I mean, when I go to Europe for grad school in a few years, this will seem downright modern."

"You want to study in Europe?" Matt turned from a wall filled with black-and-white photographs against textured wallpaper. "I do, too."

This surprised me. I felt a twinge of guilt at the discovery, like I should have known this about him. But how could I? It had been an effort just to get him to the Summit House, alone.

"Where?" I asked.

"I want to go to LSE," he said. "The London School of Economics."

I grinned again. "Following Mick Jagger?"

Matt gave a half-hearted smile in return. "My grandfather."

I widened my eyes. "Mick Jagger's your grandfather?"

Matt's semi-smile turned genuine and he chuckled. Satisfied that I'd broken through his shell, I softened my gaze. "Tell me about him."

"He was a Mancunian, a Mank," Matt began. "That's what they call you over there when you're from Manchester. He probably had a bit of a chip on his shoulder going to school in London as a Northerner."

"A Northerner? Like, compared to being from London?" I asked. "Would that matter?"

"Some, yeah. To them," Matt said. "But that probably pushed him even more to do well."

"And did he?" I asked, sensing that Matt wanted to talk more about him.

"Top of his class," Matt said, his eyes shining with pride. "And an office in the Hancock Tower waiting for him when he landed from the UK."

I powered off my camera and stuffed it back into my backpack. "Wow, he moved across the ocean for good that young? He must be really brave," I said. *Please be the right thing to say*, I added silently, appealing to any of the Seven Sisters listening at the moment.

We had stepped back onto the porch, Matt and I. He took a few steps forward and leaned on the railing, taking in the Pioneer Valley below.

"He was the bravest, toughest person I knew," Matt said.

In this distance, thunder rumbled.

"Is he your mom's dad or your dad's?" I asked, deliberately changing the tense from past to present. *Is he still alive?*

"My mom's," Matt said. "My dad wasn't, uh, really around

for us, but Grandad was. He did all the father-son stuff with me, you know? Scouts, tying ties, all that stuff. He was a rock for my mom. And me. He could've moved back to England, which is something I know he always wanted to do, but he wanted to be here for us more. He was just…great. He died, though. In January."

He swallowed and shifted his gaze slightly away from me.

I touched his arm. "I'm so sorry, Matt. I really am. He must have been amazing, for you to want to follow in his footsteps like that."

Matt's face flattened a little, as if slipping on a mask. Whatever moment we'd almost had, it was gone. Stuffed down somewhere.

"Man, I'm hungry," he said, too brightly. "I'm glad there's a bus back to my car. Let's get this last leg of the trail done and get something to eat."

We descended the porch steps and began walking across the field, when Matt stopped examining the sky.

"I think it's gonna rain, Kay," Matt said, uncertain.

Rain wasn't quite the word. Rather, the sky unzipped and fat, determined drops the size of quarters fell on us. Chastened, we ran back to the safety of the Summitt House porch, gasping for breath. We glanced at each other and then out into the rain, laughing at the suddenness of the downpour.

I touched Matt's arm, and reached for the only thing I could think of to say.

"I'm sorry about your grandfather," I said, exhaling rain onto Matt's face, inches from mine. "Do you look like him?"

Matt nodded, and pressed his forehead against mine, his hands on my waist. The wind swept warm sheets of water onto us. We ignored them. Matt tilted his head slightly and

kissed me. Briefly, then deeply.
He tasted like rain.

Chapter 10

Elena Garciá was still leaning forward, glancing from my face to Matthew's.

"Holly is your daughter, yes?" She asked. I nodded. "And what happened that you almost lost her?"

"I–," I rested a hand on my husband's shoulder. "Do you mean in April?"

He nodded, his hands gripping the damp tissue.

"We almost lost her?" I asked him. "She almost *died* that night?"

He nodded again, another sob escaping his throat. A heavy numbness settled over me, like an invisible weighted blanket.

I looked at our therapist. "Holly had to go to the emergency room last April, a few days after school vacation. She had bacterial meningitis." My voice felt robotic.

"That must have been terrifying for you both," Elena said.

Matthew dropped the tissue in the wicker waste basket next to the sofa and brought his hands to his face, his fingers massaging his temples.

"They kept her there for a few days, to be safe," I added. "I had gone into Boston to have dinner and see *Hamilton*. With Anna. When Matthew called me and said he was taking her to the hospital with a fever and neck pain, we left the restaurant and headed straight back. The ride…could I have some water as well, please?"

Elena extracted another mini bottle from the dorm-sized fridge. I sipped and swished the liquid around my suddenly-dry mouth.

"The ride was…hell. It was torture. Praying one moment and imagining the worst the next. And it took so *long* in rush hour." I took another small sip from the bottle. "I was so relieved – so, *so* relieved – when Matthew met me in the waiting room and he smiled."

I shifted to face him again. "I think I collapsed when I got to you, didn't I?

He lifted his head and met my gaze, a faint smile appearing as he nodded. "You were, understandably, a mess."

"I remember sobbing, and you saying 'she's OK, it's OK,'" I said, studying him. "Then you brought me to the ICU."

I looked back to Elena. "We couldn't be in the room with her yet. The doctor wanted to wait another hour or so before moving her to a room where they could give us cots to sleep on."

Elena was silent. I re-focused on my husband.

"When they did move us into a room together, the doctors said that she was past the worst of it," I said. "I was so grateful. Grateful to be there with her, watching her sleep. Grateful that I didn't have to imagine the worst anymore, and I could focus on getting her better. But you–"

I touched Matthew's shoulder again. "You didn't imagine the worst. You *saw* it. And I never asked you to tell me about it."

He turned to me, his eyes wet. "I wouldn't have told you if

you did," he said. "I didn't want to put you through it."

"Through what, Matthew?" Elena prompted gently. "What didn't you want your wife to know?"

Slowly, he told us. The rushing of medical staff. The urgency in the doctor's instructions. The cooling blanket, the hushed talk of brain swelling, and the dizzying moment when they nearly used a pediatric defibrillator.

As he spoke, it became clear how very, very close we came to losing Holly. Even during my darkest moments as Anna and I inched north on Route 95 – Anna gripping the wheel and insisting *she's fine, Kay. She's fine. They're just being safe –* what I had been feeling was nothing in light of what Matthew had seen firsthand. And he had shielded me from all of it.

When he was finished, a fresh set of damp Kleenex crumpled in his hands, Elena leaned forward again, her voice gentle.

"Why didn't you share any of this with Kay, Matthew?"

Matthew's eyes flared. "Why *didn't* I? How *could* I? It would have destroyed her."

Destroyed? A flicker of anger nudged at the invisible weighted blanket, and I was finally able to throw it aside.

"I'm her *mother*, Matthew," I said, forcing myself not to shout. "You could have told me. I think keeping it to yourself destroyed *you*."

He winced. "I was trying to protect you."

Elena sat back in her Queen Anne. "Kay could have shared the trauma of Holly's illness with you, Matthew, and taken some of that burden," she said. "Do you think she has a point that holding it in affected your relationship?"

Matthew thought for a moment, then gave an uncertain shrug. "Not at first. We were so focused for the next week on making sure she was OK. That there wouldn't be any...

permanent damage."

How does this all lead to Anna? I wanted to scream. *That's why we came here!*

"And after that?" Elena prompted.

Matthew ran his fingers through his hair. Once, twice. He was stressed.

Just like last Friday, when he told me he was leaving.

"I stopped sleeping," he began. "I couldn't sit still, couldn't focus outside of work. Everything reminded me of that night. Ambulances. Sirens. Even just seeing other kids. And every time, *every single time*, I remembered how close my life had come to completely changing forever."

My eyes misted – for the hundredth time this week – and I swiped at them with my sleeve. "You could have told me," I said again.

My husband had been trying to be the rock. Reliable and unflappable.

Like his grandfather, I thought.

"And when you thought about your life 'completely chang-ing forever,'" Elena said. "What did that look like?"

The weighted blanket returned, heavier, and this time with a faint ringing in my ears. Once again, I shifted my focus to the abstract painting behind Elena. Those rocks weren't going to fall, and neither would I.

"It looked like…the road not taken, I guess."

Elena stayed silent, giving my husband the chance to elaborate. He didn't.

"And which road didn't you take, Matthew?" Elena asked.

The ringing grew louder. I stared at the third rock in the stack, painted in a warm shade of honey. Beside me, Matthew sat up straight and exhaled a long, slow breath.

"The one where I got together with Anna instead of Kay."

* * *

Then (Portsmouth, New Hampshire – 2006)

The June sun streamed into the kitchen, catching wisps of smoke from the not-quite burned bacon. They trailed in Anna's wake as she carried the plate to the table, neatly skirting around Joy, who was stabbing her finger at the coffeemaker.

"Just tap it once," I told Joy as I flipped the French toast. "It's temperamental."

She sighed, holding her hands up in defeat. "This is why I drink tea," she said.

I reached over and gave it a quick, single tap. The red light came on, followed by clicks and gurgles as the machine slowly rose to the task. Soon freshly ground Nantucket Blend would mix with the bacon, and our parents would know it was time to head downstairs and pretend to be surprised.

"When it's your anniversary, I'll make you tea," I offered, heaping the last of the French toast onto my mom's sunflower serving platter, her favorite. "Can you grab the fruit?"

We set the toast, bacon, and mixed berries at the center of the large round table, nestled into what my mom proudly called "the breakfast nook." The rest of us called it a corner. Except for the sunflower platter, the table was set with my parents' pale blue Royal Doulton wedding china. Every year at these "surprise" anniversary breakfasts, my mom would pretend to be worried about breakage. I suspected she was quietly delighted they were being used.

Anna was filling the creamer with half and half when the soft pat of my mom's slippered feet on the stairs – and the heavier thuds of my dad's behind her – reached us. We hurried into place.

"Surprise!" we yelled in unison. "Happy anniversary!"

Mom beamed back and hugged each of us in turn as Dad made a beeline for the coffee pot.

"Girls, you spoil us," he said, ignoring the china cup on the table and pouring coffee into his favorite New England Patriots mug, roughly the size of a rain barrel. It matched his faded navy t-shirt, which clung a little to his stocky, five-foot-nine frame.

Mom gave Anna a final squeeze. "You didn't have to do this," she said.

"Speak for yourself, Helen," Dad said, taking his seat by the window. "Let me at that bacon. Your dad pulling a long shift this weekend, Anna?"

"Yep. A double this weekend as a favor. He'll be doing a lot of that this summer. One of the other firemen is a new dad, so the others are pitching in, donating some of their vacation time and taking his shifts."

We loaded our plates. Mom spooned raspberries onto her French toast and glanced at the three of us. I smiled into my coffee cup, knowing she was going to grill each one of us on our summer plans and was deciding who would be first. Joy would be the easiest. Having graduated with a degree in nursing last year, she was the only one out of school and working full time.

"Joy," Mom said, tucking her shoulder-length salt-and-pepper hair behind one ear. "Were you able to get the time off for Sebago?"

My sister nodded, swallowing her bite of bacon. "Yep. I'll be there."

"Did you get the same place as last year?" Anna asked her.

"We did, thank goodness," she said. "How about you, Anna? Can you come?"

"Oh, hey," Dad interrupted. "What did you decide for the internship, Anna? Was the resumé draft helpful?"

Anna nodded. "It really was, Mr. B. Thank you so much. It wouldn't have looked half as good without your input."

"What internship?" Joy asked her.

I answered for her. "Anna and Matt were encouraged by their Econ professor to apply for this summer job at a consulting firm in Boston," I told Joy. "Matt's doing it. He's subletting an apartment with three of his friends south of Boston."

My mom raised her eyebrows. "Does that mean we'll actually meet the mysterious Matt this summer?"

I stuck my tongue out and gave a short raspberry in response. "Probably not. He made this big deal about how important the job is and how it could turn into something full-time after graduation. I'm hoping he might actually start to miss me soon and invite me down."

I hoped I sounded more casual than I felt. After securing a few more authentic, one-on-one dates with Matt before the semester ended in May, I was skirting the edges between "dating" and "girlfriend."

"Oh, screw that," said Joy. "You're going to wait around for him all summer? Nuh-uh. Kick him to the curb." She balled up her maple syrup-coated napkin and pitched it into the kitchen trash can for emphasis. "Like that."

"Or," my mom said, pointing her fork at me. "You could just lay low, enjoy your summer up here with us, and let him see what a supportive girlfriend you are. Make him wonder what he's missing."

"That's what I told her," chimed Anna. "We're going to leave Boston to the boys and have a girls' summer." She looked at my mother, seeking her approval. Mom nodded firmly in agreement.

Anna nodded at Joy. "But I don't disagree with the 'kick him to the curb' part. More girls time for us."

Joy leaned forward. "I'm guessing you're not doing the internship, Anna?"

Anna shook her head. "I could have. And I was offered a room in the apartment they're all subletting, but I turned the job and the room down. I just decided it wasn't what I wanted."

"What do you want, hon?" Mom asked.

Anna smiled. "Sebago. The beach. Hot Dog Thursdays and Pancake Sundays," she added, looking pointedly at my dad.

He raised his mug to her. "I'll have the grill – and the griddle – ready for you."

My mom scooched forward in her seat to hug her. "That sounds like a perfect summer to me."

"Plus," I added, with unreserved pride. "She scored a much cooler summer job at UNH."

"Is that right?" my dad asked, interested.

Anna nodded. "Yeah, a math professor is starting up a new course in actuarial science – evaluating risk like insurance companies do. I'll be helping with research."

"And not working so much that you'll ignore me for the whole summer," I said, leaning into her.

She leaned into me in return. "You and me. That's the plan. 'Matt who?,' right?"

My dad got up from the table. "Well, that's terrific, Anna. But before one of you starts singing a Spice Girls song, I need more coffee."

Chapter 11

Elena was speaking, saying something about next steps in our counseling and signaling the end of our appointment. I didn't want to get up from Elena's loveseat, much less leave her office. I wasn't ready for the real world yet. I felt raw.

"I realize that right now, next week's session feels like a long way off," Elena said to us both. "But there are several things you can do to make the time productive. Or, at least, not counter productive."

She paused. Matthew and I stayed silent, expectant.

"Matthew, you may want to consider speaking with a separate therapist on an individual basis. To deal directly with the trauma around Holly's health scare, and how that has affected you. Specifically, the anxiety that gets triggered in the ways you referred to."

He looked down and nodded.

"Second, I'd like each of you to write a letter to the other, and bring it with you next week."

"What kind of letter?" I asked.

"It's a letter to your partner about what you feel are their best qualities. What do you love most about them? Why are they so special to you? Write it, but don't share it. Not yet."

In my peripheral vision, Matthew was still looking down. Would he be mentally drafting a letter to Anna while writing mine? About their road not taken? My stomach clenched in equal parts anger and guilt. Anger that we hadn't discussed his betrayal. *Their* betrayal.

But also anger that suddenly I wasn't the only victim, hogging all the sympathy. Entitled to it. Matthew had unburdened himself, finally, and my first reaction was *what about me? Yoo hoo, betrayed wife over here!*

Guilt elbowed my anger aside. *Do better, Kay.* I refocused on Elena.

"When we meet again, I want both of you to read your letter out loud, and our conversation will flow from there."

She leaned back in her seat, looking from one to the other. "Does that make sense to you both?"

I nodded. It *didn't* make sense, not really. But that seemed like the wrong answer.

"Finally," she said. "I gently encourage you to refrain from discussing the infidelity until we meet again."

She shifted her gaze back to me.

"Kay, I understand that this is highly stressful for you, and it may seem insensitive to hold off for another week. But it is my belief that having someone there to guide the initial discussion will be infinitely more productive. I hope you agree."

I nodded again.

"Should we still be living together?" Matthew asked.

I glanced at him, surprised. *Still?* He hadn't slept in our bed in six nights.

"Not that I've…Um, I'm not home at the moment. She

thinks I'm traveling for work. Holly, I mean," Matthew stammered, face reddening. "Should I be at home? For Holly? What should we tell her?"

I studied him, taking in this new vulnerability. Matthew rarely sounded unsure of himself. When the armor did slip, though, it tugged at me. It always had. I felt my body slowly softening, as if being zippered out of a too-small dress.

Elena appeared thoughtful for a few moments before answering. "Ultimately, only you and Kay can answer that," she began. "That said, I can offer some guidance based on my experience and what you've told me this evening.

"You've both indicated that you are not sure of how – or if – you want to move forward in your marriage. Given this early stage in our process, it seems to me that discussing the possibility of divorce" I flinched a little at the *d*-word "with your daughter right now would cause her unnecessary stress. As for your living situation, again, only you and Kay can determine whether that would be beneficial or detrimental to our therapy sessions going forward. But it's an important issue to resolve."

She turned back to me. "Kay? What are your thoughts?"

I exhaled slowly and quietly, my lips forming a small *o*.

"So, a week ago, you said that you were leaving," I said to Matthew. "And just a few nights ago you brought a book about divorce to the house for our daughter."

Matthew's face reddened again. "I know. I'm sorry."

I held up my hand. "I'm not mentioning it to make you feel bad. I'm glad we're here, together. I'm sorry the last six months have been so rough for you. I really, *really* wish I had known what was going on. But I also need you to understand how awful this last week has been for *me*. If you want to come home while we figure this out, you can. I would really like you to, actually."

As I heard myself, I realized – suddenly and wholly – how much I meant it. I wanted my husband to come home. I desperately wanted to be the *aww, you guys are so cute* couple that had date nights during their daughter's dance class. Like we used to be, until recently. I'd somehow missed the abrupt, downward trajectory of my husband's mental health, and then our marriage. He'd hidden it from me, yes, but I should have seen it. At the very least, I shouldn't have taken *it's nothing, Kay, just work* at face value.

I'd also missed the equally sudden implosion of my decades-long friendship with Anna. That particular *screw you* still needed to be unpacked, but I was in no hurry to do it. All I knew right now was that I loved Matthew, and that I'd never be made the fool again.

"You can stay in the guest room if that makes you more comfortable. But listen – don't do it for Holly – at least not entirely. I want you to do it for me. Do it because you want to keep the door open for *us*. For this marriage. If you can't do that, if you're as firm in your decision to leave as you were a few days ago, then don't come home."

I paused, allowing Matthew a chance to interject. He didn't. I took another deep breath, steeling myself for what I had to say next..

"And if you *do* come home, there's no Anna," I said. "You don't see her. You don't talk to her. You don't text her. Or this–" I gestured between him, Elena, and me. "The road that you *did* take? Is done."

Matthew swallowed. I waited.

"I want to come home," he said.

I searched his eyes, unsure of what I was looking for. Then I nodded.

"I'm glad," I said.

Outside Elena's office, we walked the short flight of steps to the parking area. I spotted his Audi in the back of the lot. I had parked in the front. We stopped and looked at each other.

"Will you come tonight?" I asked.

He nodded. "I'm packed. I just need to grab my bag and check out. I'll be an hour or so."

An hour. Enough time to call Anna. Or even see her, albeit briefly.

"Will Joy still be there in an hour?" Matthew asked.

"Probably not," I said. "Why?"

He shook his head. "I'm sure she hates me. I hate myself enough for the both of us tonight."

We stood in the October dark for another moment.

"See you at home," I said, and took a step towards my car.

He nodded, spun on his heel, and walked quickly to the back of the lot.

I drove in silence. Halfway home, I reached into the glove compartment with my right hand. Eyes on the road, I dug my Spice Girls *Greatest Hits* CD from the console and rested it in my lap.

Later, crossing over the Sagamore Creek Bridge, I rolled down the window and flung it into the sea.

* * *

Then (Marblehead, Massachusetts – July 2006)

46 days and 58 miles.

That was what separated me from Matthew. Until today. Until now.

Any minute now.

I glanced across the deck to the sliding door, then to my watch: 6:45. Plenty of time for him to get here before we head to the beach for the fireworks. Maybe not *plenty*. Adequate.

As evening approached, the winds from the ocean picked up. In another few minutes, I'd have to cover up my carefully chosen gingham halter top with my zip-up hoodie from Lone Oak Ice Cream, where I was working all summer.

The deck door slid open, but it wasn't Matt. It was Jenna, bringing me another margarita.

She closed the door with her elbow, keeping a careful eye on the nearly-to-the-brim solo cups, and made it to the table without sacrificing a drop.

"Impressive," I told her, accepting the cup. I immediately sloshed a teaspoon of liquid over the brim and onto my hand.

Jenna laughed as she eased into her seat next to me. "It's a gift. I would've totally aced Fluid Dynamics."

"It's barely *July*," I said. "I'm only just getting my tan nice and even. No school talk."

"Sorry," Jenna said between sips. "But just one more school thing; I'm *so* happy you and Anna are going to be right across the hall from me again this year."

"Me too, babe," I said. "And *I'm* so happy you decided to throw this little soirée. This is great, and I love your house."

Behind us, a cacophony of cheers cut through the otherwise mellow gathering of Holyoke friends and their plus-ones. I turned to see Anna high-five a sunburned guy in a pink Polo shirt, a cornhole board on the lawn between them. She turned to the opponents at the other end of the small yard, her cup raised in victory.

"That's how it's done, bitches!"

More cheers.

Jenna stood and pointed at someone on the losing team. "I warned you, Mick. You wouldn't listen."

Mick grinned and gave her the finger. Jenna laughed and sat back down and peeked into her cup.

"I'm glad we're walking to the beach," she said. "You 'n' Anna are crashing here, right?"

I nodded. "Yeah. Well, unless by some miracle Matt actually wants me to come to his place after."

"Why wouldn't he?"

"How much time do you have?" I joked. "He has to work tomorrow. He's on a deadline. His sublet is too messy, too crowded, too loud. Take your pick."

Jenna looked at me. "Are you cool with that?"

"Yeah, yeah. 'Course," I said. "I mean, it's a big deal for him, this internship. I'm good."

Jenna looked skeptical. I smiled at her.

"He's worth it. Plus, he'll be here any minute. I'm good, Jenna."

Was I good, though?

46 days and 58 miles. An hour's drive. And that was if I drove like my grandmother. I could do it in 45 minutes, easy. But I hadn't seen him. Not once. I was being the patient almost-girlfriend. And my patience was running on fumes.

I snuck a look at my watch. 6:52.

"Well, *I'm* glad to see you, so I win and he loses," Jenna said, draining her cup. "And before Matt the Magnificent gets here and takes you away from me, tell me all about your summer so far. Anna gave me some oddly cryptic instructions to ask you if you've seen any good movies lately?"

I snorted – laughing and dribbling margarita onto my chin – then launched into the story of a drunk Anna accidentally ordering *Pulp Friction* instead of *Pulp Fiction* from the On Demand menu of our hotel room in Montreal. And not realizing it wasn't John Travolta and Uma Thurman until much, much later. The weekend jaunt had been Anna's idea, one of the many "Matt who?" diversions we'd planned for the summer.

I stood, mimicking Anna's attempt to do the twist like Thurman, and her growing frustration and confusion over why the *Friction* actors weren't following the script. I did a spot-on drunk Anna, and she knew it. Which is probably why she'd left the storytelling to me.

Finishing my story – and dance – I caught Anna watching me, a wide grin on her face. She pointed at me.

"It's only July, Kay Kay," she yelled. "We're just getting started!"

Mick draped an arm over her shoulders. "What're we getting started? And whatever it is, will you be my partner?"

Jenna stood and joined me at the deck railing. "Mick! No groping my friends. At least not without their express permission. And what we're getting started is the trek to the beach. Blankets and coolers, people! Blankets and coolers."

7:01.

"We're heading out now?" I asked. "Don't we have, like, two hours until the fireworks?"

Jenna shrugged. "We have to get a good spot before it gets

too crowded," she said. "Call your Romeo and tell him to step on it."

I drifted to an empty corner of the deck and pulled my phone out of the back pocket of my shorts. No call, no text. I brought up his number and pressed *Call.*

"Hey! How's your fourth?" Matt said when he picked up. The background was loud.

"Where are you?" I asked.

"On the Esplanade with some of the guys from work," he said. "Where are you?"

I bristled. "I'm in Marblehead at my friend Jenna's, remember? You were supposed to come meet me here?"

Silence.

"I said I *might* come," he countered.

"No, you said you'd come," I replied. "And why haven't you?"

"Well, jeez, Kay, it's the Esplanade!" Matt said. "I've never had a fourth in Boston. And I have to work tomorrow…and you know, it was just easier to stay here."

"Dude, I'm like less than a half hour away," I said. "It's not like you're taking a pack mule over the Appalachians."

"Kay, you knew what this summer was going to be like…"

I tuned out, scanning the yard for Anna. She was bending over a canvas beach bag, stuffing a fuchsia fleece blanket inside. Behind her, Mick used the opportunity to give her a swat on the ass. She glanced over his shoulder, smiling, then her face turned hard. I recognized the look. She'd probably thought it was me, and was pissed to discover it wasn't.

She whipped around, grabbing Mick's wrist and slinging it away from her, then leaned in, her finger inches from his face. I couldn't hear her words, but I knew what they were.

That was not cool, OK? So unless you want to lose that hand, don't do that again without an engraved invitation. Are we clear?

Anna took no shit. She never had.

"…Kay? Are you there?" Matt asked.

Why did I?

"Yeah," I sighed. "I'm here."

"Anyway, I'll call you tomorrow after work," he said. "Maybe Friday you can…."

Anna slung the bag over her shoulder and looked around, finally spotting me in my new spot on the deck. She beckoned, smiling.

"…but call me Friday morning first, 'cause there's a chance I'll have to work late on–"

"Actually, it's fine," I said. "You know what, Matt? There are plenty of people who actually *want* to hang out with me. Let's just forget it, OK?"

A pause. "Forget this weekend?"

"All of it. This. Us," I said. "It's totally fine, Matt. Have a great summer."

Another pause. "When we get back to school–"

"Nope," I said. "Not then, either. See you."

I hung up, then skipped down the steps to the grass to Anna, feeling light.

"I just dumped my not-boyfriend," I said gaily.

Her eyes widened. "Really?"

I nodded firmly. "Yep. I'm single for the summer…and then some."

"Yes!" Anna pumped her fist. "And I'm here for it. We'll be unstoppable."

She stooped to pick up the cooler of Zima we planned to smuggle to the beach. "Here. I've got the blanket and food. Let's go meet some rich Marblehead guys."

I took the cooler and we headed out after the others. Anna stole a sideways glance at me.

"You OK?"

"Absolutely," I said. "No one puts Baby Spice in a corner."

Chapter 12

"Where's daddy?" Holly asked me, as she hop-scotched along the family room, following a route visible only to her.

"He's running an errand," I said. "He'll be home soon."

My sister looked at me, eyebrows raised. *He will?*

"Holls," I called. "It's almost time to get ready for bed. Is your homework done?"

Hop, hop, jump. "Yup!"

"Is your homework folder in your backpack?"

Jump, hop, jump. "Yup!"

"Have you read? At least one chapter?"

Hop, hop, stop. "*Two* chapters," Holly responded proudly. "Can I watch a SpongeBob before bed?"

"All righty, then," I said. "Auntie Joy and I will be in the kitchen."

Holly hopscotched to the sofa and grabbed the remote.

"Quick, sis," I said to Joy. "Let's get out of here before that theme song comes on. You'll never unhear it."

Holly giggled. Her fingers flew over the remote. "It's gonna sta-aa-aart."

I cupped my hands over my ears and jogged out of the family

room, chirping *lalalalala* as my daughter shrieked with glee.

"Glass of wine?" I asked Joy, once in the kitchen. She nodded.

We sat, and I recapped the counseling session for her. Matthew's revelation about the severity of Holly's illness, his apparent PTSD, and our cautious agreement to move forward with more therapy. When I finished, Joy refilled both our glasses. She swirled her wine for a few moments and took a sip before responding.

"How…I don't know…*authentic* is this abrupt change in Matt, do you think?" Joy asked me. "I mean, there's last Friday, and then today, you know?"

I nodded. "That's exactly what I said in the session. I told him point blank not to come back if he had already made up his mind to leave," I said. "I was very clear on that, and he said he's willing to work on our marriage."

"And he's been staying in a hotel?"

I nodded again.

Joy bit her lip. It was her *I'm mulling something over* look.

"Look, please don't take this as me being unsupportive, because I'm *totally* in your corner," she began. "But doesn't that worry you? Do you think it's possible that Anna finally grew a conscience and called the whole thing off? And now he's realizing that he might end up completely alone?"

I paused, listening for movement from the family room, then leaned closer to my sister, my voice an octave lower.

"I know you're in my corner, and I'm not offended by the question," I said. "But I'm not an idiot, Joy. At least, not anymore. I've thought about that possibility ever since I found out he was staying in a hotel and he agreed to go to couples therapy so quickly. *Of course* it occurred to me."

Joy reached across the table and squeezed my hand. "You were never an idiot."

I shrugged and took a sip of my wine. "Debatable. But there's another possibility, too. Maybe he still loves me. Maybe he left, and as soon as he wasn't sneaking around anymore he realized what he was giving up."

Joy was silent, mulling.

"Maybe both can be true," I added, my voice even lower.

My sister looked at me. "What do you mean?"

"Maybe he and Anna realized that they weren't going to work in the long term, or maybe she kicked him out after he put his feet on her precious little plum-colored chaise. Whatever. As soon as he came clean with me, it was over in a matter of days. And he's thinking, *I could be happy with Kay again. We could get back to where we were.*"

"And you'd be OK with that?" Joy asked. "Again, not judging, just asking."

"Joy, I love him. Until six days ago I was living under the impression that we were going to spend the rest of our lives together, and I was all in for that. Maybe I'll change my mind after this sinks in a little more, but he's my husband and I still love him. At the very least, I have to be willing to *try* to be OK with it."

Joy bit her lip again, then nodded.

"So you didn't discuss their affair at all tonight?" Joy asked.

"No. We'll get into that next time."

"Do you know why he chose last week to finally tell you?"

I shook my head. "No. We haven't gotten that far. We've barely talked about it at all."

"Then there's something you need to know."

My insides twisted. The wine suddenly felt sour in my

stomach. I looked at my sister warily.

"About 10 days ago, I saw them. I saw Anna with Matthew."

I held my breath, waiting for her to continue.

"It was mid-week. I had worked at the hospital the weekend before, so I had a Tuesday-Wednesday break. One of the other nurses – Beth, you know her – got tickets to see Indigo Girls at Harborlights in Boston, and invited me to go."

Ten days ago. My mind scrolled back. He'd told me it was a quick overnight trip to New York. For that big new client. That big new *fake* client.

"We went to this new place in the seaport for dinner beforehand, and there they were," Joy said. "Leaning against the deck railing with martinis and, well, basically making out."

She took a deep breath before continuing.

"They looked so...*familiar*, Kay," she said. "Like they went back a long, long way."

"Did they see you?" I asked. The heavy numbness I'd felt in Elena's office was back.

Joy uttered a humorless laugh.

"Oh, definitely," she said. "I walked up to them, pointed to Matthew and said 'fuck you, you fucking asshole,' and then turned to Anna and–" Joy paused, getting emotional for the first time since I'd crashed into her apartment the week before. "I looked at her and said something like 'I don't even have the words for you; they don't exist. You were *family*, you bitch.'"

My sister swiped at her eyes and drained her glass.

"I texted them both an hour later, and told them they had to tell you by the weekend, or I would," she said. "That was Tuesday. By Friday morning, when you still hadn't called me, I was afraid they were going to chicken out. I called Anna. She told me that Matthew was going to tell you about them that night, so I made sure I'd be home."

The penny dropped. "With dumplings."

She smiled softly.

"Look, I'm sorry I'm just telling you this now. When Matthew was gone it was one thing, but now that he's coming back I really wanted you to know. You can…use this however you need to."

"You mean, keep it to myself and see if Matthew mentions it in therapy?" I asked.

Joy nodded. "Something like that."

I glanced at the clock, more aware now of why my husband didn't want to run into my sister.

"Well, he'll be back soon," I said.

I walked her to the door and we hugged tightly.

"I love you, sis," I said. "Thank you for having my back."

"Always," she said.

"What kind of martinis?" I asked suddenly.

"I don't know. Dirty ones, I think. Why?"

I shrugged. "Eh, if they were cosmos and you threw them on her, the cranberry might stain."

Joy chuckled, then left.

I closed the door, amused by the image of Joy reaming my former best friend. *You were family, you bitch*, when the cloudy memory from Sunday night reemerged.

Are you family?

My body tightened in alarm. Somewhere inside me, my subconscious screamed *not yet, not yet*.

Shoving the thought away, I walked purposefully to the family room. If anything could force this echo back into hiding, it was *SpongeBob*.

* * *

Then (Holyoke, Massachusetts — Spring 2008)

I woke to weak morning sunlight filtering in through the dorm window. Rolling onto my left side, I peeked at my digital clock. 7:27AM.

Too early, I thought, and nestled back into the pillow. It triggered an internal warning that took me a few seconds to place. My final art history paper was due tomorrow, and it needed serious work. Time to rally.

Dang.

I swung my feet out from under my cranberry-colored flannel covers and glanced over to Anna's bed. It was empty. And still made. She had gone to an off-campus UMass party at her friend Shelley's apartment, and apparently it had been a good one.

"In. Ter. Es. Ting," I drawled to Cokie, the *Coca-Cola* polar bear plush I had given to Anna in ninth grade. "Did Anna get some action last night, Cokie?"

Cokie stared back from Anna's pillow, keeping her secrets.

I yanked off my t-shirt and sleeping shorts and pulled on a pale yellow tunic over a pair of black cropped leggings. I slid my feet into flip flops, opened the door, and walked the handful of steps to Jenna's room, my sandals slapping my heels with a dull *thwack.*

I thumped on Jenna's door. After a few seconds, she opened it. Ever the early bird, she was already dressed. She looked more awake than I felt.

"You're up early," Jenna said.

"Art History paper," I explained. "Bane of my existence. I need coffee. You eat yet? Want to come with?"

She nodded. A minute later we stepped into the brightening May morning.

"Where's Anna?"

I smiled at Jenna. "*That* is a very good question," I said. "She didn't come home from Shelley's last night."

Jenna frowned. "Who's—oh, wait. Is Shelley the girl from UMass?"

"Yeah. Finance major."

"That's random," Jenna said. "When did she start hanging out with Shelley again?"

I shrugged. "Just this semester. Anna's taking some advanced stats class there."

We reached the dining hall and loaded up on waffles, bacon, and coffee. It was early for a Sunday, and less than a third of the tables were filled. We grabbed an empty one by a window and sat.

"Did you go to Shelley's too?" Jenna asked.

I wrinkled my nose. "No. To be honest, Shelley and her friends were never my cup of tea," I said. "I was kinda glad when we stopped hanging out with them."

"How come?"

I wiped bacon grease from my fingers as I considered Jenna's question.

"I don't know, exactly," I confessed. "I guess I never really felt welcome around them. Like they tolerated me because they knew Anna and I were a set, but they only wanted her."

"Their loss," Jenna said. "They don't know what they're missing."

She swallowed her bite of waffle and grinned. "So you think

Anna got some last night?"

I grinned back. "I don't know, but we can give her shit about the walk of shame anyway, right?"

We chuckled together and then fell quiet, finishing our food.

I glanced out the window at the campus. "Can you believe we're *graduating* in a few weeks?"

Jenna pushed her chair back and stood, gathering her breakfast dishes. "No. It's so surreal. When I go back to the newspaper this summer it won't be my summer job. It'll be my *job* job."

A smile broke across my face as we returned our trays and headed back outside.

"Speaking of jobs..." I said.

Jenna looked at me, expectant.

"I got the Strawberry Banke job," I said. "They called me yesterday afternoon. Exhibit Caretaker. I start in August."

"Oh my God!" Jenna said, grasping my arm. "That's amazing! I'll come and do a story on you. Front page feature."

I laughed and shook my head. "Weirdo. I'm really, really excited. I'm thinking two, three years there and then grad school."

"That's–" Jenna stopped and nudged me. "Look who's back."

Anna was cutting across the lawn towards our dorm, clad in black jeans and an oversized gray UMass sweatshirt.

"She was so not wearing that sweatshirt last night," I told Jenna, grinning. "And there's no way Shelley would wear something bigger than an extra-small on general principle."

"Let's get details," Jenna said, quickening her pace.

Anna was entering our room when we arrived in the hallway. Jenna broke into a jog, reaching her arm out to stop Anna from closing the door. I, my flip flops threatening to fly off my feet, continued to walk.

"And just what have you been doing all night, young lady?" Jenna said from inside my room. "Or should I ask *who* have you been doing?"

I rounded the corner. Inside our room, Anna was turning her face into her shoulder, as if attempting to hide her wide, semi-bashful smile. I knew this look. It was the look she gave her mom when she was accepted to the University of Chicago. When her secret crush, Jamie Burke, asked her to junior prom. I'd witnessed lower-wattage versions of this look hundreds of times, but only a handful of the full-on ones. It was her *finally – thank God – it happened* look.

"Spill it, Sporty," I said, pushing the door closed.

Anna's eyes widened briefly upon seeing me. A blush creeped across her cheeks.

I laughed at her reaction. "Don't look so guilty," I said. "You're allowed to enjoy yourself. Who is he?"

"Oh, you know. No one, really," Anna said. She peeled off the sweatshirt – revealing a sheer, blush-colored bra underneath – and stuffed it into her hamper.

I watched her as she yanked an emerald green tank over her head and then stepped out her jeans. She climbed into her bed, tucking Cokie under one arm.

"C'mon, Anna," I said. "We've been in a sexual dry spell. Let me live vicariously."

"Speak for yourself," Jenna chimed.

I motioned between myself and Anna. "*We* as in the ones who live in this room," I said to Jenna, then turned back to Anna. "Well?"

She sighed. "A friend of Shelley's. Also in my stats class."

"Are you going to see him again?" I prodded.

She fixed her gaze on the plush bear, stroking the synthetic fur between its plastic eyes. "Maybe. I don't know yet."

I studied my friend for a moment, sizing up her mood. She clearly didn't want to talk about it. Perhaps not in front of Jenna.

"OK, inquisition's over," I said. "You want to get some more sleep?"

I sensed Anna's relief. "God, yes. Will that mess up your plans?"

"Nope," I declared. I adjusted the blinds, darkening the room for Anna, and slung the strap of my messenger bag over my shoulder. "I have a hot date with my art history paper. I'll wake you for lunch. We'll use that gift certificate my parents gave me to the Thai place we like, and afterwards I'll proofread your lit paper. I haven't forgotten."

Jenna opened the door and we left. I glanced back into the room as I pulled the door shut. Anna was curled on her right side, gaze to the floor, that same smile returning to her face.

Finally – thank God – it happened.

Chapter 13

They looked so...familiar. Like they went back a long, long way.

My sister's words gnawed at me as I sat up in bed, attempting to read. I was hyper aware of Matthew's presence in the house. Small sounds I knew so well – the cadence of his walk, the low murmur of his voice as he read to Holly – were suddenly distracting. Even now in the quiet, with Matthew in the guest bedroom, I was struggling to focus on the words in front of me. My mind kept swerving from the plot to the unknowable.

Is he asleep or awake? If he's awake, is he feeling weird about being in the guest room? Is he listening for me? If he's asleep...no, he can't be asleep already. That would be weird. How could he be asleep?!

Frustrated, I closed the book and allowed myself to wallow in Joy's revelation. It made sense that he and Anna would look...familiar; they'd known each other since college. Still, I didn't think that was what my sister had meant.

I thought back to Sunday night, when I asked Matthew when it had started. What had he said?

Sebago wasn't the first time the thought had occurred to me. It was just the first time I acted on it.

Was that true?

I tossed the comforter aside and swung my legs out of bed. I sat, thinking. What was I going to do, walk into the guest room and ask him? When Elena Garciá had expressly advised us not to discuss it?

I glanced at the door to his closet, a little surprised.

Why haven't you been snooping in there this week?

I stood, then sat back on the bed. What exactly was I looking for? A shoebox of hotel receipts? Secret photos?

Photos.

I got back onto the bed, kneeling over to slide open the drawer of Matthew's nightstand where he kept his tablet for reading in bed. I slid my legs back under the duvet and leaned against my reading pillow. I paused for a moment to listen for his footfall, then powered it on.

It automatically logged in as Matthew. I tapped the pinwheel Google Photos icon and scrolled through his stored cell phone camera pictures. Most were of me and Holly. A handful from family vacations. There was none of Anna alone, or of them together. I scrolled quickly, not wanting to lose myself in the images of a happy, adoring family.

The timeline ended in 2016. I thought for a moment, recalling a memory of a 20-something Matthew with a bright blue digital camera. I exited the Photos app and tapped the triangular Google Drive icon. There it was. A folder named "Photos," which led to a series of folders categorized by year. I offered up a silent thank you to the patron saint of suspicious wives that my husband's data and spreadsheet prowess at work translated into meticulous photo archiving. The oldest one was called "2010 and pre."

My finger hovered over it. Did I want to do this?

I listened, again, for sounds of movement in the house, then opened the folder.

In spite of myself and the state of my marriage, I smiled at the sight of my husband from when I first knew him. Wide grin, shaggy blond hair, lean and muscular. The images showed hikes in the White Mountains, tables littered with beer bottles and surrounded by laughing, tipsy people. I recognized the faces of his high school and college friends, many we were in touch with, some we were not.

And then I saw her. Anna.

The series of pictures was taken at a beach. In one, she and Matthew were posing for the camera. He was standing behind her, his arms wrapped around her and hands resting on her exposed stomach.

Very familiar, indeed.

She was wearing a small red bikini, the front of the top and the sides of the bottom were held together with gold bangles. I remembered this suit. She bought it from the Victoria's Secret swim catalog with her first paycheck the summer we graduated from Holyoke.

After graduation.

In another photo, Matthew still had his arms around her, but Anna had turned away from the camera to kiss his cheek. Behind them, a thin redhead was pointing at something in the water.

Shelley.

More photos. A Red Sox game. Backyard parties with *Congratulations, Grad!* decorations. Anna alone. Anna and Matthew together. Group pictures. In the group pictures, they are always next to each other, cheek to cheek or her head on his shoulder.

Then, pre-graduation. UMass parties. Anna and Shelley stretched out on a blanket by the campus pond. Anna and Matt, fingers intertwined.

I returned to the photos taken, I assumed, from the fall of 2008, examining each one carefully. That had been our first fall as college graduates. Real adults. She wasn't in any of them. Nor did she show up in 2009 or 2010. She stopped appearing in mid-summer. They were inseparable, it seemed, for at least a few months. And then they weren't.

I thought back to that summer. My first one at Strawberry Banke. Had Anna been gone a lot? I didn't know. She'd been working, again, on the UNH campus. But while I remembered missing her presence acutely during the Field Hockey Experiment in eighth grade, I couldn't remember missing her then. She'd been around.

The last photo of Anna I could find was of her grinning, eyes closed, holding a floppy pink hat to her head. Her chestnut hair was being blown across her face. She was leaning against a railing, the ocean behind her. A memory tugged at me.

It blew right off. It's halfway to Iceland by now. I'm sorry, Kay.

The hat had been mine. She'd grabbed it from the coat hooks near my back door that morning. We'd just gone to a spin class and had eaten breakfast sandwiches at my house.

She was going on a whale watch that afternoon, she'd said. With UNH co-workers. Could she borrow my hat?

I scanned the images before and after the pink hat photo. Whales. Flukes. Breaches. Splashes. And my now-husband.

But she'd said UNH co-workers. Of that I was certain.

Slowly, methodically, I went through the rest of the folders. My stomach twisted in nostalgia at the pictures of our engagement party at my parents house. Our honeymoon in England and Scotland.

Anna appeared in very few of them, and when she did, I was right next to her in every single one. The only anomaly was the spring and summer of graduation.

She lied to me. She'd lied to me, at the very least, for weeks that summer. More likely, she'd lied for months.

And then they *both* lied, withholding their short-lived post-college tryst from me years later. When it mattered.

I shut down the tablet and slid it back into the drawer. I switched off the light and lay in the dark. At some point this week, I'd have to compose a letter to Matthew sharing everything I loved about him.

Right now, it was going to be a damn short letter.

* * *

Then (Sebago Lake, Maine – July 2008)

Sploosh.

I dove off the short pier and sliced cleanly into the lake. Opening my eyes, I ran my hands over the sand-and-rocks texture of the lake bottom. The day was clear, and shafts of sunlight streaked through the surface and into the depths.

I surfaced, shaking wet strands of hair from my eyes, and breaststroked to the square, floating dock anchored 25 yards from shore where Anna was waiting for me. By the time I climbed up the three-rung ladder, Anna was nearly finished unpacking the waterproof tote she'd brought, towing it on an inflatable ring buoy. Towels, sunglasses, a butter yellow wide-brimmed hat Anna had given me to replace the pink one she'd lost the week before, a jumbo-sized bag of Goldfish and two bottles of Mike's Hard Lemonade.

Anna expertly twisted the cap off a lemonade and handed it to me. We clinked bottles and looked out over Sebago Lake. I took a sip from my bottle and studied the pine trees of Spider Island.

"Remember how far away Spider Island seemed when we were kids?" I asked Anna.

She glanced over her shoulder at the island and then back at me, bemused. "Not really. We were 14 when I started coming here with you."

I leaned back on my elbows, stretching my legs out on my yellow and white striped towel. "True," I said, then grinned. "I guess it just feels so much longer."

She flicked a Goldfish at me. It bounced off my chin and nestled into my cleavage. I plucked it from my skin and tossed it into the water, where it was promptly gobbled by one of the bass that frequently cruised under the dock.

"I'm glad you could come, Sporty," I told Anna. "Now that we're real adults and all."

She held her lemonade up for another *cheers* clink. "This real adult is always glad to be invited here."

"Dude, you're not *invited*," I said. "You're a fixture. This lake would suck without you."

"This lake would never suck," Anna said.

"OK, it would be slightly less perfect," I countered.

I turned back to take in the modest white cottage we'd been renting since I was a baby. The screened porch. The stone chimney. The tiny window of the loft where Anna I alway slept. We'd spilled countless secrets up there: boy-crushes, gossip, future plans, hidden fears, and cautious dreams.

"Remember when we broke that glass-fronted bookcase?" I said, chuckling.

Anna giggled. "Oh my God. Why did we think slam dancing with sofa cushions in front of that thing was a good idea?"

"Because none of us could drive yet and it had been raining for two days," I said. "Joy still has a little scar on her back."

"Speaking of, when is Joy getting here?" Anna asked, reclining onto her back and adjusting the inflatable ring under her neck.

"Soon, I think," I said. "When she gets here we'll do happy hour and cards on the pier before dinner. My dad's doing his steaks."

Anna groaned with pleasure. "Oh, man. I'm salivating," she said. "So, how *is* she? Joy?"

I shrugged. "Better, I think. At least, better than I would be in her situation."

Anna turned toward me, lifting her sunglasses to make eye contact. "What do you mean?"

I took another swig of my hard lemonade and laid down on my towel.

"Well, think about it," I started. "Can you imagine showing up at my house with, like, Reg in tow?"

She mock shuddered. "Gross. Don't even."

I made a face at her. "Pretend for a second you liked him, just for the sake of argument," I said. "My point is, even if you *did* like Reg, and you wanted to start seeing him, you would at least *come* to me first, right? Not just show up at a random event?"

Anna rested her head back onto the dock. "I promise you,

Kay, I will never show up unannounced with Reg."

I knew she was joking, but she was missing my point.

"Forget Reg, OK? Joy and Carlos went out for like, almost a year, and then her friend Grace shows up at this fourth of July party with him? With no heads up? It's not OK."

"No, I get that," Anna said. "So, like, what if Grace *had* talked to her ahead of time? And said what? 'I kinda dig Carlos now? You guys broke up six months ago now, so is it OK if I go for it?'"

I felt defensive of my sister suddenly. Why did I have to explain this?

"Well, *yes*, pretty much," I said. "That's not so hard, is it? I mean, it's not like Joy would have said '*no*, you can't go out with him.' That's dumb. It's the fact that Grace didn't have enough respect for their friendship to mention it. She just blindsided her in front of everyone. That's low. And now she's all 'why is Joy mad at me?'"

Anna stretched her arms in the air. "But she's not that mad, it sounds like, from what you just said."

"No, she's not really *mad* anymore," I said. "But I have to think things are going to be weird between Joy and Grace from now on. How could they not be? She handled that like crap, to be honest. *I* would be pissed at Grace."

"Yeah. I get it." Anna said quietly, examining one of her fingernails.

We laid side-by-side, bobbing gently on the float, for the next hour, talking. What we would wear to Jenna's graduation party next week. My nervous excitement over my impending first day at Strawberry Banke. Anna's contentment at securing a full-time job at UNH as a teaching assistant for the professor she'd interned for during the summer.

Gradually we fell into a familiar silence, until the *beep-beep* of Joy's Jeep signaled her arrival. Anna and I sat up, yanking our towel from underneath our bottoms and repacking the tote.

"I'm going to go for a quick run before cards," Anna said, when we waded back onto shore. "I have time, right?"

"Of course," I said over my shoulder, as I walked up the pebble driveway to greet my sister.

Anna waved to Joy and disappeared into the cottage to change. I gave my sister an extra squeeze and then grabbed the two canvas bags of groceries she'd brought.

"Where are Mom and Dad?" Joy asked me, hefting her suitcase out of the trunk.

"Picking up the steaks for the grill."

We walked into the house, and I sneaked a glance at her.

"How are you?" I said cautiously. She shook her head at me and smiled.

"I'm *fine*, Kay, seriously. Don't look so worried."

"OK, Saint Joy," I said. "But don't bring up Grace in my presence. That bitch is dead to me."

Joy laughed, then looked beyond my shoulder. "Hey, Anna! Ready for a cocktail?"

Anna was standing in the doorway to the tiny kitchen, her phone in her hand. She smiled and shook her head.

"In a bit. I'm going out for a run. But I'll take you up on it then."

"Well, c'mere first. I feel like I haven't seen you all summer," Joy said, enveloping Anna in a warm hug. "What's going on? Any guy gossip I should know about?"

Anna chuckled and extracted herself. "Nope. None at all."

As Joy and I brought our drinks to the porch, I watched Anna shrink from view up the dirt road, tapping away on her phone.

Chapter 14

I laid awake in the murky pre-dawn, thinking. My thoughts careened from self-righteous to self-flagellating, shrieking.

He lied to me. She *lied to me.*

I'm an idiot. A willfully blind idiot.

I don't need either of them. They deserve each other. Let them skip off into the sunset.

Seriously. How could I not know?

Then, quieter. *Why did they break up?*

The question snapped me out of my current *they suck/no, you suck* mental loop. I glanced at the clock on my bedside table. 6:20. Ten minutes until the alarm. I padded to the master bathroom, turning the question over in my mind.

Why *did* they break up?

The logical answer, of course, was that they were 22. How many flash-in-the-pan relationships – if they could even be called that – had I burned through in my 20s? The question was a welcome distraction. Bemusing, even. As I lathered my hair in the shower, I counted.

Before Matthew, there'd been Jake, a grad school classmate. Liam, whom I'd unceremoniously dumped just before grad school. Andrew, my first serious post-college boyfriend, who'd decided that moving to Las Vegas to DJ was a much better life path than eventually moving in with me. His face, when I'd cautiously suggested it as a possibility "down the road," had had the same frozen, deer-in-headlights look as Reg when I'd suggested following him to Kent for my junior year abroad.

I chuckled suddenly, thinking of my overeager college self, and inhaled a small mouthful of shampoo suds. Poor Reg. Poor Andrew, for the matter.

I finished rinsing and worked a bead of conditioner through my hair, my mind ticking back through my college flings and smiling in spite of myself. Reg. A semester and a half with Jonathan the lacrosse player. And Matt, of course. Sort of.

Matt.

I stood under the hot stream, allowing the memories to flood in with the water.

Matt and I were sophomores when we met. Matt, who'd been so hard to pin down. Exasperatingly so. It was why I broke up with him.

And Anna had been delighted.

Matt who, right?

I turned off the tap and slid the glass shower door open just enough to yank my lavender towel from its hook. I patted my body dry, thinking. No longer smiling.

The Matt of our senior year hadn't been hard for *Anna* to pin down. He'd been more than happy to hang out with her. Internship or no internship.

Jealousy flared in me as I wrapped my wet hair in the towel and shrugged into my robe. Through the bathroom door, in my bedroom, Holly was talking softly to someone.

I opened the door. "Good morning, Holls," I said brightly.

She was sprawled on my bed, alone, maneuvering a series of toys around my comforter and frowning in concentration.

"Hi mom," she said, focused on a pink plush kitten.

"What are you working on, there?" I asked.

"A puzzle. Mrs. Dwyer said we could get a homework pass if we can figure it out."

"Oooo, I love puzzles," I said, giving my head a final rub before depositing the towel into the wicker hamper. I picked up a comb from the dresser and began the process of detangling my hair. "What is it?"

Holly glanced up from her plushies. "You can't help me. It won't count if you do."

"I won't, I promise. I'm just curious about it."

"OK," Holly said, importantly. She held up a Barbie. "She's on an island with a duck, a fox, and a sack of grain." Holly pointed to the pink kitten, a bright yellow chick with an Easter bonnet, and a deck of Uno cards.

"She has to move to another island, but she can only take one thing with her at a time in the boat."

"Small boat," I said, smiling at my daughter.

"She can't leave the fox and the duck alone, because the fox would eat the duck," Holly continued. "And she can't leave the duck alone with the grain, because the duck would eat all the grain."

"Are you sure it's a duck? Sounds like a pig to me," I said. Holly grinned.

"I know the first move," she said. "It's the duck, 'cause the fox and grain can be alone together without anything bad happening, but the duck can't be alone with either of them. I just can't figure the rest out in my head. That's why I'm using these."

"Smart," I said, impressed with her problem-solving tactics. "How about you crack this case in the kitchen over some cereal while I get dressed?"

"Pancakes," Holly said, scooping up her toys and marching toward my door. "Daddy's making them."

"Yum," I said, dabbing cold cream onto my cheeks. "I want bananas and chocolate chips in mine."

Alone again, my thoughts drifted back to Anna and Matt, mingling with Holly's puzzle.

The fox, the duck, and the grain. Matt, Anna, and me. A riddle to be solved.

I slipped a chocolate brown knit dress from its hanger and shrugged into it, smoothing it over my body. I returned to the bathroom and pulled the hair dryer from the vanity drawer.

If Matt and Anna were inseparable that summer, why did they break up? And why didn't Anna tell me?

Because I dated him first, I thought. *Of course she wouldn't want to tell me.*

"I wouldn't have been *that* mad," I muttered over the hum of the motor. I met my gaze in the mirror and sighed in resignation over the lie. I was kidding myself. I was 22. Of *course* I would've been mad. And hurt. And jealous.

I brushed my now-dry hair. "So she didn't tell me," I reasoned.

My hand froze mid-stroke. I lowered the brush to the vanity top.

Did Anna *break up* with Matt to avoid hurting me? For our friendship?

"No," I whispered to my reflection. She looked unconvinced.

Anna had subtly steered me away from Matt when we were

sophomores, but when she had him for herself two years later, she – maybe, possibly – ended it rather than tell me?

"She chose me," I said to the stunned woman in the mirror. "She chose me over him back then."

"MOM!" Holly yelled from the stairs. "PANCAKES!"

My hands shook as I worked the clasp on Matthew's locket. Anna had chosen me, and then much later she'd – clearly and spitefully – chosen my husband. Then, last night, he'd chosen me.

At least, he'd told me he had.

The fox and the grain can be alone together without anything bad happening, but the duck can't be alone with either of them.

"Coming!" I called. I stole a final glance in the mirror, hoping I didn't look as unsettled as I felt.

Who was the duck in this scenario?

* * *

Then (Marblehead, Massachusetts – August 2008)

"You're gonna wanna put your hands up, my friends," the DJ crooned into his headset. "Not only is there a party here in Marblehead, Miley says there's a party…in… the…U…S…A-aaay!"

Cheers – shrieks, really – erupted in Jenna's backyard, largely from the gaggle of her teenage cousins already on the portable dance floor that covered the grass, surrounded by strings of fairy lights.

Leaning against the deck railing with margaritas, Anna and

I rolled our eyes at the DJ's cheesy introduction.

"He's like Bill Murray's lounge singer from *SNL*, only not as subtle and charming," I said, flicking a mosquito away from Anna's shoulder.

"You shouldn't talk about your new boyfriend that way," Anna said, wagging her eyebrows.

"Bleegh," I said. "Can you imagine?"

She nodded and emptied the contents of her red Solo cup. "Yup, I can. 'Ka-aaay,'" Anna trilled, breathing tequila into my ear. "'Forget Lady Gaga and come to Papa, 'cause this here's…no….bad…romaaaaaaance!'"

I giggled and then pig-snorted, causing both of us to laugh harder.

I had Drunk Anna tonight, and I was happy to see her. It had been a while. I felt the summer rushing away from me and I wanted – *needed* – for it to slow down. In a matter of weeks, I'd step firmly across the threshold to real adulthood. While the idea didn't exactly scare me, the loss of my annual transitions from school life to summer life left me feeling wistful.

On the dance floor, Jenna made eye contact and beckoned. I drained my cup Anna-style and turned to my best friend.

"C'mon, Sporty," I said. "We secretly love this song."

Anna was frowning at her phone. She swiped the screen shut and stuffed the device into her back pocket.

"We do indeed," she said, smiling again. "Let's dance. I'll get us more drinks."

We joined a circle of Holyoke friends and moved with the music, as we'd done so many times over the last four years. Some, like Jenna, I knew would stay in my life. Others would likely move to New York or California, or simply drift away with the years. And then there was Anna. My chosen sister. She was forever.

A sudden rush of love for her washed over me, and I felt an urgent need to do something with it. Whirling around, I moved through the tangle of dancers to the DJ. He was accepting a bottle of water from his assistant, a plain looking dark-haired boy about my age wearing a Beatles t-shirt.

He isn't a boy; he's a man, I thought, correcting myself. *We're* adults *now. How scary is that?*

"Gotta request?" The DJ asked. He was pale, with eyebrows so light they appeared invisible.

"Yes," I said earnestly, hoping that my last margarita didn't make it come out as *yesh.* "I need you to play 'If You Wanna Be My Lover' by–"

"The Spice Girls, yeah," the DJ said. "Uh, I'm not sure if I have that."

His dark-haired friend stepped forward. "We do. We'll put it on next. Hope you're having a good time."

He smiled, and his previously nondescript features rearranged into something quietly appealing. I smiled back.

"Thank you, uh–"

"Andrew," he said, offering his hand.

My smile widened. "Kay. The song's for my friend Anna."

"Great, thanks for letting us know," Andrew said. He nodded at the dance floor. "Better get back there. Your song'll be up next. But come back if you want to hear anything else, OK?"

I zigzagged my way back to Anna for the last half of a Taylor Swift song. She was swiping at her phone again.

"The DJ is deceptively sexy," I said.

She looked at me, horrified, returning the phone to her pocket. "Are you high?"

"What? I–no. Ew! No, not *him*," I said, swatting her on the arm. "His friend or helper or whatever. Andrew. Don't turn around."

She turned around.

"You're the worst wingwoman, you know that?" I declared. "The absolute worst."

She turned back and winked at me.

"Yeah, I see it," she said. "I'm not going to entertain his buddy while you go off and make out, though, so don't even ask."

On the speakers, Taylor's voice faded away.

"This next song goes out to Annaaaa, from her friend Kaaaayyyy," the eyebrow-less DJ bellowed. "I guess we know who we need to get with if we wanna be *her* lover, right guys? It's....The....Spice Girrrrrrrrrrls!"

Over Anna's shoulder, the DJ gave me a thumbs up, grinning. Andrew covered his eyes with his hand, shaking his head slightly.

Anna and I strutted to the center of our circle of friends. We owned this song, and we knew it. We slipped into the choreography that we had added to and perfected over the last decade, the one only the two of us knew. For the next three minutes, we moved as one. No one even attempted to keep up, and by the time the last refrain was being sung, we were the only ones on the floor. As the song faded, our friends hooted and clapped for us.

We bowed to the crowd, and I pulled Anna into a fierce hug.

"I love you, Sporty," I said, over the sound of the next song.

"I love *you*, Baby," she replied.

She held onto the hug for an extra moment. "I can see Andrew watching you," she whispered conspiratorially. "I think you should go talk to him."

"In a bit," I said, leaning back and grinning at her. "I'm having too much fun with you."

In Anna's back pocket, her phone chirped.

"I gotta pee," she said. "Go talk to that deceptively sexy DJ."

She ran lightly up the deck stairs and through the sliding glass doors into Jenna's kitchen. I drifted to the bar table, grabbed a bottle of water and cracked it open. The tipsiness of the tequila had subsided, sweated out on the dance floor. In my peripheral vision, Andrew stood a few feet away from his DJ partner's booth, alone.

Why not, I thought.

I meandered over to him. "There's something I'm curious about," I said. "Maybe you can help me."

Andrew raised his eyebrows. "I can try."

"Did that song's introduction break the Top Five Cringe-worthy Moments, or does your friend have a long and storied history of inappropriate ad libbing?"

"Ah," Andrew said. "Let me tell you about the request for 'You Can Leave Your Hat On' at a recent bat mitzvah."

I laughed, touching his forearm with my hand. I liked him.

I was about to beg for what I hoped would be hilariously awkward details when I spotted Anna sitting on the far steps of the L-shaped deck, alone. Had Drunk Anna crossed over to Too Drunk Anna?

"I'm sorry, hold that thought," I said to Andrew. "I need to check on my friend."

I jogged across the grass to the stairs. Anna was hunched over her phone.

"Hey," I called, when I was a few yards away. "You OK?"

Anna swiped at her face. "I'm fine. Just a little, you know, woozy."

I sat next to her, concerned. "What's wrong? Who keeps texting you?"

She shook her head. "It's nothing."

I leaned into her shoulder with my own. "I don't care if it's nothing. If it's bothering you, I want to know about it. I want to help."

Anna looked thoughtful. "I don't want to lose you."

I was surprised. "Why would you lose me?"

"Just, you know, life. Adulthood. The real world."

"What about it? The real world isn't going to change *us*," I insisted. "I hate to break it to you, Anna, but you're stuck with me. The minute you told Billy Arthur to go screw himself in sixth grade homeroom, you were stuck with me."

She smiled at the memory. "I was a badass back then."

"You're still a badass. You're *my* badass."

We sat in silence for a few moments, then Anna stood up.

"Go back to the DJ," she said. "He's into you."

"If he's into me, then he'll wait," I reasoned, standing up to join her. "I'd rather hang out with you than some guy."

Anna smiled, the happiness – was there a touch of relief in there as well? – contrasting with her red rimmed eyes.

"Me, too," she said.

Chapter 15

Holly and I sat side by side at the breakfast bar, munching on our chocolate chip and banana pancakes. Between us lay Barbie, Uno, and the plush kitten and chick, abandoned for the better offer of chocolate, butter, and maple syrup. Matthew stood across from us, where he could keep a trained eye on the last batch in the skillet.

It was surreal for the three of us to be sitting here, nonchalantly eating breakfast and sipping tea, when my world had imploded a week ago.

Six days and 12 hours, to be exact.

Matthew leaned over and speared a syrup drenched square from my plate.

"Stop, thief!" I said, smiling.

Matthew flipped the cakes in the pan and smiled back at me. "I'll give you a bite of mine."

"Two," I said. "One, plus interest."

He pretended to think it over. "OK, but no chocolate chips."

He turned back to the stove, and I snuck a lingering look at him. He was dressed for his office's casual Friday, wearing khaki pants and a navy long-sleeved polo shirt. He looked good, but not quite rested, which oddly satisfied me.

He doesn't know you know about their first fling.

I felt a little thrill of power, though I didn't know what to do with the information. Not yet, at least.

I clocked Holly's progress on her breakfast. "More bites with banana, Holls," I said, as Matthew sat his plate on the counter top. He dug in, still standing.

"It's Friday," he announced. "What night is Friday, Holly?"

"Family-dinner-but-no-one-cooks night," she said. "Where're we going?"

Matthew looked at me, eyebrows raised. "I think it's Mom's turn to pick."

The feeling of unreality washed over me again. There was no way I could play happy family tonight. Not after the Google Photos revelation of the night before. I needed to debrief with Joy.

I looked at Holly. "You know what I think? I think you've missed Daddy this week, and you both deserve some time together, just the two of you. Anywhere you want," I added, leaning closer to my daughter. *"Anywhere."*

She brightened, getting the message. "I want to go to Pooley's Playground. Will you take me, Dad? Pleeeeease?"

I smiled, triumphant over my brainstorm. Pooley's – all flashing lights, shrill gaming sounds, and cardboard pizza – set my teeth on edge. I hated the place, but they loved it.

"I don't know," Matthew said, feigning uncertainty. "I'm just worried how you'll react when I–" he pointed a forkful of pancake at her. "Win *all* the tickets in skee ball."

They chattered happily for the rest of the meal, comparing strategic ways to roll the ball and reminiscing about the day Holly scored three 100 shots in a row. I watched, bemused yet cautious. This felt so normal, and yet it was anything *but* normal.

"It's about that time, family," I said, tapping my watch. "Shoes and backpack my young friend."

Holly leapt down from her stool and turned to leave.

"Whoa," I said. "Bring the duck, the fox and the grain back upstairs, please."

She ran upstairs, toys in hand. I stacked our plates and walked around the breakfast bar to load them into the dishwasher.

Matthew poured coffee into his UMass travel mug.

"Did you sleep OK?" I asked him.

He screwed the lid onto his mug and tilted his head at me. "You know, I don't think I've ever actually slept in that room before," he said. "It felt weird."

I softened. "I know. It was weird for me, too."

He paused, as if listening for Holly, then took a step towards me. "I'm sorry if you felt put on the spot about dinner tonight."

I shook my head. "It's fine. I just….can't yet," I met my husband's eyes. "Pretending in front of Holly is exhausting."

He winced, then nodded.

"But I meant what I said," I added, quickly. You two should have some one-on-one time."

"Thanks," he said, smiling. His smile turned a little wry. "But did you have to plant the Pooley's seed? God, I hate that place."

My eyes flew open. "Seriously? You do?"

He chuckled. "I mean, I did. When I was Holly's age. My grandfather would take me to the one near where I grew up. My mom couldn't stand being in there for more than five minutes, so it was our thing." He paused again, thoughtful.

"Huh. You know, it just occurred to me that *he* probably hated it too."

I looked at him with wonder. "I totally thought you enjoyed it. Like, for real enjoyed it."

He shrugged. "It makes Holly happy."

"How come you never told me you hated it?" I pressed.

He shrugged again. "I don't know. It didn't seem like that big a deal."

I drained my cup of tea and added it to the dishwasher, frustrated. What a dumb thing to keep to himself.

"That's actually not true," Matthew said suddenly.

I waited, silent.

He sighed, his head lowered. "I didn't want Holly to know I didn't like it because I was afraid it would make *her* not enjoy it as much," he began. "And I thought if I told you, you'd feel guilty about encouraging me to take her when it's just the two of us. I didn't want you to feel bad about that."

He looked up at me. "I'm making this out to be a way bigger deal than it actually is. It's really not that big of a deal."

I nodded. "I know."

"I just felt like I wanted to be honest, even about the small stuff."

I nodded again, slowly. "I'm glad."

We stood in the kitchen, the few feet between us feeling, to me, like a mile.

I stepped closer to him. "You don't have to shield me from every negative emotion, you know."

He stiffened.

I closed the gap between us and rested my forehead on his chest. I breathed in his scent. Pancakes, and a hint of sandalwood from his deodorant. The cotton of his shirt was smooth. I turned and rubbed my cheek against the fabric as he wrapped his arms around me, his chin resting on the top of my head.

He couldn't do that with Anna; she's too tall.

I pushed the thought away, snaking my arms around his lower back. There wasn't room for her in this moment.

"I'm so sorry," Matthew whispered.

I held him tighter. He was here again, right here in our kitchen. By choice.

Holly clattered down the stairs. Matthew and I pulled apart.

He kissed my forehead, lightly and quickly. "Now you know. It was a stupid thing to hide from you," he said, echoing my own thoughts mere moments ago. "I'm sorry."

I smiled. "You're a good dad," I said. "Just like your grandfather."

* * *

Then (Portsmouth, New Hampshire – May 2009)

"I have to say, you look amazing," Jenna told me. "I'm proud of you and I hate you at the same time."

We sipped our coffees, Anna, Jenna and I, having scored a table at The Friendly Toast after our Saturday morning spin class. I pulled the scrunchie out of my hair and shook the strands loose, where they clung to my shoulders, still damp from the exertion. I felt pleasantly spent, and eager for some warm food and a catch-up with my friends.

"You don't have to sound *that* surprised," I joked, pouring another glug of cream into my mug. "I guess the break-up diet really works."

"That's not what I meant. Not entirely, at least," Jenna said. "You look, you know, happy. Zen, even. Andrew left for Vegas, what, a month ago? You're doing way better than I was a month after Sal and I broke up."

"You should have seen me a month ago," I said, looking to Anna for confirmation. "Right?"

She smiled and reached over to squeeze my forearm. "It was nothing a few pounds of caramel corn and some rom coms couldn't fix."

I smiled back and turned to Jenna again. "She's downplaying it. I wouldn't be the sweaty and Zen woman before you without her. She inspired my epiphany."

Jenna raised her eyebrows. "Which was?"

I leaned back to let our server lay our plates on the table. Veggie omelets with sourdough toast for Anna and Jenna, and a short stack of pancakes for me.

"That Andrew was great, but not The One. That my time with him wasn't wasted, and that who I am now *because* of him will make it all the more clear when I *do* meet The One."

Jenna blew on her coffee and took a short sip, looking at Anna over the mug.

"No offense, Anna, but that doesn't sound like your brand of Yoda-isms."

"No? And what does my brand of Yoda-isms sound like?" Anna challenged.

"Yours is more like 'enough with the moping, already. He's a douche.'"

Anna spluttered, sending a flurry of sourdough crumbs onto the front of her bright orange sports tank. She wiped her lips with her napkin and held up a finger. *Hang on, I have something to say but I haven't finished chewing.* I jumped in before she could swallow.

"I think that's pretty much *exactly* what you said after Reg dumped me," I said.

Anna lowered her hand. "Well, A, Reg *was* a douche, so there's that. And B, that was Young and Foolish Anna's brand of advice. Before you now is Wise Adult Anna."

"And Wise Adult Anna gently leads her flock to relationship epiphanies?"

"Kinda, yeah," I interjected, feeling a need to come to Anna's defense. "It was really just her letting me talk *ad nauseum* about him, and asking questions. Like free therapy."

Anna smiled.

I turned more to face her. "It was the questions you asked that helped. Like 'what are some things about Andrew that you'd want to have in your next relationship,' and 'what are some things you'll do differently next time,'" I told her. "I think it got me to see that there *would* be a next time, with someone else, and that I should focus on who and what I want that person to be instead of being stuck on someone I couldn't have."

"Huh," said Jenna, nodding and raising her mug slightly in salute. "That's some Wise Adult stuff, Anna. Where'd you learn that breakup recovery trick?"

Anna shrugged. "I don't know," she said, vaguely. "Probably from some weird afternoon talk show a million years ago."

"When you were home sick and no doubt high on Nyquil," I added.

"Don't talk smack about Nyquil," Anna quipped.

"So who is he?" Jenna asked, suddenly.

Anna's hand, holding her coffee cup, froze midway to the table. "Who?"

"This someday guy. The One," she said. "Who is he for each of you?"

Anna lowered her cup and turned to me, expectant. "You first."

I swept my now-dry hair onto one shoulder, thinking. "He has to have a good sense of humor, tolerable taste in music, and love books," I began.

Jenna made a face. "Come on, that's on every girl's list. Dig deeper."

"*Fine*," I said. "He *can't* make fun of my undying love of girl pop, and he can't be one of those people who only reads nonfiction and is smug about it. That's a dealbreaker," I said.

"Fiction haters lack imagination and are bad in bed. These are facts," Jenna said, making a *keep going* gesture. "This is good. What else?"

"OK, so this one is a contradiction. He has to like having family traditions – keeping them and making new ones – but at the same time I'd secretly love it if he had a small family, so I wouldn't be obligated to miss time with mine that much," I added. "That's awful of me, isn't it?"

Anna clinked my mug with her own. "Since I'm part of that family, I say no. Cheers to that."

I swirled a perfect square of pancake into a streak of syrup and melted butter and held up my fork.

"And he *has* to love pancakes. Bonus points if he makes them from scratch."

"Is he tall, dark and handsome, like Andrew or Reg?" Jenna joked.

I shrugged. "I think The One will be blond. All my movie

crushes are blond," I reasoned.

Our server stopped at the table, and when we declined his offer of more coffee he slid the check onto the table.

Jenna laced her fingers together and stretched her arms over her head. "This was so great, you guys. I'm glad Wise Adult Anna was able to convince you to come out after your month of mourning," she said, then looked at me, worried. "Sorry, that came out wrong. I didn't mean for it to sound so, you know, callous."

I waved away her concern. "It's fine. I'm glad this one–" I looked at Anna. "Brought me out today, too. Which is also exactly what she did when Reg dumped me. Dragged me out to UMass."

A memory began to form in my mind. Anna's Ford Focus. Crunching down a hill of snow to a dorm. Overly sweet bocce ball cocktails. And a sandy-haired boy who fixed them for me. A boy who intrigued me, but never quite let me in, save for that one moment on the Summit House porch.

I chucked quietly. "Speaking of that night," I began. "Whatever happened to Matt–"

"Hey, I have an idea," said Anna, leaning forward and grabbing my forearm.

"What?" Jenna and I said in unison.

"Are either of you up for hitting that consignment shop?" She gathered up the check and stood. "I think we pay at the counter," she said brightly.

"Ooo, spin, breakfast *and* shopping," I said, rising from my chair and slinging an arm around her shoulder, all thoughts of Matt forgotten. "I love Wise Adult Anna."

"*Namaste*, Baby."

Chapter 16

"How about a fire?" my dad asked.

I nodded, as he'd clearly known I would. The fireplace was already set with my dad's signature perfect proportions of newspaper, kindling, and logs.

Dinner had been a subdued affair. While Matthew and Holly were, no doubt, being assaulted by noise at Pooley's, Joy, my parents and I quietly made our way through platters of dumplings and steamed broccoli. Between bites, I filled them in on our first session with Elena Garciá. There had been a walking-on-eggshells undercurrent to the meal at first, with Joy and my parents exchanging concerned, empathetic looks with me and furtive *does she seem OK to you?* looks with each other.

I settled into my preferred corner of the mushroom colored sofa and watched as Dad lit the paper in various spots with a long kitchen match. The flames consumed the newspaper quickly, hungrily, building up the strength to take on the layer of thin wood kindling above it. I took comfort in the logic and reliability of it.

My back sank deeper in the sofa as the tension I'd kept locked away while at work slipped out, a teaspoon at a time. I felt safe here, in the home of my childhood. As Joy and my parents took up their usual places on the sofa and chairs around me, I felt secure enough to let my *everything's fine* mask slip off. Nourished. Letting Matthew and Holly have their evening together was definitely the right call. I would, I decided, use the opportunity to build up my own strength. I had things far more challenging than kindling to take on.

Joy handed me a mug of herbal tea and drew her knees up, hugging them loosely while she rested her back against the arm of the sofa. My family was silent, perhaps waiting for me to set the tone for the post-dinner conversation.

I took a tentative sip of tea before beginning. "So, um," I stammered, feeling nervous. "Matthew and I are going to try to work through this. Not just for Holly, but for us."

My mother nodded, her face neutral. Joy and my father were still, waiting.

"I just hope that, if and when we do, the three of you can find a way to forgive him, too."

A few moments of silence. Then my mother cleared her throat.

"We're going to support you in what you want and need to be happy," she said. "And if that means working things out, then we're with you on that." she made a circling motion with her finger, including my dad and sister in her sentiment.

"I can't say it's going to be easy to act like it never happened, and I know you're not asking us to do that," she added quickly, as if sensing my protest. "It will take some time to rebuild that bridge, but we'll get there."

She looked from Joy to my father for confirmation, and they murmured their agreement.

"Thank you," I exhaled, relieved to have addressed that particular elephant in the room. I turned my gaze to the fire and relaxed even further.

"I saw Craig Becker today," my dad said.

I glanced at him, surprised. Though actually, it made sense. Of course he'd run into Anna's dad. *I'd* likely see him, too, eventually.

"Where?"

"As I was picking up dinner," he said. "It was…weird."

I let out a short, mirthless laugh. "Well, *yeah*."

"No," he said, shaking her head. "Not weird in the way you think. I…he doesn't know, Kay. He doesn't know about Anna and Matt."

I looked at Joy, incredulous, then back at my father. "What was he like? What did he say?"

He scratched the back of his head absently. "He was completely normal. Big smile, big handshake" he said, frowning a little at the memory. "He brought up Thanksgiving, and asked me if he should bring his usual beer and wine."

"Oh my God," Joy muttered, more to herself than to us. "What did you say?"

"I told him that if he wanted to come to Thanksgiving, he'd have to tell his daughter to stop screwing my son-in-law."

My eyes widened. For a moment, I relished the image.

"You did not," Joy said. "Though that would have been pretty great."

"Oh, sure," I added. "My cratering marriage blurted out to everyone at Taste of Shanghai."

"Which is exactly why I didn't say it," my dad said, pointing at me. "I played along, like everything was normal."

I thought about this. Why wouldn't Anna tell her dad?

"Maybe he was playing along, too," I suggested. "He could've been surprised to see you, and just didn't know what to say."

My dad crinkled his eyes, thinking. "I really don't think so. I saw him before he saw me. I think I would have seen it on his face. He doesn't know."

This unsettled me. If Anna hadn't told her dad, had she told anyone? I couldn't believe she had told Jenna; Jenna would have reached out to me if she had. Besides, Anna wasn't as close to Jenna as I was.

"She's alone," my mother said quietly.

Tension crept back into my neck. I placed my mug of tea on the coffee table and rolled my head in a slow circle. Clichés flitted through my mind – *You reap what you sow. She's made her bed* – but I didn't have the stomach to say them out loud. My body, on muscle memory alone perhaps, shifted into protective mode at the thought of Anna vulnerable and alone. Joy and my parents, I knew, were feeling varying levels of the same. Each one of us had had flashes of rage and disgust since the affair – I threw a beer bottle at a *wall*, for heaven's sake – but flashes were all they were. Quick to dissipate, like newspaper in the fireplace. Underneath the grief and the anger and the uncertainty and the longing to go back in time, there was a deep and powerful love for my friend. The well-maintained bed of embers that can glow for a long, long time.

I thought of my mom, placing a gentle hand on my dad's forearm at Mrs. Becker's funeral. *We have to step up and really be there for her. Craig is going to be lost without Elizabeth when it comes to Anna.*

"How come she hasn't talked to her dad, do you think?" I asked.

Joy exhaled slowly, her head tilted slightly to one side as she thought. "She could be waiting to see how things turn out with Matthew," she suggested. "Or, I don't know, she could be trying to figure out *how* to tell him. I can't imagine it's going to be an easy conversation."

"She may feel ashamed of what she did," my mother said.

Doubt briefly clouded Joy's face; presumably she was picturing her run-in with them at the bar in Boston. But she hadn't told Jenna, and Matthew was home. At least for now.

An image of Anna's father, his face closed, rose in my mind. *What would your mother think, Anna?*

Pain pierced me, as if Anna and I had suddenly swapped places and it was me who was forced to reckon with a deceased parent. I lowered my head into my hands and wept. Huge, guttural waves of grief, both for my friend and our broken friendship.

My mother slipped in between me and my sister and held me, like Joy had not long ago.

"She's all alone," I sobbed into my mother's purple cotton sweater. "I hate her right now, but I love her, too. I don't want her to be all alone."

"I know, honey," she said. "I know you don't."

The intensity of my outburst ebbed. I shifted slightly, untangling myself from my mother. Over her shoulder, my dad handed me a small packet of tissue.

"I–I'm worried she's not OK," I hiccupped. "I don't like that she didn't tell her dad."

"She could have someone else she's talking to," my mother said. "A friend at work, or a therapist."

Joy stood and walked around my mother, crouching down in front of me.

"Do you want me to find out?" she asked.

I pressed a tissue underneath my eye. *I must look like a raccoon*, I thought. *A blotchy raccoon.*

"You mean, talk to her?"

"Yes," she said. "I'll invite her for coffee, just to talk. And to listen."

From a rational point of view, it made no sense. Why was I sitting here crying over the idea that Anna had no one to confide in about *sleeping with my husband?* Yet it made perfect sense. She was Anna. Concern for her wellbeing was instinctual, coded into my DNA.

I nodded, swiping at my eyes again. "Yes," I said to my sister. "I want you to do that."

* * *

Then (Portsmouth, New Hampshire – November 2009)

The plates were stacked in the dishwater, and the Waterford crystal wine glasses rested, drying, on a tea towel spread carefully over the breakfast table. The aroma of turkey gravy lingered. Despite my pleasantly full stomach, I breathed it in, already looking forward to tomorrow's leftovers.

We were sprawled on the sofa and chairs in the living room, my parents, Anna, and I, nursing fresh glasses of red wine and listening to the fire crackle. The last of our Thanksgiving gathering – two grandparents, a great-aunt, two aunt/uncle combos, three cousins, and Anna's dad – had left a half hour before. Joy had traded kitchen clean up duty in favor of driving our grandfather's sister, Aunt Mary, home.

"Even though my hands are now chapped from scrubbing pans, I still think I got the better end of the deal," I announced to the room.

"Stop. Aunt Mary loves you," my mother said, smiling.

"Yes. She loves me so much that after taking pictures of me getting into the limo before the prom, she showed up *at* the prom so she could get a picture of us getting *out* of the limo," I said, turning to Anna. "Remember?"

Anna waved her hand high in the air, imitating my great-aunt's Yankee accent. "YOO HOO! KA-AY!"

My mom let slip an involuntary cackle, then clapped her hand over mouth, shaking with laughter.

"She was so pleased with herself," my dad said, chuckling. "Dropped off copies for us the next day and everything."

"*Your* smile looked natural," I said to Anna, gesturing to her with the hand holding my wine glass. "Mine looked like Jack Nicholson frozen at the end of *The Shining*."

Anna giggled again.

"You're not working tomorrow, are you, Anna?" Dad asked, while pointing at me. "Not like this one."

Anna shook her head. "Nah, UNH is closed until Monday."

"I actually don't mind working tomorrow," I said. "We'll be officially kicking off the holiday season at the museum. It's fun. Everyone's always in a great mood."

"Don't ever say that in front of someone who works in retail in December," Mom offered.

I raised my glass to her. "Helpful, thanks."

My year and a half at Strawberry Banke had been a happy blur. I loved being around the history of the place, and spending my days with people who were as enthusiastic about it as I was. It had ignited something in me, a drive.

"I just love it," I had told Anna over drinks at The Press Room a few months ago, shouting over the rock music coming from the bar's sound system. "I don't think I've been this excited about something since…I don't know."

"Since *Spice World*?" Anna said, eyebrows raised.

"Won't you miss it when you're in London?" Mom asked me now, while nudging my dad to add a log to the fire.

"Well, sure. But it's *London*," I said. "If anything, working at the Banke has made me want to go even more and see the *really* old stuff."

"Make sure you say it that way in your grad school applications. 'I want to see the really old stuff,'" Anna offered, using air quotes.

"Helpful again, thanks," I said.

"When will you hear from them, do you think?" Dad asked me.

"Probably March, maybe earlier," I said, feeling the familiar stirring of excitement at the thought of living and studying in London. "God, I can't believe it's so soon."

"How about you, Anna?" Dad asked. "I heard you talking about MBAs with Kay's uncle earlier today. What's going on with that?"

Anna looked thoughtful. "Well, my professor isn't sure that I *need* one, necessarily, for actuarial science, as I already have the math," she began. "But since I want to make the move over to the private sector, it feels like I'd be at a disadvantage without one, you know? And my dad is all for it."

"Oh, that's great," I said. "You–you'll do amazing, I know it."

You won't have any loans, like me, I'd been about to say, but stopped myself. Mr. Becker being "all for" an MBA meant that he'd pay for it. The same way he'd paid for her Mount

Holyoke tuition in full: with the payout from Mrs. Becker's life insurance policy and the settlement from the wrongful death lawsuit against the company of the driver who killed her. And I had been this close to pointing out what a fortunate thing that cash-on-hand was.

My stomach soured at the thought. I considered an alternative, but my mom beat me to it.

"Your mom would be so proud of you, Anna," she said quietly.

My dad nodded firmly. "She *is* proud. She's watching and she's proud."

Anna smiled. It was an authentically grateful smile, and not an *I'll-let-them-think- they've-comforted-me* smile. I knew the difference.

"Will you do that at UNH while you're working there?" Mom asked.

Anna shrugged. "I haven't thought that far ahead," she said. "There are so many great Boston schools, it's not like I have to fly across the ocean for *two years*." She looked at me pointedly.

"Hey, really old stuff, remember?" I said. "You'll visit and talk about how old it all is with me."

In truth, I did feel a little bad – a *little* – about how much I'd been going on about England. This wasn't the first pointed remark she'd made.

I reached over and squeezed her forearm, clad in maroon silk. Our eyes met.

I got you, sister-I-chose.

The color of her sleeve sparked something. Anna's mother, spraying maroon and white Silly String over her head. *You got in!*

"What about Chicago?" I asked suddenly.

"What do you mean?" Anna asked.

"The University of Chicago," I said. "For your MBA. You could go *there*."

Anna looked wistful for a moment, and it hurt me to see it.

"I don't know," she said. "I think the Chicago ship has sailed."

I opened my mouth to argue with her, remembering the joy, the energy, the sheer *Anna-ness* of her reaction when she'd been accepted five years ago. But again, my mom beat me to it.

"Well, thank goodness we're not losing *two* daughters next fall," she said to my dad.

Anna's hundred watt smile in response was clear. I swallowed my words along with the rest of my wine.

Chapter 17

Ping!

The text notification seemed overly loud in the gym's locker room following my run on the treadmill. Mindful of the NO CELL PHONE USE IN CHANGING AREA signs screaming in all caps, I fought the urge to pull my phone out of my fleece jacket pocket.

It might not be from Joy, I reasoned. *It's probably a promo code from Jockey.*

Still, I hurriedly toweled myself dry and dressed, nearly tripping when my foot got caught in the leg of my jeans.

I'll let my hair air dry for once, I thought, and rushed to the gym lobby, reaching into my pocket for my phone as soon as I had cleared the locker room door.

It *was* from Joy.

I'm about to text A., it read. *Are you still at the gym? Can you meet me at The Works?*

I glanced at my watch. I still had 20 minutes before it was time to pick Holly up from her swim lesson. I gave her message a thumbs up emoji and strode to the exit, bumping the door open with my shoulder as I typed.

I'll be there in 5 mins.

Minutes later, I was in line at The Works, accepting a large hot coffee with cream and one raw sugar. Joy was seated at a table in the corner, stirring a packet of honey into what I assumed was her usual green tea. Her phone lay on the tabletop, the screen dark. She was dressed in her nursing scrubs, her hair in a neat ponytail.

"Hey," I said, breathlessly. "Thanks for meeting me before work. I know you don't have much time."

"I have a few minutes," she said, unlocking her phone and tapping at the screen. "This is what I've written. I haven't sent it yet."

She held the phone out to me. I took it gingerly, afraid an errant pinky will send the message before I have the chance to read.

Hi Anna, it began. *I'm reaching out to see if you wanted to meet up sometime soon to talk. Our dads saw each other the other day and it seems like yours doesn't know what's going on. We go back a long way, and I wanted to make sure you were OK. It would be just the two of us.*

I slid the phone back to her across the table, my stomach fluttering. "OK, send it."

"Are you sure?"

I nodded. "I don't want to overthink it. Send it."

Tap.

"It's done," Joy said, leaving her phone on the table. "Now we wait. What're you doing today?"

"I'm picking up Holly in a few minutes, and then we're going to Plum Island for a hike."

"That sounds nice," she said, evenly. "All of you?"

"Yeah," I said, taking a sip of my coffee. "We like it there, especially in the fall. We haven't been there in a while, so I thought it'd be nice…" My voice trailed off, mentally adding *Plum Island hikes* to the list of things Matthew sacrificed during his months-long indiscretion.

"Is it…weird?" Joy asked me, leaning forward. "Being with him and not being able to talk about, you know, *it* yet?"

I exhaled. "God, it's *so* weird," I said. "There'll be these moments that feel so normal, you know? And I almost, *almost* forget what they did. It's like–"

Ping!

We both froze for a moment, then looked down. Even upside down, I could read that the message was from Anna.

Joy looked at me, a question in her eyes.

"You read it," I said. "It's for you, anyway."

I busied myself while Joy and Anna sent rapid fire texts to each other, staring out the window onto Congress Street. Joggers, shoppers, parents pushing infants and toddlers in strollers. The babies tugged at my heart.

Joy sent a final text and then retrieved her bag from the seat beside her.

"She agreed to meet with me. We're having breakfast next Sunday."

Sunday? A week? My heart sank, and I tried to keep the disappointment hidden. Instead, I nodded.

"OK. Did she say anything else?"

Joy scrolled through the text messages. "She appreciated my reaching out, and she's grateful to Dad for not telling Mr. Becker what happened. She wants to do that herself, and she's working out how and when…with her therapist."

Joy and I looked at each other, taking this in.

"Did you know she saw a therapist?" Joy asked.

I shook my head. "Anna's never been in counseling, not even

when her mom died," I said. "And it's 'her' therapist, rather than 'a' therapist. I think she's been seeing this person for a while. I'm…I'm glad."

"So, what do you want me to ask her?" my sister said.

I thought about this. Anna knew that anything she told Joy, Joy would tell me.

"Mostly just make sure she's OK," I said. "But if she's willing to tell you, I want to know her side of things. How it began."

"And who ended it?" Joy prompted me.

I flinched. *Did* I want to know who ended it?

"I have the feeling you're going to get that info, regardless of whether I want it or not," I said, with a wry smile. Joy tilted her head in acquiescence.

"What do you want me to say if she asks me about you?"

I gazed back out the window, where a redheaded woman was assisting her daughter – about four, I guessed – with the zipper of her Hello Kitty windbreaker. Next to them, the girl's father spoke into a cell phone, his free hand absently stroking her head. I idly wondered if he had ever had – or considered having – an affair.

"Kay?"

I turned back to my sister. "I have no idea," I said. "I mean, it's impossible to know what to tell her until you see how she'll be with you. Those messages–" I gestured to her phone. "They may *seem* calm, but they're just words. Maybe she'll be contrite, or she could be defensive. Maybe she'll come in with an ironclad poker face. You…you'll just have to do what feels right in the moment. I trust you, Joy."

"What if she wants to reach out to you?"

My stomach soured at the thought. I shook my head again, slowly, but stayed silent.

She reached over and squeezed my hand, then returned her phone to her bag.

"I have to go," she said. "We'll talk later this week,"

"Thank you for doing this," I added quietly.

We left the cafe together and hugged goodbye. I spotted the family of three a half-block in front of me. Their little girl – zippered snugly into her windbreaker – was between them, clutching their hands and lifting her feet so she could swing. I smiled, suddenly eager to be on my own family walk.

It would be a picnic, I thought, spinning on my heel and heading back into The Works. *With their favorite sandwiches for lunch.*

A *family* picnic.

* * *

Then (Portsmouth, New Hampshire – September 2011)

"Is this seriously all you're bringing?" Anna asked me. "You sure you're not going to monk school?"

"Ha ha," I said drily, picking up a pink fleece scarf from the *not going to England* pile and tossing it at her. "If you want to fly to Heathrow with me and help me lug everything on the Tube, I'll bring more."

Anna batted the scarf away and burrowed deeper into the black bean bag chair. "You're supposed to say 'ha bloody ha,' now, I think," she said.

I shuddered. "Gross. I still gag every time Joy slips in 'blood' when she's talking about work. If I start using that word in everyday conversation, you need to smother me with that scarf, because I'm clearly not me," I said. "It means they've smuggled me to Scotland and cloned me along with Dolly the sheep."

"Who's they?" Anna wondered.

"The Duke of Edinburgh, obviously," I said, and we both snickered.

We were in my room. Outside, rain slashed against my bedroom windows, making the Thursday afternoon preternaturally dark. My departure for the two-year Masters in Architecture program at the Royal College of Art was four days away. Anna's first week of classes at MIT's Sloan School of Management began the same day. We had both left our jobs – the first real jobs of our adulthood – the Friday before, and had spent the week enjoying the last of the summer weather, studiously avoiding any talk of being separated for two years. By an ocean, no less.

I took a fresh glance around the room. "I might – *might* – be done," I said, cautiously. "What am I forgetting?"

"The new journal you bought at RiverRun," Anna said, twirling a kelly green scally cap around her index finger for a few rotations before placing it, backwards, onto her head. "I'm keeping this, by the way."

"Sure," I said, striding over to my bookshelf and retrieving the forgotten journal. I nestled it into my oversized Travel-Smith suitcase and zippered it shut.

"There," I said, sighing and climbing down to the floor and leaning against my bed frame to face Anna. My legs stretched out to meet hers, our shins resting together slightly.

"I'm going to miss you, you jerk," Anna said, nudging my leg with her own. "Why'd you have to go all the way to London?"

I looked at her. "Can I tell you a secret?"

She raised her eyebrows.

I swallowed. "I'm nervous."

She smiled, a little sadly. "It would be weird if you weren't."

"Well, maybe terrified."

She tilted her head at me. "Why terrified?"

I shrugged. "Just…everything. A new city – a new *country*, even. The program's going to be really tough. I mean, not that it's MIT or anything," I added, quickly.

Anna scoffed. "Don't do that," she said. "Don't minimize what you're doing. Not to me. Not to anyone."

"See?" I said. "*That's* why I'm terrified. I'm not going to have you there to call me on my crap. Or be my wingwoman."

"I hate to break it to you, Baby," Anna said. "But you knew that when you filled out the application."

Of course I had. I was so excited at the prospect of two years in London that I didn't let the fact that I'd be doing this on my own fully sink in. I'd be Kay, with no other qualifier than *the American*. Not Kay, *Joy's sister* or Kay *Anna's friend*. Just Kay. Who would she be, with this new slate wiped clean by the Atlantic Ocean?

"We'll be bordering on our late-twenties when we're both done with school," I said.

Anna made a face. "Are you trying to make me feel worse?"

I shrugged. "It's not a *bad* thing," I suggested. "It just makes me feel curious about it all. Look at how many weddings Joy's been to in the last six months. I could come back and you'll be engaged to some rocket scientist and looking at houses near 'the right schools,'" I said, making air quotes.

"Well, said rocket scientist shouldn't be holding his breath for *me* to have his babies," Anna said, definitively. "That's not going to happen."

I looked at my friend, surprised. All of our pie-in-the-sky conversations about true adulthood had included our kids – vague shadows of fog that they, as yet, were – growing up together.

"You don't want kids?" I asked her now. "Since when?"

Anna's face took on a quietly defiant expression. "For a while now," she admitted. "I just didn't admit it out loud until now."

"How come?" I asked, genuinely curious.

A cloud flitted across her face. "Do I need a reason?" Anna challenged me. "Maybe I just don't want them."

A small flare of defensiveness shot through me. I let it burst and die out, confident that this new revelation of hers wasn't worth poking the bear I knew was below the surface, semi-dormant.

I shrugged again, hoping for an air of nonchalance. "You don't owe anyone anything," I said. "But if you're going to tell *someone* about this seemingly new development, I hope it would be me."

My approach worked. Anna's shoulders, tense against my bean bag chair, slumped. "Sorry," Anna muttered. "I've been having this debate in my head for, like, a year."

"With who?" I asked.

"My dad. Future boyfriends. Society at large," she confessed. "I always end up yelling."

"Well, screw them," I told her. "You don't have to convince anyone, least of all me. I'm just honestly curious. Explain it to me. I promise I won't try to change your mind."

It was her turn to shrug. "I don't know if I can," she said. "I know you and I have always said stuff like 'when we have kids, we're gonna blah blah blah.' But it never felt real, you know? And now that we're actually at an age when it's not, like, out of the realm of possibility, I just realized that it's not what I actually want."

"There's nothing wrong with that," I said. "Frankly, I'm relieved."

Anna looked at me, curiosity sparking in her eyes. "Why?"

"Well, I mean, look at you," I gestured. "Miss MIT math genius. How's my kid supposed to compete with yours? You're much less intimidating as an auntie."

She grinned at me. "I'll take that as a compliment, I think."

I smiled back. "You should."

Anna stretched, her gray Holyoke t-shirt exposing an inch of tanned stomach. "So what about you?" Anna asked me. "Are you going to come home engaged to a duke or an earl?"

I stood, reaching my hand down to pull Anna to her feet. "Only if said duke or earl is prepared to live in New England," I said. "With my *family*."

Chapter 18

"Holly, look!" I called.

She paused midstep, about 10 yards ahead of us on the boardwalk, and turned back. I watched her expression as she searched where I had pointed, relishing in her surprise and joy when she spotted the swooping great blue heron over the saltmarsh. She stood stock still, tracking the bird as it skimmed the water and came to rest in a patch of golden grass.

The day was beautiful. Crisp and sunny, with just enough bite to the offshore wind to make me grateful for the armful of fleece jackets I'd remembered to toss into the car. I was in my favorite, a light gray with a full zipper and a tiny Scottish flag on the hood.

Holly studied the heron for a few more seconds and then continued to skip ahead on the Hellcat Trail. Beside me, Matthew chuckled quietly. I waited, knowing he'd share whatever Plum Island memory had surfaced, making him laugh.

"Remember when the Hood blimp flew over the island?" he asked.

I laughed. It was a genuine one, not bracketed by caution or inauthenticity. It felt wonderful.

"Oh, my God," I explained. "I thought she was going to lose her mind."

"She was *obsessed* with blimps," Matthew said. "What was she then? Three?"

I nodded. "I think her first real word was 'blimp.'"

Matthew took a sip of the coffee we'd bought in Newburyport before continuing on to the trailhead parking lot. He seemed lighter today. Calmer. *Unburdened* wasn't quite right, I thought. Maybe it was the fact that he was no longer being slowly poisoned by a secret.

He held the cup in his right hand, leaving his left arm free for me to link mine through. It was what we usually did during these walks. Today, though, I felt shy. I was overly aware of his free arm. Was I supposed to take it? For the last half mile, I'd kept my hands loosely gripping the shoulder straps of my backpack that held a blanket and the sandwiches I'd impulsively bought after meeting with Joy. My fingers were starting to tingle uncomfortably.

"You knew it would be there," Matthew added.

"Huh?" I asked, dropping my arms to my sides and giving my hands a small shake.

"The blimp," he said. "You knew, didn't you? That day?"

I smiled. "Yeah. I had checked online. It was going to be flying over Fenway that afternoon, so I knew it would be close by," I said, calling the image up in my mind. "I figured we should try to spot it while her fixation was at its peak."

Matthew laughed again. "You timed it right," he said. "Wasn't she hooked on unicorns after that?"

"Narwhals," I corrected.

Matthew shrugged. "Same thing."

I laughed again, and suddenly my right arm snaked through

his left, on its own accord. It was pure autopilot. Once my mind stopped obsessing over it, my body took over.

Is this OK? I wanted to ask. Then Matthew slid his left hand into the pocket of his midnight blue fleece, creating a shelf for me to rest my wrist. Like he'd done so many times in the past. I relaxed. It *was* OK.

"I love that you did that," he said, softly.

I swallowed and gave him a sideways glance. "The blimp research…or my arm?" I asked, giving his forearm a gentle squeeze.

He used his left elbow to press my arm a little closer to his side. "Both," he said. "But I have to give you special mom points for the blimp research. That was something."

I didn't do anything, just spent about three minutes on a computer. The words were forming in my mind and about to be spoken out loud, but my husband preempted me.

"And before you tell me it was nothing," he said, scanning my eyes briefly to confirm that I had, in fact, been about to say that. "I want you to understand that it's not."

We slowed and turned to face each other, coming to rest against the railing. I slid the backpack from my shoulders and placed it at our feet. Ahead of us on the boardwalk, Holly was examining an interpretive sign, glancing now and again at the marsh, trying to spot whatever flora or fauna was in the images.

"You planned that whole morning so that our daughter would get a real, live glimpse of the thing that she loved most in the world at the time," he said. "And you've done things like that – for Holly, for me – a million times. You can point to one example and say 'oh, that was nothing,' but you do it *every single day*. That's not nothing. Just like the food that I suspect is in that pack isn't nothing." He nudged the bag with his foot.

He placed his paper cup on the railing and held his hands up, a signal for me to lace my fingers through his. I did.

He leaned closer. "You are kinder, more thoughtful, more loving than anyone I've ever known. Ever. And certainly more than I deserve," he said.

My stomach fluttered a little at the second *ever*. A dozen questions – some pleading, some accusatory – tried to bubble to the surface. *Then how could you... But why did you...* I forced them back down, mindful of Dr. Garciá's advice to not discuss the affair outside of counseling yet.

He drew in a deep breath. "I got…lost, Kay. Really lost. And I can make some bad decisions when I'm…in the dark like that. As you know."

"Mo-om!" Holly called. "I see the beach! Can we have a picnic? I'm hungry!"

"We'll be right there!" I yelled back. "Wait for us."

I turned back to Matthew. He drew me closer.

"You saved me, once," he whispered, his fingers playing with the frayed hem of my sleeve. "We both know you did. I guess I thought I couldn't ask you to do it again."

"That's what we signed up for, Matthew," I protested. "For better or for worse, you know?"

He nodded. "It was a mistake. A huge one. But we'll get to all of that, I guess. Yeah?"

He let go of my hands and bent down to pick up my backpack. He slung it over one shoulder and took a step forward, holding a hand back out for me to take.

I studied him. *We'll get to* all *of that.* Would that include his first dalliance with Anna as well? If he didn't bring it up, would I?

"Yes," I said, quietly and steadily, slipping my hand into his. "We'll get to that. All of it."

* * *

Then (London, England — January 2012)

Hello, Italian Gardens! Hello, Peter Pan!

I greeted the statues, bridges, and trees of Kensington Gardens and Hyde Park like old friends. I beamed, ridiculously happy to be back in London. I'd booked my flight home for Christmas late, arriving on the 21st. To keep the peace with my disapproving mother, I'd stayed back in the U.S. for a few days into the new year. Reluctantly.

Hello, Queen Caroline's Temple!

Oh, how I loved London. I loved its history, its bustle, its heartbreakingly gorgeous buildings, and its people. I loved the roommates – *flatmates* – that I'd stumbled upon in my quest for semi-affordable housing. I loved the pubs, and I was committed to experiencing as many as I possibly could in the next year and a half, while staying true to my local one.

A breeze kicked up. Around me, walkers tucked down their caps and re-wrapped their coats. I smiled wider, leaving my pea coat unbuttoned and allowing myself to feel like the smug New Englander. *This? This is nothing.*

Hello, Serpentine Gallery!

I stole a glance at my watch. I didn't need to be in my advisor's office for another half hour. I'd be early. With luck, she'd be running ahead of schedule. We'd meet, she'd sign off on the change to my schedule, and then the day would be mine. Perhaps a visit to the Tate. Or – even better – finally check out that secondhand bookshop in Chelsea for a guide to Scotland and hole up in a new pub to plan my Edinburgh weekend.

Hello, Albert Memorial!

Wait, what?

I slowed, then stopped, studying the profile of the man walking lazily down the steps of the memorial. His hands were shoved into the pockets of his forest green down vest, exposing the cable knit sleeves of his off-white crew neck sweater. At the bottom of the steps he turned, moving clockwise around the sculpture, and I saw his full face.

Matt.

He continued, gazing at the African sculptures and ambling towards the Asia set. I quickened my pace, and when he turned right onto South Carriage Drive I fell into step beside him.

"It's romantic, isn't it, Matt?" I asked, as casually as I could.

Matt flinched and turned to face me. His expression was blank for a second. Then two. Then three. I waited, smiling.

Recognition sparked in his eyes and a wide, boyish grin lit up his face.

"Kay!" Matt exclaimed, an octave too loud considering how close I was. His cheeks reddened, as if reading my thoughts. He took a half step towards me, pulling his hands out of his vest pockets and opening them. I stepped forward and accepted the quick hug.

"What're you–"

"This is so–"

We stopped speaking over each other and chuckled, each pausing to let the other go first.

I held up a finger in an *aha* gesture, remembering a long-ago conversation on a rainy porch, just before a kiss. The memory caused a brief, gentle flutter in my stomach.

"Wait. London School of Economics, right?" I said, pointing at him. "You told me about it once. At the Summit House"

"Yeah," he said, looking at me with a little surprise. "Good memory."

The flush in his cheeks deepened.

He just remembered the kiss, too, I thought, quietly pleased.

His hair had darkened a shade since college, and the scruff of what I guessed to be two days' growth covering his jawline was something I'd never seen on him before. It was sexy.

There was also the slightest shadow under his eyes. Heavy course load, or something else?

"What about you?" Matt asked me.

I pointed across the street. "Royal College of Art," I said. "I'm in the architecture program. I started last term, and I'll be here through the end of next school year. When did you get here?"

"Same. September."

"Oh," I said, pleased. "So you'll be here for two years, too, then?"

Matt hesitated, a flicker of doubt in his eyes, then nodded. He turned back to the Albert Memorial.

"So you think C-3PO here is romantic?"

I laughed, swatting him on his shoulder. "The symbol, you philistine. Commissioned by a queen grieving her late husband."

"Ah," Matt said, examining the monument with renewed interest. "Grief. Yes. That explains the funeral procession of statues here." He waved a hand at the *Frieze of Parnassus*.

"You mean the 169 composers, architects, poets, painters, and sculptors?" I asked, teasingly, showing off a little.

He turned to me, smiling. "Well, you *do* go to school across the street," he reasoned. "You're supposed to know this stuff. Talk to me about Moldova's place in the global economy."

"Blegh," I said. "Hard pass. So what *are* you doing in my part of London?"

Matt shrugged, his hands back in his pockets. "I hadn't made it over to this part yet," he said. "Today seemed like as good a day as any. I was going to take a spin through the Royal Albert Hall and grab some lunch in the cafe there."

I glanced at my watch again.

"I have a better idea, if you're up for it," I said. I motioned for us to continue walking to Queen's Gate and cross the Kensington Gore.

"I'm meeting with my advisor in a little bit," I said. "But that shouldn't take long. I'll meet you in the cafe, but if I'm not there when you're finished with the Hall, just get a pot of tea or something. I'll take you to the Gloucester Arms for lunch. It's my favorite pub near school."

"Yeah? That'd be great," he said. "You don't have to change your plans 'cause of me, though."

We strode over the crosswalk – *the zebra crossing*, I thought – and arrived on the other side of the Gore.

I smiled up at him. "Don't be silly," I said. "It's lovely to see you again."

He grinned. "*Lovely*. You're already sounding British."

"I'll teach you," I offered. "I'm afraid I can't let you run around London referring to Prince Albert as C-3PO."

He smiled – shyly, I thought. "Yeah, I guess I can't be exposed as an 'uncultured hick' over here, can I?" Matt said, putting air quotes around the phrase. He looked at me, expectant. There was practically a thought bubble floating above his head, reading *Remember the night we met? Please remember, or I'll feel like an idiot.*

I laughed. "I see what you did there, but I don't think The Arms serves bocce balls." I said. "I'll meet you in a little bit. Enjoy the Albert Hall."

I spun on my heel and started down Jay Mews, towards my advisor's office.

"Kay," Matt called.

I turned around.

"I know I'm supposed to act all cool seeing an old flame like this," he said, still smiling. "But I'm really, really happy to see a face from home."

I smiled in return and then turned back, walking briskly towards school, feeling a warm flush spread across my cheeks.

Old flame?

Chapter 19

D*ear Matthew.*
~~*I love you.*~~
~~*You hurt me.*~~
~~*I'm trying to understand why you and Anna did this. HOW could you do this? You ruined everything, you jerk.*~~
~~*Why did you come home again?*~~

I tore the page containing my latest false start from the yellow legal pad, crumpled it, and chucked it into the wastebasket next to the desk, where it came to rest with my previous attempts. It was beginning to look like a pile of tennis balls was nesting in it.

I stared at the fresh, blank page in front of me.

"Focus, Kay. Focus," I muttered.

The little office nook we'd set up in a corner of the den suddenly felt claustrophobic. I swiveled away from the desk and stood, bringing the pad and my pen to the sofa. Tucking myself into one end, I draped a beige chenille blanket over my knees and propped a square decorative cushion on my lap. Instant sofa desk.

I want you to write a letter, our therapist had said. *Write a letter to your partner about what you feel are their best qualities.*

What do you love most about them? Why are they so special to you?

It was Tuesday evening. The first floor of the house was eerily quiet, with Holly already asleep and Matthew in the guest room having a virtual consultation with a trauma counselor, as Elena Garciá had suggested.

I winced at the thought. My husband was upstairs preparing to relive the day our daughter nearly died, and I was down here scrawling *you ruined everything, you jerk* on pieces of paper. I saw, with abrupt clarity, why I couldn't write the letter. I was still seeing Matthew through the lens of what he and Anna had done. I needed to see *him.* Just him.

I closed my eyes and drew in a few deep, slow breaths, letting the memories come. Quietly but firmly, they nudged aside my current anger, pain, and fear. My body grew still, and I let the slideshow of random, non-chronological snapshots scroll, letting it go where it wanted. Finally, I opened my eyes and picked up my pen, humming with a focus I hadn't felt in a long time.

Dear Matthew,

When I first saw you, you were laughing at me for grimacing over a sickly sweet cocktail. It might seem like a small thing, but I've always kind of loved that our first exchange was a bit of an inside joke.

It was hard to get to know you in the beginning, when we were still in college. You were always friendly to everyone, but there was a guard up as well. From what I could see on the surface – the fact that we read the same books and both knew that The Who didn't name the song "Teenage Wasteland" – you were someone I wanted to know.

I remember the first time you let me in, when you talked about your grandfather. I loved how you spoke about him then. I loved how much you respected, admired, and loved him. And I love how that translated into the husband and father you became.

You love your family with a fierceness that is palpable. You would do anything for them, including shielding me from the hell-on-earth that is Pooley's Playground...and the truth of our daughter's health scare.

And it's not just me and Holly. When we came back from England, you embraced my family as yours. You could have moved west to be closer to your mom, or taken a job in Los Angeles or New York, where the firms were more prestigious and the money and perks more appealing. You chose a smaller work life for a richer family one. And you never complained about it, not once. You never made me feel like you had sacrificed anything by staying here. Instead, you made me feel chosen. Like I was the center of your world.

I paused, placing the pen down on the pad and flexing the cramps out of my hand. My words – *sacrificed, chosen* – had triggered a memory from our first session with Elena.

The road not taken. The one where I get together with Anna instead of Kay.

I mentally flicked the thought away. We'd be getting to that eventually.

I remember the day I told you I was pregnant. It wasn't planned, and I was nervous about telling you. I was nervous that the first emotion I was going to see on your face was terror, or worse, disappointment.

Instead, you smiled. One of those fast-spreading, lip-stretching smiles of yours that can only mean one thing: pure and utter joy. You said "we're going to be a family," and I was so relieved and happy that I started sobbing. I love you for making that moment perfect.

When we were on Plum Island a few days ago, you told me that I saved you once before. I like to think that–

Matthew's footfalls on the stairs signaled the end of his virtual meeting. I clicked my pen shut and rose from the sofa to tuck my unfinished letter into my filing drawer. When I returned to my seat, Matthew was in the kitchen. From my position on the couch, I had my back to him. Instead of turning around, I listened, my mind's eye imagining his movements in perfect synchronization to the sounds he made.

Two gentle *tinks* – Matthew pulling two stemmed wine glasses from the cabinet and resting them on the granite counter.

A hollow *thwock* – my husband pulling the cork out of the half-drunk bottle of cabernet we'd opened on Saturday after our hike.

Two *glugs*, one longer than the other. He'd likely poured me my usual half glass and gave himself a little extra following his session.

Finally, he appeared in my peripheral vision, one hand extending a glass – a perfect half full pour – to me.

"Thank you," I said, accepting the glass as he sat down on his end of the sofa. "How was it? Do you like him?"

He sipped from his own glass – a tad fuller than usual – and nodded.

"I do," he said. "I think he's a really good fit. I'm going to meet with him remotely. Once a week, to start."

I smiled, genuinely happy for him. "That's great; I'm really glad. Do you want to tell me about it? You don't have to," I added quickly. "I just thought–"

I stopped. Matthew was staring at a point over my shoulder, giving his best mock stink eye. I turned. Holly's small face and tousled blonde hair was peeking around the entry to the kitchen.

I chuckled softly and turned back to Matthew. "I heard on the news recently that Portsmouth has a spy problem," I said, letting my voice travel farther.

Matthew refocused on me. "Is that right?" he said, playing along. "I hadn't heard that. Is it dangerous? Should we be worried?"

"I don't *think* so," I said, studiously avoiding looking over my shoulder again. "I heard that they just quietly creep up behind you…" I paused, the tiny creak of the first board of the den floor giving Holly away.

"And then what?" Matthew asked breathlessly, also avoiding our daughter's eye.

"Well," I said. "When you least expect it…."

Holly was low on the floor, crawling toward me.

"Yes?" Matthew prompted.

"They…DEMAND TO BE TICKLED!"

Holly stood and tried to run, but I reached and pulled her onto the sofa between us. My fingers tickled her ribs, while Matthew's attacked her bare feet. She shrieked with glee.

We stopped our dual tickle assault and spent a few moments enjoying a quiet family cuddle.

"Why are you out of bed, Holly Jolly?" Matthew asked her.

She looked at me, her face pulled into an exaggerated pout. "You didn't finish my story."

I bopped her nose with a finger. "I did, actually," I said. "You fell asleep halfway through."

"That doesn't count, then."

Matthew placed his glass on the end table and stood, scooping our daughter up in his arms. "I'll rectify this travesty," he said. "But you're coming with me. And I'm keeping you close this time so you don't get into trouble."

He took a few steps towards the kitchen.

"Daddy, STOP!"

I turned. "What's wrong?"

Holly wriggled out of Matthew's hold and ran to the floor in front of the sofa. The toys representing the characters in Mrs. Dwyer's riddle – Barbie, Uno, kitty, and chick – were in a small heap on the area rug.

Holly grabbed Barbie and the chick and held them up. "The puzzle! 'Member I said that she has to move the duck first to the other island? That's 'cause the fox and the grain can be alone together without anything bad happening, but the duck can't be alone with either of them. But, if I always take the duck with me, there won't be any trouble!" Holly exclaimed.

Grinning, she moved the duck to the new island. "Now, I go back alone, and bring the fox with me," she said importantly. "But when I drop the fox off on the new island, I take the duck with me for the return trip!"

She continued to manipulate her toys, keeping the duck close, until all items were safely transported. Then she looked up at both of us, triumphant.

"You did it, Holls!" I said, proud of my daughter.

"Very clever, Miss Marple," Matthew said, holding out his hand for her to take. "The duck either causes the trouble or gets hurt by it; good thinking keeping it close."

Holly took his hand and together they headed towards the stairs.

I'll be back, Matthew mouthed to me. I nodded.

On the floor, Holly's toys were arranged in a happy circle on their new island. The duck – both a villain and a victim of the riddle – sat in the center.

For the second time in less than a week, I wondered who the duck was in my own personal riddle.

***

Then (London, England – January 2012)

I collected Matthew from the cafe inside the Royal Albert Hall, where I found him nursing a cup of tea and reading what appeared to be a brand-new *Lonely Planet* guide to Great Britain. During the 10-minute walk to the pub, he'd asked polite questions: about the meeting with my advisor, my classes for the upcoming term, and what Anna was up to. I prattled in response, happy to keep the conversation light while we walked. I sensed something heavier under the surface, but I wouldn't attempt to uncover it until we had pints in our hands.

The Gloucester Arms came into sight from Queen's Gate Terrace, its navy facade and muted gold lettering standing out against the pale stone of the larger building. Inside, patrons were engulfed in warm wood, an aesthetic broken only by the tight perimeter of black and white tiles surrounding the bar at the center of the large room.

It was early, not yet half past twelve, and the pub was quiet. Students weren't back yet, and the weekday lunch crowd was light. I knew from experience that on a day like today, the

Arms wouldn't really pick up until four, when the first wave of office workers snuck out early.

"Welcome back, Kay. 'Appy new year!" said Finn, from behind the bar. "Perfect timing, this is; the boys in the kitchen are working on a nice batch of fish n' chips. What can I get 'ye to drink?"

I felt like Norm walking into *Cheers*, and I glowed from this stroke of luck. Finn was the only person on staff at the Arms who knew my name, and the only reason he took the time to use it was because the pub wasn't bursting with students. But Matt didn't know this, and I wasn't about to enlighten him.

"Happy new year to you, Finn," I said. "I'll have a pint of Newcastle Brown." I turned to Matt, my eyebrows raised in a *what about you* question. He nodded and gave me a thumbs up.

"Make it two pints," I said. "This is my friend, M–"

"Matthew," Matt said, reaching over the bar to shake Finn's hand. "Pleased to meet you."

"Nice t'meet you, Matthew," said Finn, as he poured our pints. "Any friend of Kay's is welcome at the Arms." He gave me an exaggerated wink, as I was hoping he would.

See? I'm a regular! I'm fun!

"I'll get this round," I told Matt. "Pick out a place to sit."

I handed Finn a ten pound note, feeling suddenly nervous. Logically, I shouldn't care about impressing Matt with my adapting-to-new-surroundings prowess. But I wanted to, all the same.

Matt had opted against a table, and we slid onto stools at the bar, our foaming pints in front of us.

"Cheers," I said, clinking my glass against Matt's. "To serendipitous run-ins."

We sipped at the foam threatening to overrun the rims of our glasses and I studied him, stealthily. He looked good, I thought, save for the bluish hollow under his eyes.

"It's really good to see you, Matt," I said, when we rested our pints on the bar. "Or is it *Matthew* now?" I wagged my eyebrows at him, jokingly.

He grinned, sheepishly. "Guilty. I realized pretty soon after I got here that 'Matthew' sounded a lot more professional than 'Matt,' especially in an English accent. So I leaned into it. Is that weird?" he asked.

I shook my head. "Absolutely not," I affirmed, thinking of my own desire for a clean slate in England. I raised my glass again and tipped it towards him slightly. "Matthew it is." I took another sip of my New Castle and set the glass down.

"So, what's it like? Finally following in the footsteps of your grandfather?"

He smiled, a little sadly, I thought.

"It's…uh, great," he said. "Really great."

I frowned at him over my pint. "OK, are you auditioning for *Showgirls 3* right now? Because that was the worst acting I've ever seen in my life," I said.

Matt sputtered on his beer, looking surprised and a little resigned, as if he'd been caught in a white lie.

"Matt, *Matthew*, talk to me," I continued. "Seriously. What is going on?"

He glanced around, as if uncertain he should be speaking the words out loud, "Being here. Going to the London School of Economics. This is something I've wanted my whole life," he said.

I nodded. "I remember. And now you're here," I said. "And?"

Matthew took a deep swig of his New Castle. "And I hate

it," he said. "I hate it. There. I said it."

"OK," I said, calmly. "At the risk of sounding like a stupid, first-time therapist, *why* do you hate it?"

Matthew chuckled, but it was without any actual mirth. "You know, that's exactly what my stupid, first-time therapist asked me about a month ago. And I wasn't even honest with him."

I laughed in response, but my heart twisted a little at his joke. I couldn't claim to know Matthew all that well, but the news of a therapist, his paleness, and general lack of, I don't know, *oomph*, worried me.

"Well," I said again. "Do you want to give me the answer you couldn't give him?"

Matthew looked at me. He looked with the clear blue eyes of the boy I'd fallen for briefly during my sophomore year in college.

"OK, counselor," he said jokingly. "I guess it's because when I went looking for my new home, I lost my old one." Matthew sipped his pint and returned my gaze, a challenge in his eyes.

I blinked, but held his stare.

"All right," I said. "But, since I can't read minds – *yet*, science is working on it – what does that actually mean?"

His shoulders slumped a little.

"I'm sorry," he said, absentmindedly scratching the back of his head. "You're trying to help and I'm being a dick."

"No, stop," I said. "Look, if you don't want to talk about it–"

"I do, though," he insisted.

I waited.

"My mom got married again. Just before I came over here," he said. "And he's a great guy and I'm really happy for her. I mean, she deserves to be happy."

I nodded, but stayed silent.

He took a sip of his pint. "He's from Arizona. They met when he was on assignment in New England. He's a documentary filmmaker. Anyway, she spent the fall putting the house on the market and moving out west. It was all final just before Thanksgiving, so she lives there now."

"Did you go there for Christmas?" I asked.

Matthew shook his head. "Nah. I stayed here. One of my friends invited me for dinner on Christmas Day, which was nice, but…"

I smiled softly. "But not the same as family."

"No, not the same," he said. "And I know I shouldn't let it impact my time here, but…I don't know. I guess I just feel…lost. In between homes, I think. Like I don't really belong anywhere. I don't know if I'll stay here for the full two years, to be honest. If I finish the year, I might be able to transfer credits, but I don't even know where I'd transfer them to."

"What about your grandfather's family?" I asked, interrupting him. "Don't you have uncles, or cousins or cousins-once-removed here?"

He shrugged, adjusting the neckline of his sweater. "Maybe. I don't really know."

"You don't know?" I asked. "But you're here! Wouldn't now be the perfect time to find out?"

He looked at me, his expression softening, lightening. "I mean, *yeah*. But my mom wasn't the one who kept in contact. It was all Granddad. Would it be weird for me to reach out?"

I reached over and squeezed Matthew's wrist. The contact sent another quick flutter through me. I was here. And, suddenly, *he* was here. The one that got away. Or, really, the one that never really happened. Here in London. The place I didn't realize I would love so much. This had to be a sign. Of…something.

"I think it'd be weird *not* to," I said. "Think about it. Meeting them will make you feel closer to your grandfather, and closer to this place. I *love* it here, and I'm, like, three generations removed."

I took a resolute gulp from my pint and set my glass down firmly. "Matthew Lanning, you are my new project," I announced. "I'm going to help you find your extended family. But not only that, I'm going to show you the London that I love. And I'm not going to rest until you love it as much as I do."

Matthew blinked, then broke into a wide smile. The first real smile I'd seen in the last hour.

"You're on," he said. "I have my doubts, I'm just sayin', but you're on."

"Challenge accepted," I said. We clinked pints again and drained them.

"Wow," Matthew said, resting his glass on the bartop. "I actually feel better. And all that cost me was a pint? You're a much better deal than the campus shrink I was talking to."

I shook my head and gestured to my now empty glass. "*I* bought the first round, remember? You get the next one. Let's order a big pile of fish and chips, and then we're walking to a bookstore in Chelsea. We have a trip to Edinburgh to plan. I'm going out on a limb and assuming you haven't been to Edinburgh?"

"Nope," Matthew said, signaling to Finn for another round and smiling. "Not yet."

Chapter 20

"When we were on Plum Island a few days ago, you told me that I saved you once before," I read. "I like to think that, rather than one of us 'saving' the other, we both got stronger by being together. Like the perfect mortise and tenon joint."

Matthew smiled softly at my architecture reference. I took a calming breath and continued to read my letter.

"In all of our years together, you've never given me a reason not to trust you. There have been moments in the last few weeks when I've berated myself for this trust. I thought it made me look stupid or weak. But I don't look at it that way anymore. The way I see it now, my complete trust in you was an indication of how committed I am to you, to Holly, and our life as a family together. I *don't* regret trusting you. And it's the fact that I don't regret it that's helped me realize that I can trust you again. That I love you, and I want to be with you."

I folded the pages of my handwritten letter in half. I hesitated, then handed them over to Matthew.

We were back on Elena Garciá's taupe suede sofa for our second session. For the first 15 minutes or so, Elena had checked in with Matthew on whether he had found his own therapist, and had asked light questions about how our week under the same roof had gone. Finally, we turned to our assignments from the previous session.

I'd volunteered to read my letter first, wanting to establish early in the session that I was, still, fully committed to our marriage. I didn't know what Matthew's letter would contain, not completely. Based on his cautious affection and – seemingly – authentic apologies since moving back home, I suspected his words would be similar to mine.

But there was a small, frightened sliver inside of me that held back.

"Thank you, Kay," said Elena, shifting slightly in her cream chair and crossing her legs, which were clad in similar linen trousers as last week, except today they were duck egg blue instead of sage. "Matthew, is there anything in Kay's letter that you'd like to respond to before you read yours? Or, you can go ahead and read your letter and we can discuss them both afterwards."

Matthew nodded. "No, umm. Let's do it that way, the second option."

He held up the folded pages of my letter slightly and met my eyes.

"Thank you," he said quietly, then laid the paper down on Elena's coffee table. He reached into his messenger bag and pulled out his letter.

"It's, umm. I didn't hand write it," he stammered. "Sorry."

"Your words don't have to be handwritten to be meaningful," Elena said. "Getting your thoughts down using a keyboard and printer is every bit as valid as using a pen and paper."

Matthew nodded and cleared his throat. I shifted on the

sofa, turning my body to face him, and clasped my hands loosely in my lap to stop them from shaking.

"Kay," he began. "You have been a lot of things to me. You were a friend when I desperately needed one, and 'desperate' isn't too strong a word. If we hadn't met that day outside your school in London, I wouldn't have stayed to finish my degree. And I would never have connected with my relatives. For that year and a half in England, you were so much more than a girlfriend. You were a guide and a cheerleader. You were a reminder of home, and you helped me make a new one."

As I listened, the muscles in my neck and shoulders tensed, waiting for the *but*. The small frightened sliver in me quivered.

"You build people up," he continued. "You built me up when I needed it, and I've watched you do it with others for years, with your family, with *my* family, with your clients, and with your friends. The care and kindness and support that you offer the people you love is incredible. I am so, so lucky to have you – not someone like you, *you* – and I don't know if I'll ever fully forgive myself for losing sight of that.

"I began this letter by saying that you have been many things to me: a friend, a girlfriend, a guide, a cheerleader, a wife, a mother to Holly. I'm sure there's more that I'm forgetting. But I think most of all you're my tether. And I don't mean that in a negative 'ball and chain' kind of way," Matthew glanced up at me briefly, as if worried about my reaction. "I mean that you anchor me. You're home. You're my home, I love you, and I'm sorry. I'm so sorry for what I did."

Matthew refolded his paper and, as I had done with mine, offered it to me. I swiped at a single tear that had escaped and took the page from him.

"Thank you," I said.

Elena uncrossed her legs and leaned forward.

"Thank you, Matthew," she said. "I'm very interested to know what each of you thought of the other's letter. May I share my own impressions first?"

We nodded.

"What I heard is that there is a great deal of love and respect between the two of you, and believe me when I say that that isn't always the case in this room."

I glanced over at Matthew. He was looking at the coffee table, his expression neutral.

"Matthew, what did you think about Kay drawing the connection between your grandfather and yourself as a husband and father?"

Matthew looked at me, and then back to Elena. "I…it meant a lot. I mean, all I've ever wanted was to be someone he'd be proud of. Kay knows that."

"Do you think the fact that she took the time to include something in her letter that she knew would be very meaningful to you is an example of how she – as you put it – builds you up when you need it?"

Matthew looked down and nodded. "Yes. It's a perfect example of that. As long as she still believes it, and isn't telling me what she thinks I want to hear."

"I'm not," I said quietly, a little stung. "I may never have met him, but I wouldn't use his memory like that."

"Kay," Elena said. "How did you feel about Matthew sharing the impact you had on him during your time in England?"

I thought for a few moments before speaking. "I loved it. I love knowing that I was able to be all those things for him, and it was nice to hear it again," I said. "But it also made me feel scared."

Elena's expression softened a little, as if I had given the answer she was hoping for.

"Why does it scare you?"

"Because I want to know that he's with me – that he's in this marriage – because he *wants* to be with me, not because he feels like he owes it to me for what I did then, or because he thinks it's what a good husband should do."

"You're referring to his comment from last week, the 'road not taken,' yes?"

I nodded.

Elena sat back, appearing satisfied. "Then I think it's time we discuss the affair. Here is what I propose. I would like both of you to sit with these letters for the night. Reread them, let them fully sink in."

My heart sank. I couldn't go another week between appointments. I just couldn't.

"I don't book regular sessions on Fridays," she continued. "I like to keep them available for when topics come up that simply can't, or shouldn't, wait a full week. Would you be willing to come back tomorrow so we can meet again?"

"Yes," I said, relieved, glancing at Matthew for his agreement. "Yes, we can do that."

On the ride home, we were quiet. I felt the page of Matthew's printed letter in the pocket of my jacket. I wanted to pull it out and read it again right there in the darkness of the car, snatching a sentence at a time as we crossed under streetlights.

"Arthur," Matthew suddenly said, with a quiet chuckle.

"What?" I asked, confused.

"We just passed Arthur Road," he said. "It reminded me of when you were pregnant with Holly, and you told me if it was a boy you wanted his middle name to be Arthur."

"I think your reaction was to choke on a mouthful of IPA, you unsentimental bastard," I teased.

"Yeah, I missed the reference at first," he said. "I was too busy picturing scenes from *Monty Python's The Holy Grail.*"

We were both quiet for a few moments.

"I like the sentiment of it, though," Matthew added.

He swung the car into the driveway and we stepped out into the light evening rain. I glanced at my watch as we entered the house.

"My mom will be here in about an hour with Holly," I said, shaking droplets from my hair. "They're having dinner. Are you hungry?"

He ignored my question and pulled me close in the kitchen.

"I'm not here because I feel obligated," he said, and kissed me. The first real kiss in months.

When we broke apart, he leaned his forehead against mine. "And I'm not hungry."

I removed my jacket and dropped it onto the kitchen island. We kissed again, more deeply. Was I ready for this?

Yes, my body cried. *God, yes.*

But was I really? In less than 24 hours, we'd be back in Elena's office discussing the many months that my husband had been sleeping with my best friend.

A spark of jealousy burned in my chest. Yes, I was ready. I had to be. He'd promised to never lose sight of me again; and right now I wanted – I *needed* – to be front and center.

We broke apart again and I led my husband up the stairs to our bedroom, as the small, frightened sliver inside me earlier dissolved into territorial rage.

* * *

Then (Edinburgh, Scotland — February 2012)

"I don't think I've ever stood on an extinct volcano before," Matthew said, snapping a series of panoramic images with his blue digital camera as we stood at the top of Arthur's Seat. "Have you?"

"Once," I admitted, scanning the city below us. "My parents took my sister and I on a cruise over April break when we were in high school. One of the stops was St. Kitts."

"Oh, so this is your *second* volcano?" Matthew teased. "Showoff."

"Well, it's my first extinct volcano that also has chapel ruins on it," I reasoned.

"No way!" Matthew said, zooming in on Edinburgh Castle with his camera. "What a coincidence. Me too."

I laughed, then turned away from the view of the castle to face Matthew. "I'm officially starving. Let's find that pub your great uncle told us about and start sampling those Scottish ales."

We walked back down the path we'd hiked up. In my peripheral vision, Matthew's head was high, swiveling to take in the views. In the month since we'd met at the Albert Memorial, he'd grown noticeably lighter and happier.

Guess who I ran into?! I'd texted Anna in January when I returned to my flat after spending that first afternoon with Matthew. *Remember Matt from UMass??*

I waited as the three dots cycled, signaling that Anna was typing a reply. Once, twice.

Wow, she replied. *Small world. Gotta run, heading into class. Talk soon.*

That's it? I tossed the phone onto my bed, disappointed in her reaction, or lack thereof. I was happy and excited, and wanted Anna – or *someone* – to be happy and excited with me. For the first time, I felt the distance between us.

Well, Matthew was certainly happy and excited about it, I'd said to myself then. You can be annoyingly gleeful with him.

And that was exactly what we did. We went out at least twice a week, discovering new pubs and embracing our identity as insufferable tourists.

We'd become friends. Good friends.

Good friends, at least, until last week. When we'd kissed. Once, briefly.

With my help, and a few emails to his mom in Arizona, we'd tracked down his grandfather's brother and two sisters. Between the three of them, they'd had a swarm of first cousins-once-removed and second cousins. Finally, he'd heard from Maggie, his grandfather's niece, Matthew's first cousin once removed, who'd met and remembered her uncle, Matthew's grandfather, and was eager to meet his grandson. Could he come and have dinner with her and her family in Manchester this weekend? He'd be welcome to stay the night.

At the invitation, Matthew was exuberant. Upon reading the email, he'd whooped in the pub we were trying out. He'd shown me the message, then when I looked up at him, beaming, he'd kissed me.

"You totally made this happen," he'd said, after breaking off the kiss. "You have to come with me. Please?"

I looked at him. He was so *alive,* so excited about meeting the family he'd longed for. The family that I'd encouraged him to meet.

How could I say no?

I couldn't. And, for that matter, I didn't want to.

"Of course I'll go with you," I'd said. "I'd be happy to."

We plotted, and then booked a train to Manchester, aligning with our earlier commitment to visit Scotland. We'd meet with Matthew's family, and then if things didn't work out, we'd have the excuse of a weekend in Edinburgh to fall back on.

He'd accepted the invitation joyfully. As it happens, he'd told them, he'd be traveling through Manchester by train en route to Edinburgh with a friend.

We didn't discuss the kiss.

The visit, of course, had been a resounding success. Maggie was welcoming and lovely, treating Matthew like the long-lost cousin he was, and me as if I was already family. I stood at a distance, watching Matthew melt into the circle of his late grandfather's love.

"This is my friend Kay," he'd said, proudly showing me off to his newfound family. "She's coming with me to Edinburgh."

They talked. They laughed. They shared stories about Matthew's grandfather.

I'd been more than happy to delay our arrival in Edinburgh, had Matthew wanted to stay in Manchester. The next morning, however, he'd been intent on continuing on with me to Scotland.

"If I'm going to be here for another year and a half," he'd said to me, now firmly committed to the idea of completing his degree in England. "I don't want to overstay my welcome. Not just yet."

And here we were, in the capital of Scotland. We'd arrived

at the Royal Mile a few hours ago and – casually – checked into a small hotel. We were offered a room with a queen bed, was that alright? We looked at each other and shrugged. It would save money, we reasoned.

We still didn't talk about the kiss.

After dumping our backpacks in the room and scaling Arthur's Seat, we were now searching for a pub using a map drawn by felt tip marker on a paper towel. During the meandering walk to the pub, I'd tried to take in Edinburgh's sandstone buildings. But instead of awestruck, I was feeling nervous.

We were just friends, weren't we?

We'd kissed. But we were *together*? Was I still just "his friend Kay"?

"Here we go," Matthew said, steering me through the arched iron gate of the Pear Tree pub. "Find us a place to sit and I'll grab us some pints. You want to try the McEwans first?"

I nodded, and he disappeared to the bar.

I slid into one seat of an empty table for two and watched as Matthew strode confidently around the bar and signaled to the bartender. The difference between the man now ordering pints in a strange city and the one I'd bumped into outside my school a month ago was staggering. This Matthew was so confident, accepting the pints of deep red ale. He was a different person altogether.

"I ordered a couple of burgers," he said. "Hope that's OK."

"Thanks," I said, accepting the pint and scanning the crowd of students. "Do you think your cousins are here?"

Matthew laughed. "Who knows? I'm not about to question each person with a passing resemblance to my great uncle Fred," he said, raising his pint of McEwans to me. "Besides, we're finally here. Let's have a drink."

I smiled at him, relaxing and clinking my pint to his. He was right. I was overthinking this. We were just two friends spending a weekend in Edinburgh.

"No! Na-oo, ye BASTARD!"

Over Matthew's shoulder, a woman with a thick, dark braid pushed past, knocking his coat to the floor as she rushed for the exit. A ginger haired man chased after her, pleading.

"But 'Annie, I luuurve you!"

Matthew and I locked eyes and chuckled.

He retrieved his coat and hooked it over the back of his chair. "Ah, young love."

I laughed again. "Says the guy in his mid-twenties."

He flashed a grin at me and looked over his shoulder towards the entrance to the pub. "Have you ever chased someone out of a bar for love?"

I considered his question, a slow blush creeping onto my cheeks. "Sort of," I confessed. "But he was heading for Vegas, so it would've been a long jog if I'd really wanted to pursue him."

Matthew raised his eyebrows. "I'm intrigued."

I told him about Andrew, beginning with his co-worker's embarrassing song introductions at Jenna's party and ending with his rented UHaul driving west.

"His loss," Matthew said. "And not for nothing, but…a Vegas DJ? I feel that would age me a full year in about two weeks. But hang on, I think I might know who he is."

He picked up his phone and tapped on it for a few seconds before turning the screen to me. "Isn't this him?"

I peered at an image of the skeleton from *Tales from the Crypt* and laughed. "Mean."

He put his phone down and leaned back in his chair, giving me a *keep going* gesture. "Tell me more. How many other exs left for Vegas to become famous DJs?"

I smiled. This felt like familiar territory, swapping stories about former relationships. I filled him in on Jake, Liam, and Jonathan, wrapping up with Reg.

"He dumped me not long before you and I first met, sophomore year," I said, chuckling. "God, I was so heartbroken. Or thought I was."

Matthew took a final pull from his pint.

"Being dumped is hard," he said quietly. "It doesn't matter how old we are."

I nodded, studying him. Was he being kind to me, or was he holding a torch for someone?

We were interrupted by our server, who deposited two plates heaping with burgers and chips.

"Well, you know all *my* secrets," I said, standing up and gathering our glasses. "Now it's your turn. I'll get us another round. Do you want the same, or do you want to try the Belhaven?"

"Belhaven," he said. "I'll go to the bar with you; we should try a shot of Scotch, too."

"Do you need fortification before opening up your can of exs?" I teased.

He held my eyes for a few seconds, as if searching them for something, then smiled.

"Always."

A minute later we were seated at our table, tucking into our pints and food.

I swallowed a chip. "So go ahead, then," I prompted. "Give me the notches on the bedpost. I showed you mine."

Matthew wiped his lip with a napkin. "It's not a long list," he said. "I had one girlfriend in high school, Becca. We broke up before college, and then got back together about a year after graduation. We broke up again about six months before I left for London."

"I'm sorry," I said. "That's a long time. Are you OK?"

"I'm fine," he said. "I probably shouldn't have gotten back together with her in the first place."

"Why not?"

He sipped a glass of water that had arrived with our food. "I think we got back together out of habit rather than genuine feelings," he said. "I should've ended it long before I did."

So Becca wasn't the one who'd dumped him.

"What about at UMass?" I asked. "Anyone serious then?"

He looked at me, and again I got the feeling he was trying to read my mind. He suddenly smiled, sheepishly.

"Well, there was *you*," he said. "But you dumped me. Over the phone, too."

I gaped at him. It never occurred to me that he would think of our short-lived...*whatever* as me dumping him.

I lifted another chip and pointed it at him. "Maybe I wouldn't have dumped you if you'd shown any interest in actually hanging out with me," I said playfully, popping the chip into my mouth.

Matthew, to his credit, grimaced at the memory. "Yeah. I was...stupidly preoccupied back then. I guess you made the right call," he said.

I shrugged. "Water under the bridge," I said. "You've been doing a good job these last few weeks at making it up to me."

He picked up his shot of whisky and held it out to me. "To second chances?"

"Second chances," I said, smiling.

We took the shot, the whisky burning in my throat for a few seconds before settling warmly in my gut, mingling with the food and the beer. Matthew and I studied each other quietly, mulling over our shared memories.

"Want to head back to the hotel?" Matthew asked. "Dinner's on me."

I nodded.

He placed a short stack of pound notes on top of our bill, and we walked into the February evening. Outside, the city was in darkness. I stopped on the sidewalk just beyond the iron gate entrance and turned to Matthew.

He held his hands out to me, palms up; I intertwined my fingers with his.

"So," I said, the whisky summoning my courage. "Are we giving us a second chance?"

He pulled me to him and we kissed, more deeply than the week before.

"Yes," he said.

He dropped one of my hands and held tight to the other, leading me back to the hotel.

Chapter 21

I was nudged gently awake by something, but my semi-conscious brain couldn't place it. Rolling onto my back, I snaked my right arm to Matthew's side of the bed.

It was empty. The clock on his nightstand read 5:38.

I glanced over my shoulder to our bathroom. The door was open, the light off. Not there, then.

I propped myself up on my elbows and listened. The house was still.

Where was he?

I slid out of bed and walked softly to the door, easing it open quietly and hating myself for the stealth of it. Last night's lovemaking had been tender, if a little tentative. Like we were getting to know each other's bodies all over again and were treating them carefully. The intimacy had left me feeling an odd mix of victory and sadness. Last night I had reclaimed another piece of my marriage, and had taken another definitive step farther from Anna.

And yet here I was, creeping silently to the top of the stairs. I descended the first three steps and paused.

A low murmur in the kitchen. Matthew.

"…talking about it tonight."

I sank onto the stair, goosebumps spreading across my bare arms. It was too early to be talking to his therapist, and far too early for his mother in Arizona.

"I don't know…" Light footsteps covered the next few words as Matthew walked to the far side of the kitchen. "…tell Joy?"

I stiffened, straining to hear. It could only be Anna.

"No…no, you're right. I'm sorry." A long sigh. "Yeah, OK. I should go too."

I held my breath for an *I'll call you later*, or worse, *I love you*. There was neither.

His phone clacked onto a hard surface, the metallic *tink* giving away that he'd placed it in its usual spot in the corner next to his keys and wallet.

Perhaps this was my cue to creep back up the stairs to our room. Or continue down the rest of the stairs to confront him. Instead, I sat.

The kitchen was silent. A split screen appeared in my mind. On one side, I was seated on the stairs, debating which direction to move. On the other, Matthew stood in the pre-dawn kitchen, doing…what? Gazing out the window?

It's a movie poster for a D-list drama, I thought. *Only feet from each other, but miles apart.*

The freezer door opened. There was a rustling of bags as my husband began the ritual of making coffee.

I stood and backed slowly up the stairs and into our room. Back under the covers, I considered the snatches of conversation.

"…talking about it tonight."

We're talking about his – their – affair tonight with Dr. Garciá.

"…tell Joy?"

Anna's meeting Joy for coffee tomorrow, and he knows that. So they've been talking. He's asking her what – or how much – she's going to tell Joy. So they can get their stories straight.

"No, you're right. I'm sorry."

What had Anna said?

Stop worrying about what I'm going to say to Joy and start focusing on what you're *going to tell your* wife.

Classic Anna. Brief and to the point, with just enough bite to let you know that to her, the subject was closed.

I folded the comforter back and stalked into the bathroom, closing the door just loudly enough for Matthew to know I was up.

I stared at my reflection with detached curiosity. The woman in the mirror was seething, a high pink flush on her face.

"We had sex last night," I whispered to her, grabbing my toothbrush. "And now he's talking to *her*. He's *been* talking to her."

I scrubbed at my teeth, taking my aggression out on whatever microbes were responsible for morning breath.

"He went on that hike with me and told me it was a mistake. A *huge* mistake," I said, the frothy toothpaste turning the words into *huuth mithake.*

I spat and rinsed, then looked back at my fresher, slightly calmer reflection.

"Three things," I muttered to her, idly tapping the toothbrush against the sink. "He needs to say three things to me tonight."

I tossed the toothbrush into its stainless steel holder and held up my fingers. I paused, listening for Matthew, then returned to the mirror.

"One," I whispered. "That he dated Anna in college and

never told me. Two, that he's *still* talking to her. If neither of those things come up, then we don't even need to get to number three."

The woman in the mirror gave a decisive nod.

I swiped at my mouth with my hand, erasing a stray fleck of Crest from my bottom lip.

"And three," I said. "He needs to pick a goddamn road to take, once and for all."

I turned and yanked open the bathroom door, half-expecting to find Matthew standing in the bedroom, a deer-in-headlights look on his face and a proffered cup of coffee in his hand. I was almost disappointed to find it empty.

I pulled on my fleece pajama bottoms and headed downstairs, rearranging my features into what I hoped was ignorant sleepiness. Matthew was sitting at the breakfast bar with his coffee and a thick slice of cinnamon raisin toast. He was dressed in a zip up windbreaker and his black nylon running pants.

"Morning," he said.

"You're up early," I said. "How come?"

"I'm going to the gym before work," he said. "I was going to bring you a cup of coffee before I left."

I forced a grin as I poured myself a cup. "You weren't going to skulk out and do the walk of shame?"

He gave a half-hearted chuckle. "No..of course not."

I stole a glance at my husband as I poured cream into my coffee. His face was slightly turned away. He was avoiding eye contact with me. I approached the breakfast bar opposite him and placed my cup down.

"Matthew," I said. "You're being weird."

The deer-in-headlights look I'd imagined upstairs lit across his face. He looked at his toast and then back to me.

"I'm nervous," he said. "I'm nervous about tonight. Tonight…tonight's going to be hard. Especially after last night." He reached over to touch my hand, as if to reassure me. "I loved last night. I did. It just…I don't know…makes it harder to talk about, you know, *it*."

"Was last night a mistake?" I asked.

"Not for me," he said. "Was it for you?"

I shook my head.

"Are you nervous about our session tonight?"

Three things.

"Actually, no," I said lightly. "I mean, I know it's going to be hard, but because there's so much I don't understand about what happened between you two. I'm relieved to be finally getting…enlightened."

"You know, you've been pretty great at not asking about it, like Dr. Garciá told us," Matthew said. "I appreciate it."

I looked at him. "You sound surprised."

He blanched. "No, that's…that's not what I meant. I'm just acknowledging that not talking about it must have been hard."

"It wasn't easy at first," I confessed. "But it gave us the chance to make the last few days nice for Holly."

I took another sip from my cup and then waved at the door.

"Go," I said. "I'm working remotely today. I'll get Holly to and from school and then to my parents' house."

Matthew stood and slung his gym bag over his shoulder. "Should I meet you here or at Dr. Garciá's"

"Dr. Garciá's," I said.

He walked around the bar and gave me a quick, light kiss.

"I'll see you tonight," he said, and turned to the side door.

"See you tonight," I echoed to his retreating back. I watched as he stepped outside the mudroom door and onto the driveway to his car.

Tonight is your last chance, I silently warned him.

* * *

Then (London, England – May 2012)

"The Isle of Man, huh?" I asked.

Matthew nodded. His *Lonely Planet* guide, brand new when we'd bumped into each other at the Albert Memorial in January, was positively battered.

"That's where they filmed *Waking Ned Devine,*" he said. "Granddad loved that movie."

We were sitting on a sunny patch of grass in Lincoln's Inn Fields – just a few steps from the London School of Economics – on a warm Friday afternoon. I'd arrived a half hour before, waiting for Matthew's last seminar of the week to let out. I'd been stretched out on my side, lazily sketching the scene at the bandstand, where a pair of caramel corgis were industriously sniffing the perimeter of a trash bin. Their owner, a posh-looking man with silver hair and a herringbone jacket, let them linger while he relished the last inch of his cigarette. *Silver Fox,* I thought. Beyond the bandstand, a noisy group – LSE students, I presumed – gathered on a patchwork of blankets, snatches of The Clash wafting through their chatter.

"Hiya," Matthew had said when he'd finally arrived. "You wanna get a pint?"

"Mmmm, let's hang out for a few," I said, scribbling, not

taking my eyes off the man in the herringbone jacket. Our classes were done for the week, and the feeling of freedom was delicious. "I'm kind of into this whole sunny afternoon thing."

"Sure," Matthew spread his fleece on the grass next to me and flopped on it. He rested his head on my calf and opened his *Lonely Planet.* "I want to check out this section of the Isle of Man."

Last night, Matthew's cousin Maggie had invited him to join them on their summer holiday; two weeks in a little cloister of cottages near Lhen Beach, owned and managed by another member of his extended family.

I was delighted for him, of course. The holiday was in late June, long after our terms ended. The fact that Matthew was seriously entertaining the offer was proof that he was staying in the UK for the summer, and *not* transferring back to the States. When I came back to London for the fall term of our second year, Matthew would still be here.

"Have you seen it?" Matthew asked me, breaking me from my attempt to capture the creases in Silver Fox's sleeve as he curled the last of the cigarette to his lips.

"Seen what?" I asked absentmindedly, my pencil quivering across the pad.

He swatted my feet with his *Lonely Planet,* causing a few pages of the index to slip out of the book's broken spine. I blinked and refocused on my boyfriend.

"*Waking Ned Devine,*" he said, smiling at my concentration. "And it's Friday, enough of the books already."

"Yes, I've seen it," I said, flipping the cover of my sketch pad closed and shaking it at him. "And this is *fun,* not school. Because 'all work and no play makes Jack a dull boy.'"

He grinned at my reference to *The Shining*, another harkening back to our date at the Summit House.

"It just sounds like a great trip," Matthew said. "The Isle of Man, I mean."

"I know it does," I told him. "I totally think you should go. Why wouldn't you?"

"Well, of course *I'm* going," he said. Matthew climbed to his feet and tucked his guide into his backpack. "I'm asking you because I want to know if *you're* going. I'd love for you to come with me."

I looked up at him, surprised. *Me?*

He smiled and reached his hand down to me, clearly pleased by my reaction. I accepted his hand and he pulled me up, his hand snaking around my back once I was off the grass.

"Did you think I'd want to spend the summer here without you?" he asked, pressing me close to him.

"I...I don't know," I said. "I guess I haven't had time to really think about it."

This wasn't precisely true. Naturally, I'd idly entertained ideas of staying in England for the summer. Accepting Finn's offer of under-the-table bar work at Gloucester Arms. Getting a head start on my second year's portfolio. Traveling to the continent.

And being with Matthew, of course.

These first few months together – in a real, honest-to-God relationship –had been heady and fun, if not entirely real. Everything in England, to me, still seemed tinted with a surreal pink haze. Like it wasn't actual adulthood, but practice.

So sure, I'd thought about it, but each time the images flitted through my mind, I was transported back to my sophomore year at Mount Holyoke, standing in front of a panic-stricken Reg as I pitched the idea of following him to Canterbury.

Or watching the back of Andrew's beat up Toyota Tercel as he headed West to Las Vegas, instead of moving in with me. I'd always pushed too far, too fast.

Never again, I thought.

And so I let the images float away, content with my plan to spend the summer back home. My parents. Sebago Lake. Joy. And Anna.

Not that I'd see much of Anna. As my video chats and text threads had been increasingly peppered with *Matthew this* and *Matthew that*, hers had introduced a steady stream of details about a burgeoning summer research cohort involving a midwesterner named Leo. The prospect of a summer in New Hampshire had seemed comforting, if a little subdued. But it was better, miles better, than frightening off yet another boyfriend with half-baked *wouldn't it be nice if* monologues.

Now, the slightly-darker-than-sandy-haired young man in front was offering to upend all my plans. And it was *his* idea, even!

Across Lincoln's Inn Fields, the party of LSE students turned up their speakers, still blaring The Clash. Or, maybe they had all gone silent simultaneously, as mesmerized by my new dilemma as I was. At any rate, the song drifted across the grass to where Matthew and I stood.

Should I stay or should I go?

Matthew's hand was still wrapped snugly around my back.

"Just so we're clear," I said, placing my free hand on his chest and steadily meeting his gaze. "You're asking me to go on holiday with your family to the Isle of Man, *and* stay in England for the summer instead of going home."

So you gotta let me know...should I stay or should I go?

Matthew's eyes didn't waiver.

"Yes and yes, my little Kay of sunshine," he said. "Will you do me the honor of staying on this side of the Atlantic with me?"

A thousand thoughts flashed through me. *What will my mother say? Could I stay in my flat? Would Finn still let me work off the books?*

And, over all the other noise, *does he mean it? He means it, right?*

"Are you sure?" I pressed. "I mean, I don't want you to feel obligated to ask."

"Kay," Matthew said, tipping his head forward closer to mine. "In case you haven't noticed, I'm in love with you."

"You are?" I asked, praying the words hadn't come out like a squeak.

"Yeah," he said, blushing. "Is that OK?"

He's in love with me! And he said it first!

"It's more than OK. And I love you, too," I said, my own blush creeping over my cheeks.

"So stay. Stay for the summer. Will you?"

"Yes," I said, reaching behind me to clasp the hand that gripped my back. "I'd love to. On one condition."

He kissed the tip of my nose. "And what would that be?"

"You can never, ever, call me your little Kay of sunshine again," I said. "At least not in public."

Chapter 22

"There are a few ways we can begin," Elena Garciá said, once we'd settled onto the sofa in her office. "I can facilitate by asking questions that will guide you, Matthew, through sharing your experiences with Anna. Or, if you'd prefer, you can walk us through the details, and Kay and I can ask follow up questions."

Elena paused and waited for Matthew's response, her face a mask of polite inquisitiveness. For tonight's session, she'd foregone the pastel linen suits in favor of tailored black trousers and a light sweater in geometric patterns of white, black and rust. I sat in my usual spot, clad in the pink cashmere sweater and charcoal yoga pants I'd worn the night Matthew first brought *Two Homes* into our family room.

Get the hell out of my house, I'd told him then. If I needed to be that version of me again, I was already dressed for the part.

Matthew cleared his throat. He was leaning forward, his elbow resting on his knees, hands clasped tightly together. "Let's…uh. I'd like your help, please, Dr. Garciá. Let's do it that way."

She nodded. "I'm interested in knowing more about your history with Anna," she said. "I'm aware of her history with

Kay, but not you. Tell me about your friendship with her."

Matthew squeezed his hands together again, then sat back, letting out a long exhale.

"I actually met Anna before I met Kay," he said. "We took a class together in college and there was a group of us that started hanging out. Kay would come along sometimes, and that's how she and I first met."

I winced at *come along*, but stayed silent. I couldn't argue that it wasn't true.

"Were you and Anna close?"

Matthew paused to consider the question. "I wouldn't say close, exactly, but…I did have a crush on her. For a while I thought it was mutual, but nothing ever came of it. Not then."

An image floated by. Me, in a borrowed shirt of Anna's – one even she hadn't worn yet – barging in on their conversation at UMass' Blue Wall.

I'm going for it, Sporty, I'd said to her.

"We fell out of touch for a while after that," Matthew said.

I waited, my senses on heightened alert.

"Until England?" Elena prompted.

Matthew ran his fingers through his hair. Once. Twice. He exhaled again.

"No. Senior year."

He looked at me. "Anna and I were together second semester senior year. And for a little while after graduation."

I kept my face deliberately neutral. "Like, *together* together?" I asked him.

He nodded. "I considered her my girlfriend," he said. "I told her I loved her. Once."

I looked down at my lap, bitterness rising in the back of my throat. It hadn't occurred to me that they might have exchanged *I love yous*.

"Why did you break up?" I asked.

He took a sip from his water bottle and rested it back on Elena's coffee table. "She didn't want it to ruin her friendship with you," he said. He turned to Elena, who was quietly observing us from her Queen Anne chair. "Because Kay and I had gone on a few dates when we first met," he told her.

I felt myself shrinking. He'd gone on *a few dates* with the girl who would *come along sometimes*. When the one he'd wanted – had *loved*, even – was Anna.

Elena nodded neutrally. "And Anna told you this herself?"

"Yes," Matthew said.

"At the time of the breakup, or later?"

Matthew reddened. "After. She told me, ah, recently."

"When you were seeing each other," Elena said. Matthew nodded.

"What did she tell you at the time of the breakup, then?" Elena asked.

Matthew gazed around the room, as if the right answer was written on one of its walls. "Nothing, really," he said. "She just said it wasn't going to work, but wouldn't tell me why."

"How did you feel about the way it ended?" Elena asked.

He gave a small chuckle. "I was 22," Matthew said. "I felt like she broke my heart."

"So when you spoke previously about your trauma over Holly's illness leading you to reconsider, as you put it, 'the road not taken,' were you seeking a more definitive closure from your earlier relationship?"

Matthew paused to consider the question, then nodded. "That was part of it, I think. Our history was kind of the elephant in the room; it had been ever since Kay and I came back from England."

"Once Anna knew that you and Kay were committing to each other, did you never talk with her about it?" Elena said.

"Yeah, briefly. Once," Matthew said, his cheeks reddening again. "We just agreed that it was all in the past and it was probably better if Kay didn't know." Matthew turned to me again. "I…I'm sorry. I wish I'd told you."

"But agreeing not to speak of it again isn't the same as closure, is it?" Elena asked.

I was beginning to find Elena's facilitation irritating. *Poor Matthew. You didn't get* closure. *No wonder you cheated on your wife. Here's your pass.*

Matthew turned up his palms in an *I don't know* gesture. "At the time I didn't feel like I needed it anymore," he said, still looking at me. "I was in love with *you*. I *am* in love with you. And I was so happy to be marrying you, it didn't seem to matter."

I knew he would be hoping for a small, soft smile in response, but I couldn't give it to him. Right now, it was not my job to reassure him. There was too much at stake.

"And then Holly got sick," Elena prompted. "She recovered, but you did not. How did that lead to your turning to Anna?"

Matthew shifted in his seat, turning slightly away from me. He picked at the label on the water bottle in his lap.

"We were up at the lake, at our rental," he said. "Anna had arrived the night before. It was the first time I'd seen her since the hospital. The four of us spent the day outside, then had a cookout at the fire pit."

I remembered that day. We'd attempted to build a sandcastle replication of Hogwarts, and Anna and I had taught Holly snippets of our Spice Girls dance. She was a quick study, spinning in her neon yellow bathing suit.

Matthew paused. Elena and I waited.

"Holly had gone to bed, and then Kay went to bed. Anna and I were going to stay out by the fire a little longer, so I went inside to get us more drinks."

Don't you dare blame this on alcohol, I thought.

"She came inside with me; there's this screen porch with a beer fridge," he said, clarifying the scene to Elena. "She said that Holly seemed completely recovered, and then she looked at me and said 'you, on the other hand, look like shit.'"

A short bark of laughter escaped me, despite everything. Of course Anna would say that.

Matthew gave me a sidelong glance before continuing. "I know, right? Classic Anna. But she was serious. And I *did* look like shit. She wanted to know what was going on, that she was my friend, too, and that I could talk to her. And…I lost it a little."

"How so?" Elena asked.

"I…broke down, just started bawling. I told her that Holly almost died, but that Kay didn't know. I admitted how exhausted I was, how I couldn't get past the night at the hospital, how I felt anxious and unfocused all the time thinking about how my life could have changed that night. All of it."

Guilt pierced my chest. I'd missed the signs of Matthew's mental deterioration for months, and Anna had spotted it in just a few hours.

"And then I just blurted it out," Matthew continued. "I asked her why she broke up with me."

He paused, and swiped at his hair again. Once. Twice. He looked down, focusing on the curl of paper he'd begun to shred from the water bottle label.

"I said 'we were so good together, and you broke my heart.' And then I broke down again."

He paused again.

Just rip off the goddamn Band-Aid, Matthew, I thought.

"And then we kissed. Things…escalated really fast and we, ah, made love on the porch."

My stomach soured. He'd already confessed to starting the affair at Sebago, but the thought of the two of them going at it on the porch while I slept upstairs was more detail than I had been prepared for.

I thought back to that night. A new memory surfaced. Matthew, sliding into bed with me, his hair wet.

Wood smoke from the fire, he'd said, when I asked him why he'd showered so late. *I didn't want to stink up the sheets.*

"You left the next day," I reminded him. "You both did."

He nodded. "I thought we needed to talk about what had happened, and I didn't think it could wait until we were back from vacation."

"But instead of talking, you had sex with her again," I said. It wasn't a question.

Matthew nodded, not looking at me.

"And again. And again." Anger was clawing its way from the pit of my stomach and into my chest. "And again, until you were caught by *my sister.*"

"Kay," Elena said, gently. "What do you need to know from Matthew, right now?"

I leaned over, forcing myself into Matthew's field of vision.

"I want to know how you went from 'Anna and I are moving in together' to staying at a hotel. I want to know why you moved back home after our first counseling session. And I want to know *exactly* when you spoke with Anna last."

* * *

Then (Edinburgh, Scotland – June 2013)

"Oh, my God," I groaned, stretching my arms over my head and taking in the view from Calton Hill. "I'm going to miss this place so much!"

I glanced over my shoulder at Matthew. While I'd been gazing at the cityscape of Edinburgh below me, he'd climbed onto the National Monument and was standing between two of its Greek Revival pillars, smiling at me.

"We'll be back," he assured me, patting the stone affectionately before hopping back down to the grass. "No question; we'll be back."

We were on the tail end of a three-week farewell tour. With our respective degrees completed and some networking interviews already lined up for Matthew in Boston, there'd been just enough time to take a final spin through the country. We crossed off the "must do" item of hiking Hadrian's Wall with my soon-to-be ex flatmate and her boyfriend, spent a few days with Matthew's cousins in Manchester, and were now relishing a final-for-now visit to Edinburgh. We'd been back here several times. The sentimentality of our first stay here tugged at me, and I'd grown to love it deeply.

Now, we were leaving. Our flights departed in just two days. The Real World was waiting.

Matthew would stay with me at my parents' house for a

night before continuing on to Arizona for a long overdue visit with his mother and stepfather. While I'd spent winter break of our second year back at home, Matthew had chosen to stay in England.

"Are you sure one night at my house is enough?" I'd asked, when we were huddled around the computer last month booking our flights. "You're welcome to stay longer."

"I know," he said, kissing my temple. "But I haven't seen my mom in almost two years. If I delay another day, she'll kill me. Besides, if I'm going to be living on the East coast, I better get a good long visit in now."

I felt a little thrill at *living on the East coast*. I'd terrified Reg in college. I'd chased away Andrew not long afterwards. Now here was Matthew, actively choosing to live a continent away from his mother to be near me. To be *with* me. It was a revelation.

But could it survive The Real World? Could it survive adulting?

I was so used to my love interests running away at commitment, real or imagined, that I'd prepared myself for his inevitable casual announcement of a job opportunity in New York or Los Angeles. It hadn't come. Just the opposite, in fact. It was Matthew who'd begun scouring finance and consulting firms in Boston, exhausting his network to secure his upcoming appointments.

The Matt I'd chased in college was hesitant and guarded, aloof even. The Matthew I'd fallen for in England was vulnerable, candid, and happy.

And he *loved* me. Of that I was sure.

The sky beyond Calton Hill was turning pink. I closed my eyes and breathed in the Scottish air. *We'll be back*, Matthew had said moments ago. *We.*

Wafts of bagpipes drifted from somewhere behind me. I recognized the tune as "Flower of Scotland." We'd seen a performance during the Edinburgh Festival last summer - that happy, heady summer I'd blown off going home and stayed in Europe with Matthew - and this particular song had left me awed and breathless. That I was hearing it now, on my final day in Edinburgh, was almost too serendipitous to be real.

"Kay," Matthew said. I turned.

He was on the grass, kneeling. A midnight blue velvet box in his hand.

The world hummed around me. I took it all in, the green of the grass. The small patch of clover just beyond his right knee. The tickle of my hair as a breeze pushed a few strands across my cheek.

The bagpipes grew louder. I looked past his shoulder; a lone piper was marching towards us, slowly and deliberately. I watched for a few moments as he staked out a spot at a discreet distance and played on. Beyond the piper, a handful of people who had been scattered around the hill a minute ago were craning their necks to see what was happening.

I looked back to Matthew. He raised the lid of the box and revealed the ring. It was exquisite. A round, brilliant solitaire diamond set on a platinum band.

My hands went to my face involuntarily, covering my mouth. *Get it together, Kay,* I thought, lowering my hands and clasping them loosely against my chest.

Matthew was beaming. He cleared his throat, and a small laugh escaped.

"I–I want this to be all serious and romantic, but I can't stop smiling," he confessed.

"So don't stop," I told him. "And believe me, this *is* romantic."

He took a deep breath. His hands, I saw, were shaking slightly.

"Kay, this has been, beyond any doubt, the best year and a half of my life," he said. "And it's all because of you. With you, I found my family. With you, I stayed here and honored my grandfather. I've never been happier than I have been with you. I don't know what would have happened if I hadn't decided to hang around the Albert Memorial that day you found me, but I *do* know that I don't ever want to find out."

He raised the box higher.

"Kay, I love you. I will always love you, and I'll spend the rest of my life trying to make you as happy as you've made me. Will you marry me?"

"Yes," I said gently, leaning in so that only Matthew would hear it. So that he would know my answer first before I shared it with the rest of Calton Hill.

I tilted my head back. "YES!" I said again, this time shouting.

He slid the ring onto my finger, then stood and hugged me, lifting me off the ground. People clapped. The bagpiper bowed to us and switched into the celebratory bars of "Scotland the Brave" before turning and marching away.

"Thank you for saying yes," Matthew whispered into my ear and placed me back on the ground. "Thank you thank you thank you. I love you."

I pulled back and smiled at him, tears in my eyes. "You remembered 'Flower of Scotland,'" I said.

He beamed again. "I did."

He lifted my left hand and we studied the ring. Now that it was closer, I saw the delicate engraving of a flower and its leafy stalk running throughout the band. The detail, so personal to me, brought a fresh wave of emotion.

I looked at my fiancé – my *fiancé!* – and beamed back at him.

"I love you, too," I said. "Now kiss me."

Yes, I thought, as he complied. *We* would *survive the real world.*

Chapter 23

I was still leaning forward, staring my husband down. My breath was coming in short, shallow gasps. I shifted backwards into my side of the loveseat and forced myself to slow down, to breathe deeply through my nose.

Elena Garciá watched me intently for a few moments, then gave a small nod and moved her gaze back to Mathew.

"Matthew, Kay's just told you what she needs to know. Let's start with what seems, to me at least, to be the easiest question. When did you last communicate with Anna?"

Matthew exhaled and tossed his empty water bottle back onto the coffee table.

"This morning," he said, looking at me directly. "I called her this morning and told her that we were going to be talking about our affair tonight."

"And before that?" I prompted, willing my relief at his honesty to not show on my face.

"Last weekend," he said. "She texted me and told me that she was meeting with Joy."

"Why did you feel the need to tell Anna about our session this evening?" Elena asked.

Matthew sat back, a look of resignation on his face. "I wanted to find out how much she was going to tell Joy."

"And why should her conversation with Kay's sister have any impact on what you share in this room, with us, tonight?"

Matthew looked down, shaking his head slightly.

"You wanted to know if Anna was going to be completely honest with her," I interjected. "Right?"

He nodded, still looking down.

"What part were you hoping she would leave out?" I asked.

He lifted his head to look at me, and his eyes misted over. "Having sex on the porch while you and Holly slept upstairs."

"What good would it do to leave it out?" I asked, already knowing the answer.

"I knew how much it would hurt–"

"Stop," I said, raising my palm. "Just stop."

I turned to fully face Matthew.

"I'm so *tired* of you both trying to protect me from everything," I continued. "Who do you think you're protecting? It's *me*, Matthew. I'm the girl who flew halfway around the world to where she didn't know a soul and goddamn *crushed* living in London. I'm the one who held Anna for *three days straight* after her mother's funeral when her father couldn't. I'm a functioning adult, Matthew. When did I become someone who needed so much protection?"

Matthew stared at me, blinking.

"Is that what you want?" I asked. "Do you want someone you need to protect? Someone you need to be strong for because she can't? Or when it gets down to it, do you want to be someone your grandfather would be proud of? Because guess what, Matt, *you already are*. You have been since the day I met you. Save for the last few months, that is."

Matthew's face crumpled, and he put his head in his hands. "I just want *you*, Kay. You and Holly. I want my family."

I was still. I couldn't bring myself to comfort him yet.

"Both of you underestimated me," I said. "Anna should have told me you were dating when we were still in college, and you *both* should have told me about it when we got engaged."

He raised his head and nodded. "I'm sorry."

I massaged my temples for a moment, then looked at Elena. "Two weeks ago he told me he was leaving me. Two nights later he was prepared to tell our daughter we were getting a divorce. He wanted to sell our home so he could buy something new with Anna. Just a few days after that he was staying at a hotel. And then–"

"That *was* the night I went to a hotel," Matthew said.

"What?" I turned from Elena to look at my husband.

"That Sunday, when you threw me out after I brought that stupid book over, I left Anna's and went to a hotel."

I stared at him, my mind reeling.

Elena cleared her throat. "Matthew, I think you can agree that your words and actions over the last two weeks have been inconsistent. Rather dramatically so," she said. "You can't fault Kay for her earlier question as to why things changed so radically."

He nodded.

Elena lifted her hand in a *proceed* gesture and waited.

Matthew coughed and leaned forward again, his forearms on his knees.

"Before we were found out by Joy, it was…it was like it wasn't the real world. We were sort of in this bubble," he said.

"And when Joy discovered the affair, it was no longer a 'bubble,' as you put it, but part of the real world," Elena prompted.

"Yeah, and I fought that," Matthew said. "I was in denial.

I knew Joy expected me to tell Kay right away, and I kept putting it off. I…didn't have the guts."

"Until Joy gave you the ultimatum," I said. "Tell Kay or I will."

He nodded.

"And you chose to say 'I'm leaving,'" I reminded him. "Why?"

Matthew reached for my hands. I pulled back.

"Just tell me," I said. "I don't need protection."

"I knew I'd screwed up badly," he said, running his hands through his hair again. "I thought about asking you to take me back that Friday night, but I was terrified. Like, really terrified."

"Of what?" Elena asked.

"That she'd say no," Matthew said. "I'd nearly lost my daughter, and now I was about to lose my wife."

"So you thought doing the leaving would somehow be easier?" Elena said.

He nodded, and rubbed one hand across his forehead. "I think so. I figured I'd blow up the bridge back to my marriage instead of trying to cross it and failing," he said. "God, I'm such a shit. And I was *awful* to you that night, Kay."

"You were awful to Anna, too," I said. "You told her you were leaving me."

A corner of my heart, the part that still flickered with love for my best friend, broke. The same way it did when I discovered she hadn't told her father about the affair.

"What made you change your mind?" Elena asked. "What made you move out of Anna's that night after seeing Kay?"

Matthew sat back and exhaled. "I started driving back to her place, and…I realized that I just didn't want to go there. It wasn't home to me. *She* wasn't home to me. She wasn't *you*.

We weren't going to survive the real world. So I packed the few things I'd brought and left."

How did she take it? I wanted to ask this, but couldn't bring myself to.

"So when Kay arranged for us to come here, when she did what I was too scared to do and booked these sessions with you," Matthew said, looking at Elena. "I knew I had to do everything I could to get her back."

"You didn't *seem* like you wanted me back," I said, thinking back to that night at The Water View. "You seemed trapped."

"I *was* trapped," he said quietly. "I had torched that bridge, and I wasn't on the side I wanted to be on."

The three of us were silent for a few moments.

"Kay," Elena said. "Is there anything else you'd like to know tonight?"

I thought, and then turned to Matthew.

"If Joy hadn't caught the two of you in Boston that night, would you still be sleeping with her?" I asked.

Matthew gazed up at the abstract art of balanced stones, and shook his head, turning up his palms again.

"I…just don't know, Kay," he said. "But I do know that it *was* going to end. The bubble wasn't going to last."

* * *

Then (Portsmouth, New Hampshire – June 2013)

"Forget 'forever,'" Joy said, nudging me and handing me a pot to dry. "The slogan should be 'a diamond is distracting.'"

She winked at my sheepish grin. I accepted the pot and swiped at the inside with a tea towel, watching as the ring sparkled in the early evening sun streaming through the kitchen window.

I couldn't stop looking at it. I studied it when I brushed my teeth, when I folded my clothes, as I poured my final cups of tea in England, and as I buckled my seatbelt for my flight home. I noticed when other women noticed it, and beamed when they took the time to make eye contact and offer a knowing smile.

"What do you think they're talking about?" I asked Joy, nodding towards the window. Beyond, Matthew and my parents sat on the patio, nursing the last of the champagne we'd popped in celebration before sitting down to dinner.

"Dad's chewing him out for not asking his permission," Joy said.

I gaped at her.

"Kay, I'm *joking*," she said. "They're getting to know him, is all. Stop worrying."

I returned the pot to its place in one of the lower cabinets and peered out the window again. "I just want you all to like him."

"We do," she insisted. "If he loves you, then I love him. That's how it works." She rinsed soap suds off a set of salad tongs and passed them to me.

"That simple, huh?" I asked, smiling at my sister.

She nodded firmly. "It's that simple. As long as you're happy, I'm happy."

I stowed the now dry tongs in the crowded ceramic jar on the counter and glanced at the clock. "Anna should be here any minute," I said. "I can't wait to tell her."

The back door opened and my parents entered the kitchen. My dad had the empty bottle of champagne in one hand and the stems of three champagne flutes in another. My mother set the two crystal flutes she was carrying down on the counter gingerly before relieving my dad of his.

"When did you get champagne glasses, by the way?" I asked her.

"Mrs. Harkins next door," my mother replied. "I wanted to give you a champagne toast, and knew she had them. And they're called flutes, dear. These are things you'll need to know as a married woman."

Joy and I made gagging noises in response.

She waved our smirks away. "Fine, don't register for *flutes*, then," she said, cupping my face in her hands. "I can't believe my little girl is getting married." She released my face and enveloped me in a hug.

"Do you like him?" I whispered into her shoulder.

She pulled back to look at me, her hands on my arms. "I *love* him. He's sweet."

"And just nervous enough to be respectful," my dad added. He clapped his hands together. "Now, that fine young man of yours is interested in one of my dirty martinis. I'd hate to disappoint. Who else?"

Joy and I raised our hands.

He nodded. "Post-dinner happy hour in the family room, then. The bugs are coming out."

I turned to the window again, but couldn't see my fiancé. I listened for his footsteps at the back door, but there were none. Where was he?

"I'll get Matthew," I said over my shoulder as I walked out the door.

Once outside, a low murmur wafted from the breezeway next to the patio. I took a few more steps and glimpsed around the corner.

Anna had arrived. She was talking to Matthew; they were standing about two feet apart. Her arms were folded across her chest, while my fiancé was making downward motions with his palms.

"Sporty!" I shrieked, and ran the remaining paces, flinging myself at her.

She flinched, looking at me in surprise, then fixed her face into a smile. We hugged tightly, swaying from side to side for a few moments, and then pulled back to grin at each other.

"You're back for good now, right Baby?" she said.

"You're stuck with me," I confirmed. "Forever."

I looped an arm around her back and faced Matthew, who'd been watching with mild bemusement. "I see you're following the cardinal rule and getting with my friends," I said, pointing from him to Anna and back.

Matthew's eyes widened in alarm. "Uh, what-"

"It's a Spice Girls song," Anna said quickly. "It's a song lyric, dude."

He scratched the back of his head. "Yeah. I'll, uh, I'll be inside." Matthew flashed me a quick smile and left.

"Dirty martini?" I asked Anna gaily.

"Definitely," she said, turning to face me and lifting my left hand. "But is there anything you want to tell me first?"

My face fell. "He told you already?"

She paused, then shook her head. "Nah, you blinded me a minute ago. That thing is hard to miss."

I laughed and hugged her again. "I've missed you."

"You saw me for a month at Christmas," she said, giving me

another squeeze.

"It's not the same," I protested. "I missed having you in my daily life. Let's not do that again."

She pulled back. "So, again. Is there anything you want to tell me?"

I grinned, then said the words she already knew out loud. "I'm getting *married*, Anna. Matthew and I are getting married."

She raised an eyebrow. "Is it Matthew now?"

I nodded. "He'd started going by Matthew in England, and I guess it stuck with me. And since 'Matt' and I never worked out," I said, making air quotes. "I'm kinda happy about the clean slate."

I sighed happily. "He's not the same guy we knew at UMass, Anna. He's so much more open with me now. You'll see." I searched my friend's eyes hopefully.

Anna's expression softened. "I'm happy for you, Kay. Really, really happy."

I lifted her left hand, the way she had just lifted mine. "Anna Becker, will you be my bridesmaid?"

She smiled, the smallest hint of sadness in her eyes. "Of course."

I squeezed her hand. "I've asked Joy to be my maid of honor, because, well..."

She nodded. "She's your sister. I totally get it."

My heart cracked a little for her. A part of me wanted – desperately – to have her immediately next to me on my wedding day. But Joy...Joy was my *sister*.

Anna gestured towards my house. "So is Matt staying here with you?"

I shook my head. "Just tonight. He leaves for Arizona in the morning for two weeks. His mom moved there."

She exhaled slowly and gave her shoulders a little shake. She brightened and clapped her hands together.

"Well, then. Let's not waste any more time out here," she said, linking her arm through mine. "We've got martinis to drink and a wedding to plan."

We strode towards my back door. "What were you and my fiance talking about back there?" I asked her.

She smiled at me, the hint of sadness gone. "You, of course."

Chapter 24

Elena Garciá's office was silent. My fingers were back to my temples, trying to massage out the first stirrings of a headache. I was cagey, claustrophobic, and tired. So incredibly tired.

"I know this has been rough for both of you, but please trust me when I say that you have done excellent work here tonight," Elena said.

I looked over at my husband. "I think I'm beginning to understand how this started for you," I said, choosing my words carefully. "I don't forgive you for it yet, I don't agree with it, and I'm still mad as hell at you. But I think, I *think*, I get it. A little."

I held up my finger, preventing interruption while I picked over the thoughts swirling through my brain. "But I don't get why *Anna* would do this to me. Do you?"

Elena cleared her throat. "I don't think Matthew can speak for–"

"I don't know why," Matthew said, ignoring our therapist and looking at me with frank honesty. "I never asked her. It didn't even occur to me to ask, and I probably wouldn't have even if it did."

"It would have popped the bubble?" I asked him.

He nodded. I exhaled and turned back to Elena, aware that our hour was up.

"Where do we go from here?" I asked her.

"We get back to it next Thursday," she said gently. "And every Thursday after that, until it's resolved, whatever resolution looks like for you."

We walked down the short flight of steps outside Elena's office together, then stopped and looked at each other, much like we did more than a week ago after our first appointment.

Has it really only been two weeks since everything imploded? Another surge of exhaustion washed over me.

"Holly's at my parents' house," I reminded Matthew.

He nodded. "I'll see you both at home in a little bit?"

I shook my head. "I'd like you to pick her up."

Naked panic rose in his eyes. I put a hand on his arm.

"Matthew, you have to see them eventually," I reasoned. "Just get it over with. You loved them once."

"I still do," he said, the panic morphing into hurt. "Of course I still do."

"Then show them," I said. "Go to their house and talk to them. Stay for dinner, even. Then bring our daughter home."

"What about you?" he asked.

I looked up at the sky for a moment, then back at my husband. "I need some time to myself right now, Matthew."

He studied me, searching my eyes, then nodded. "OK. I love you, Kay."

"I love you, t-too," I said, the words catching in my throat as my eyes filled again. I turned away and strode quickly to my car. Once inside, I took deep, gulping breaths, ridding my body of the tension that had built up over the last hour, the last day, the last two weeks.

I drove aimlessly, certain that I didn't want to go home but unsure of where I should be. Eventually, I pulled into an empty parking spot near Strawberry Banke and got out. The mid October evening was chilly. I kept my hands in the pockets of my brown leather jacket as I walked alongside the outdoor museum's sixteenth century houses.

I'd been so happy when I was working here. Life was easy. A fun day job, then an endless string of evenings with Anna. Bars, concerts, movies, or curled up at my parents house, talking. Always talking.

When did that change?

I circled back to my car, then stopped. I left it where it was parked and walked the handful of blocks to The Press Room, one of our regular haunts. Once inside, the wall of sound – currently U2's "Where the Streets Have No Name" – sent me into blissful anonymity. I slid onto a free stool at the long polished wood bar and ordered a burger and a vodka martini, extra dirty. The din of the Friday evening crowd was strangely soothing, allowing me to disappear into my thoughts.

I pulled out my phone and opened my messages, sipping my drink while scrolling through the thread of my and Anna's text messages. The most recent one was about three weeks ago.

Sporty! You're alive, right? It feels like it's been forever.

Ha ha, was her response. *Alive, but barely. Just busy.*

I kept scrolling. A month ago:

Jenna's free, too! See you at mine on Friday? Matthew's at a work thing, so it's a girls night. (confetti emoji)

Was it THIS Friday? Gah, I can't. Show tix in Boston. Sorry, Baby. Kiss Jenna for me.

On and on it went. Slowly but surely, Anna had pulled away from me, and I hadn't fully noticed. I was too busy passively worrying about my equally distant husband.

My index finger landed on a text from the middle of April. *Glad to hear Holly's on the mend.*

I drained my martini and popped one of the olives into my mouth, frowning at my phone as I chewed. The previous text had been from Anna as well, confirming our tickets for *Hamilton* in Boston. That was the day Holly got sick and Anna drove me through the painfully slow traffic to the hospital, assuring me that my daughter would be OK. Beyond April, our messages were frequent and light, filled with the banter that had defined our friendship.

Glad to hear Holly's on the mend.

I must have called and left her a message from the hospital the next day, gushing with relief.

I must have.

I placed my phone face down on a napkin and tried to remember a message or a phone conversation with Anna. I could picture the hospital room perfectly, Holly's still feverish body in bed, and me – still clad in the black velvet pants and cream silk blouse I'd chosen for the theater – lying next to her, stroking her hair. Matthew dozing in the chair, his face pale and pinched with what I now knew had been the first stirrings of post-traumatic stress. But for all the details I could easily recall, down to the way the pat of cold butter refused to spread over Holly's lukewarm pancakes the next day, I couldn't remember talking to my best friend.

I paid for the drink and food, left a tip for the bartender, and headed back into the night. Instead of trying to shake off the feeling of unease that had settled over me, I picked at it.

There was something there.

Anna hadn't started pulling away from me after Sebago. She'd started earlier, months before the affair began. Either Matthew hadn't been honest about when it started, or Anna had had another reason to keep me at a distance.

What was it?

I drove home to find the house quiet and in near darkness. Matthew had left the kitchen light on for me, but both he and Holly were already in bed. I crept up the stairs and paused at Holly's half-open door. Her breathing was deep and even.

I continued to the room I shared with Matthew and eased the door open. Undressing silently, I pulled on my old, soft cotton Holyoke tank and slid under the covers.

"Hi," Matthew murmured, his back to me.

"Hi," I responded. "How did it go?"

He rolled over to face me. "It was awkward at first, but it got better. You were right; I needed to get it out of the way. Thanks for the push."

I reached over and brushed a lock of dark blonde hair from his eyelids, which were closed again. "You said it started at Sebago," I said. "If it was before, you can tell me. I want you to be honest."

"I was being honest," he said, his eyes fluttering open to meet mine before closing again. "That's when it started."

I chewed on my bottom lip for a few seconds. "OK," I said. "Go back to sleep."

I laid on my back, staring up at the ceiling and thinking about Anna until sleep finally came.

* * *

Then (Portsmouth, New Hampshire – May 2014)

I whirled in place on the dance floor, relishing the way the layers of crepe organza fanned out as I spun. The ruched, sweetheart bodice of my strapless gown freed my arms and shoulders and I took full advantage, exaggerating my "Vogue" moves and causing Jenna and Joy – dressed in pale yellow chiffon – to peal with laughter.

"I'm never taking this dress off," I declared, curtseying as the song came to an end. Across the floor, Matthew finished twirling Maggie's giggling daughter Fiona, who'd served as our flower girl.

We met in the middle of the floor just as the *tink tink tink* of forks against crystal erupted from a nearby table. The guests at the tables around them quickly followed suit.

I grinned, snaked my unencumbered arms around my husband's – *husband's!* – neck and kissed him. We pulled our faces apart, his arms still firmly holding the beaded belt at the waist of my wedding dress.

"I still need to stop by a table or two," I said. "And I want to sit with your mom for a few minutes."

He lifted me a few inches and spun me in a circle before setting me back down again, planting another kiss on my mouth.

"I'm going to visit the UMass table," Matthew said. "Meet me there?"

I nodded, a rush of joy coursing through me as I walked, the skirt of my dress whispering against my legs. *I'll never get tired of this feeling*, I thought. *Never.*

I claimed the unoccupied seat next to Matthew's mother, Carol. She and her husband Max – the documentary filmmaker – were engaged in conversation with Maggie and her husband Colin. Carol turned to face me as I sat and beamed.

"This is wonderful, Kay," she said, her eyes bright.

"Thank you, ah," I paused, unsure if I should now call her *Carol* or *Mom*, then decided to save that question for another day. "I'm having even more fun than I thought, and I was already setting the bar high."

Carol laughed easily as I reached for an untouched glass of water and drank. "Look at him," she said, leaning closer to me and pointing at her son, sitting with his college friends. "Look how happy he is."

Behind him, Matthew's best man – his former UMass roommate Sam – clapped him on the shoulders and said something I couldn't hear, but the eruption of laughter and Matthew's sheepish grin delighted me from a distance. Just beyond their table, Anna was leaning against one corner of the bar, appearing deep in conversation with Shelley.

I'd sighed inwardly when her name appeared on Matthew's share of the guest list, and again – not so inwardly – when she RSVP'd yes. *Maybe she's changed*, I'd thought. Or perhaps she would warm to me now that I had officially married into the UMass Econ crew. At least she'd had the decency to skip the shower.

"You're good for him, Kay," Carol said, snapping me back to the present. She placed her hand on mine and gave it a light squeeze. "He told me all about how you helped him connect with our family while he was in London. You saved that whole experience for him, and I'm grateful."

I squeezed her hand in return. "Those first few calls to you from overseas must have been hard."

She shook her head. "No, he hid how unhappy he was from

me. My typical tough guy," she said with a wry chuckle.

I chatted with her for another minute before getting shooed off with a "can't be caught hogging the bride!" I squared my shoulders and headed towards Shelley and Anna, determined to make nice.

"...you're a better person than I am," Shelley said, her back to me.

Ain't that the truth, I thought, as I signaled one of the bartenders for a glass of champagne.

"Hi Kay," Anna said, straightening up and taking a few steps my way, which forced Shelley to turn towards me.

"Hi," I said, accepting the flute and raising it a inch to Shelley. "It's good to see you again, Shelley."

She gave me a thin smile. "Congratulations," she said. She was wearing a straight-necked sheath of olive silk. It looked good, unfortunately.

"How are you?" I asked, undeterred. "I mean, it's been forever...since before we graduated, right?" I looked at Anna for confirmation.

"Mmmm," Shelley said in what I assumed was agreement. She took a sip from her cosmo, then gestured to Anna. "Though I see this one all the time."

Really? All the time?

"Ah," I said, taking a longer draw of champagne to mask my hurt and surprise. "That's nice."

Anna's smile was guarded, inauthentic. "We reconnected while you were away."

"Yes," Shelley said. Her left arm was folded across her chest to prop up her right elbow, her hand swirling the last of her cosmo. "While you were in England with Matt."

I couldn't be certain whether she'd placed the tiniest emphasis on *Matt* – not Matthew – but I didn't care. I was the bride, goddamnit, and I was done with this shrew. What did Anna see in her? I caught my husband's eye and gave him a quick *I'm coming to you* gesture. I decided we'd have to come up with a "save me from this person" code phrase now that we were married.

"I'm going to thank Sam for his great toast. Good to see you, Shelley," I said. I gave Anna a conspiratorial smile, and hoped it annoyed Shelley. "I have something planned for us in a bit."

I turned away from them and approached the table where Matthew was sitting with his friends, heading for the lone empty seat.

"That's Sam's wife's seat," Shelley offered. "But go ahead, just take what was hers."

I threw her my best false smile. What was her *deal*?

"Thanks, I will," I said. *And you're not getting invited to dinner at our place anytime soon.*

She arched an eyebrow in response.

I slid into the seat, praying for the DJ to queue up my Spice Girls request as soon as possible. I couldn't wait to pull Anna away from her and put on our show.

I'll show you who sees Anna all the time, I thought, feeling smug.

Chapter 25

"Bye, Holls!" I called as Holly slid out of the car, balancing the brightly wrapped present carefully on one hand. "And happy birthday, Monica!"

Monica grinned at me as she handed Holly a glittery pink party hat. They ran into the house, holding hands. Monica's mother, Cindy, gave me a thumbs up and waved me off.

I half-listened to a glib talk radio program for the rest of the drive to my office. I'd told Matthew that I needed to catch up on some work, which wasn't *precisely* a lie. The event my boss, Tom, and I had gone to hosted by the League of Historic American Theatres had turned out to be more than just the mental distraction I'd needed at the time; it had resulted in a request to pitch the organization on what Dawson & Tilman, Restoration Architects felt were the five theaters that should be prioritized for preservation. I had some ideas for the Pickwick Theatre in Park Ridge, Illinois that I wanted to sketch. Today – sandwiched between the day I'd delved into Matthew's affair with Anna and the day she would meet with my sister – seemed as good a day as any.

As if I could have focused at home, anyway.

I parked, then made my way to the front door of the wharf warehouse that now housed a variety of businesses, including the offices of Dawson & Tillman. Before I could reach my own office, I caught sight of Tom in his.

His door was ajar. Tom Dawson was sitting at his desk, frowning over a set of papers. The collar of his Polo shirt was askew and his monk's ring of pale brown hair rumpled, as if he'd been at this particular task longer than he wanted to be.

"I hope you haven't slept here," I said.

He looked up and laughed. "No. I got here about an hour ago. Lance's band is rehearsing at ours this afternoon." He shrugged in a what-can-you-do manner. Much like I'd shrugged to him over the years whenever I went to Pooley's Playground with Matthew and Holly.

I smiled. I knew Tom adored his husband, even if he *didn't* adore his banjo. "You're a saint, Tom."

He waved the compliment away. "What are you doing here on a Saturday?"

I raised my sketchbook. "I have some ideas for Pickwick. It seemed easier to get them down on paper here."

He looked surprised, and then looked embarrassed at being surprised. "That's terrific, Kay. Do you want to run through them with me this week? Our proposal is due the following Thursday."

His expression triggered a spark of insecurity. Was Tom *surprised* that I was showing initiative?

"Sure," I said, pretending I didn't see the conflict on Tom's face. "I'll find a time on Tuesday that works for both of us."

I turned to leave, then faced him again. "What do you know about Godzilla?" I asked him.

Tom looked at me, his face blank, which oddly gratified me. "You mean, the Japanese monster?"

I nodded.

"Uh…not much?" he conceded. "Why?"

"Because Godzilla Fest, or G-Fest, as it's known, is the largest international convention on Godzilla and the kaiju film genre." I said. "And it's held just outside of Chicago every year. The Pickwick Theatre is a partner. They host a film festival during the convention."

Tom looked at me shrewdly. "Every year?" he asked.

I nodded. "Nearly 30 years and counting." It was something I'd stumbled upon when researching Pickwick's history.

Tom rubbed one side of his chin, thinking. "And how would one incorporate this into a restoration design?"

I shrugged. "That's one of the things I'm kicking around. Easter eggs are a huge draw for the new generation, I'm told," I said vaguely, and left.

Once inside my office, I closed the door behind me and exhaled. It was unlike me to show off. *Here's what I've learned, keep up!*

Who was I? What was I doing?

For the last eight years, I'd been the reliable associate. I was the one who happily turned the partner's sketches to real drafts. The one who rarely used all her vacation days, but whose sick and personal time were routinely gobbled up by family needs. Matthew had taken Holly to the hospital that Friday evening when she was so ill with meningitis, but it had been me who had burned through a week's worth of sick hours to see her through her recovery.

As Matthew's career flourished, it had been me who had stepped up at home, year after year, when he couldn't be present.

When he'd had his *big new client,* for example.

I looked around my office as if seeing it for the first time, taking in the framed sketches, the vintage industrial shelving, and my design award from the year before Holly was born. I loved my job and I loved the firm, grateful for the work life balance it provided to me. To my family. But just a few weeks ago, I'd been sitting in a chair in our den, listening to my husband casually mention selling the house, or buying him out of his share. Which he'd known I wouldn't be able to do.

And why was that? Why wouldn't I be able to?

I laid a fresh sheet of paper on my drafting table and let the answer – and the anger – come.

Because I've been happily toiling away the last eight years as an associate, content to let my career remain in stasis while my cheating husband got promoted three – or was it four? – times.

I glanced at the calendar on my desk. The *Two Homes* conversation had been just over two weeks ago. *Two weeks.* The cold reality that my marriage was still on very fragile ground washed over me. I'd been so focused on the next hour, the next day, the next appointment that I hadn't stepped back to consider the larger view. As a couple we were still in trouble, and I'd put myself in a vulnerable position.

Things are going to change, I thought as my pencil made broad strokes on the paper. *Even if we stay together.*

No, especially *if we stay together.*

* * *

Then (Portsmouth, New Hampshire – March 2017)

"Congratulations, Kay," Tom said again. He raised his nearly empty glass towards me. "May this be the first of many."

I smiled and slung the strap of my briefcase over my shoulder. "Thank you, Tom. And thanks for the impromptu celebration. I'll see you tomorrow."

The added weight in my briefcase caused me to flush with equal parts pride and nerves as I walked to my car. I rested the bag on the passenger seat and drove, bypassing the right turn towards the apartment I shared with my husband in favor of the waterfront route to my parents' house.

Anna's getting a ride with me instead of taking the train. We'll meet you there, Matthew had texted me earlier. *Traffic is tough today. I'm so proud of you!*

The flush returned, deepening at times during the short drive. When I eased my car onto their narrow driveway, it had receded. Mostly.

My parents were in the kitchen when I walked up the back steps from the driveway. I tapped on the glass twice and let myself in, smiling.

"Honey!" my mother rushed towards me, beaming. "You did it! Where is it? Can I see it? Can I hold it?"

"Of course!" I laughed reaching into my briefcase for the award, careful not to dislodge the small cardboard box underneath it. I handed her the small glass monolith bestowed to me by the Portsmouth Preservation Alliance for my work on the South Ward Meeting House. It was my first real award at my first real architectural firm. And even though the award itself – in the shape of a Colonial era steeple – looked vaguely phallic, I couldn't stop smiling at it.

My mom slid on her reading glasses to take a closer look while my dad pulled a bottle of sparkling wine from the fridge.

"I know Matthew and Anna aren't here yet, but I want to have a toast with just the three of us first," he said. "Your mom and I are so proud of you."

The warm flush returned. "Thanks, Dad," I said. I readjusted the strap on my shoulder. "I just need to freshen up; be back in a sec."

I headed to the small half bathroom just off the short hallway between the kitchen and the family room. *The family room where I'd been the child,* I thought. *Now I might be the* parent.

I closed the door and drew the pregnancy test box out of my briefcase. Turning on the faucet to mask the sound, I opened the box and tore into one of the plastic-wrapped testing sticks.

Here goes nothing.

I held the stick in my stream dutifully and capped it, draping a tissue over it as I washed my hands and touched up my hair and makeup, trying to make the two minutes go as quickly as possible, even though I was hesitant to know the result. Even though I didn't even know what I wanted the result to be.

I'm only a few days late, I thought, brushing my hair into a ponytail. *It's probably nothing.*

If it's a boy, his middle name could be Hollis, after Matthew's grandfather.

Don't be ridiculous. It's nothing.

Holly! Holly if it's a girl. That would make Matthew so happy, I think.

Are you even ready to be a mother? You just scored your first real professional success. How are you going to do this?

The last thought stopped the mental ping pong match in my head, and I paused to consider it. It was true; I had felt a little…left behind professionally since returning from England. In the two years it had taken me to land the job at Dawson & Tilman, my husband and best friend had risen in their respective ranks in Boston. Matthew was a supervisor at his management consulting firm, and just a month ago Anna had been promoted to deputy director of the actuarial department at the insurance company where she'd worked since graduating from MIT. Jenna, too, had moved on from her hometown newspaper to an upscale regional magazine. My Meeting House project – followed by my award nomination – had been the first time that I'd felt I was finally catching up. And I'd *won*, damnit.

I re-packed my makeup bag and looked at my reflection, yanking the tissue off the pregnancy test as I stared into my own eyes.

It will be OK, I told my reflection. *No matter how many lines there are, it will all be OK.*

My gaze flicked to the sinktop. Two lines.

I looked back at my reflection. I was beaming.

This is the right answer, Holly, I thought. *I know it is.*

I wrapped the tissue around the test stick, tucked it back into the box and returned the kit to my briefcase. As I stepped out of the bathroom, the pop of the sparkling wine cork pulled me out of my head and back to the present.

"Well done as always, Mr. B.," Anna said. "No spillage."

So much for a "just the three of us" toast, I thought, then smiled. "Just the three of us" suddenly meant something very different to me. I walked into the kitchen.

"There she is!" Matthew said, sweeping me into his arms. "Congratulations!"

Matthew released me and Anna stepped in for a quick and

light hug.

"The Preservation Society has some Freudian issues," she whispered. I stifled a laugh and winked at her.

My dad held out a half-full glass. I took a tiny, delicate sip. A pretend sip.

"A toast to Portsmouth's best new architect," he said.

"Hear! Hear!" Matthew said, one arm around my shoulders as we all clinked glasses. "This is the first of many."

His echoing of my boss' parting words sparked a warm glow in my stomach. I suddenly couldn't wait to get back to the apartment, to be alone with Matthew and tell me my secret. I had nothing to be afraid of. My husband supported me. He would continue to support me, and we were going to do this together.

Chapter 26

"Can I watch *SpongeBob* with Minty yet?" Holly asked me.

I gave her my best exaggerated side-eye, and she grinned. Over the top side-eye usually meant yes.

"Show me your pumpkin," I said. "If it's front-door-worthy, then yes."

We were sitting at Joy's kitchen table making paper decorations for Halloween. The table and floor were littered with construction paper confetti in orange, green and black.

Holly held up her fourth and final pumpkin for inspection. She'd given each of the other three a different expression: happy, scary, and sleepy. This one looked surprised. Or perhaps frightened.

"Hmmmm," I drawled, pretending to think it over. "I don't knooooow."

"I've done *four*," Holly pleaded. "You've only done one."

"Mine's bigger," I said. "Mine's the Mommy Pumpkin."

My daughter looked unconvinced.

"In my professional opinion…" I began, drawing out the suspense. "This is going to be the best door on the block."

She grinned again, triumphant.

"Go. You and your pumpkins earned it," I said, winking.

She bounded toward the living room, pausing to grab a cat treat from the bag on the counter. "Mintyyyyyyy!" Holly yelled for Joy's cat. "Come sit with me!"

I stacked the pumpkins, set the pile underneath my purse and set about sweeping up the paper shards, glancing at the kitchen clock as I worked. Joy was late. Or at least it *seemed* like she was. She'd met Anna for coffee an hour and a half ago. What was the etiquette on how long it took to have coffee with your brother-in-law's mistress? Or your sister's ex-best friend? I tipped the dustpan into the trash, then looked around for something else to do. My skin crawled with nervous energy. I eyed Joy's coffee maker, and decided to brew a fresh half-pot.

I was stirring cream into my first cup when the familiar whir of Joy's wagon sounded outside the window. I couldn't decide if I was relieved or reluctant.

Joy stepped into the foyer, standing on the spot where I'd collapsed just a few weeks before. She slipped out of her jacket and hung it among the short row of hooks inside the door. Her expression was neutral, and that worried me.

"Hey," I said. "I just brewed some coffee. Want some? Or are you caffeinated enough?"

She gave me a half smile in return and strode through the short hallway to the kitchen. "There's always room for one more cup," she said, lifting a banana yellow mug from the rack next to the pot and filling it.

Blowing on her cup, Joy peeked around the corner into her living room. "Hi Holly," she said.

"Hi auntie," my daughter replied in a flat voice. I pictured her glued to her favorite show, not breaking contact with the screen to look at my sister.

"Minty, you're in charge," Joy informed them, and then came to the table to sit. She raised her eyebrows to me and gave a quick jerk of the head towards the other room, which I took to mean *OK to talk here?*

I waved away her concern. "She'll have TV tunnel vision for at least another episode," I said in a low voice. "We're fine."

"Where's Matthew?" she asked.

"With Sam," I said, trying to stuff down my impatience. "His son has a soccer game and then they're going to get lunch. Joy, I'm dying over here. Tell me."

Joy sighed and cradled her steaming mug. "Well, for starters, she was late. I waited about 15 minutes before she showed up. She said that she'd been sitting in her car, thinking about turning around and going home."

"How did she look?" I asked, thinking back over the last few months. She'd been pulling away, and I'd missed it. When was the last time I really *saw* her?

"Tired," Joy admitted. "But there's a lot going on. Kay, she's leaving. Moving."

My stomach flipped. "To where?" I asked.

"New York. At least temporarily. It didn't sound like that was the long-term plan," Joy said. "She said she has a friend there."

I nodded grimly. "Shelley." *Fucking Shelley*, I thought. "When?"

"Soon. She's putting her place on the market in a couple of weeks, and she's leaving pretty much right after that."

"That's…fast," I said, more questions rushing over me. "How did she seem? Did she say what her long-term plan was? Has she told her Dad yet? Did–" I paused, tracing the rim of my now empty coffee cup. "Did she say *why*?"

Joy's eyes were soft. "She was, you know, a little closed off with me, but seemed OK. She didn't say what her plan was for after New York; for all I know she doesn't have one. She told her dad, as she put it, 'everything,' but I didn't press her for details about that. I just didn't think that was my place. I *did* offer her to tell me her side of things."

"And?" I asked, holding my breath.

Joy shook her head. "She wouldn't go into it with me," she said. "She wants to tell you herself. She asked me if you'd meet with her."

My stomach flipped again. Was I ready to meet with her?

Joy reached over and placed her hand on mine. "If you're not ready to meet in person," she said, as if reading my thoughts. "Anna said she'd either wait, or write to you. It's up to you."

I looked at my big sister. "What do you think I should do?" I asked. "What would *you* do?"

Joy sat back into her chair, thinking. "I…it's hard for me to say, Kay," she said. "To be honest, I don't know that I've had a friendship like yours and Anna's. I mean, I *love* my friends. They're wonderful. But you and Anna have always been…different."

She leaned forward again. "Remember the night you came here after finding out about the two of them?" she asked. I nodded. "I asked you that night if you'd suspected Anna. You said you didn't, that nothing had changed."

I nodded again. "And you said 'everything changed.' And you were right. I've been looking over my texts with her. She'd pulled away from me even before the affair started. Months before."

"Well, Anna did tell me one thing. She said that you hadn't been 'Kay and Anna' for a while," Joy said, using air quotes.

"But she didn't think you were aware of that."

I opened my mouth to protest, then closed it again. If this was truly how Anna felt, then she was right. I *hadn't* been aware of it.

But still, she slept with *my husband*. Regularly.

"So somehow this is my fault?" I asked.

Joy shook her head and reached for my hand again. "I don't think that's what she was saying," she said. "But you were 'Kay and Anna' for most of your lives, and then you weren't. And there's a reason for it other than their affair. If it were me, and I truly wanted to move forward from this whole thing, I'd meet her in person. *That's* what I'd do."

* * *

Then (Portsmouth, New Hampshire – August 2017)

"Oof," I said, dropping the last few inches onto the new sofa. "My feet are killing me."

I kicked off my espadrilles and rested my heels on the low glass coffee table in front of me, studying my pregnant belly. At six months, I already felt enormous.

"Here, let me," my mother said. She expertly swiveled me, moving my aching feet from the coffee table to the sofa. She placed one pillow behind me to support my back, and a second one under my knees. Perfect.

"Thank you," I said, sinking into the fabric. I drew my finger across the sofa's edge. "This is a good color, right?"

"Yes, especially when we get the leather chair in here with it," my mother said, looking around the nearly empty room. "This room will get such great light. Are you thinking of putting your desk in here?"

"Definitely," I said, pointing to an area in the far corner of the room. "Right there."

Matthew and I had purchased a wood frame house on a tree lined road off South Street in Portsmouth, complete with a winding brick walkway and an oak tree in the front yard. It looked as if the builder started with a center entrance New England colonial, and then decided to add a Victorian styled two-story addition on the left front of the house, complete with dormers and a steep roofline. While creating an unbalanced appearance from the street, it offered a high-ceilinged den/office on the first floor and additional bedrooms and bath on the second. It was quirky and strange and I loved it at first sight.

I gazed around the room, hardly believing these walls, floors, and ceilings were now mine. Were ours. *A house*, I thought. *We have a house, and we're having a* baby.

The mudroom door slid open, and my father backed in. He paused, revealing one half of the leather armchair my grandparents had given Matthew and me. "You want it in there, yeah?"

"In here, yes," my mother confirmed.

He continued through the doorway and Anna appeared, supporting the other side of the chair. They maneuvered it to its new home and stood back, inspecting its placement.

"All right-y then," my dad said. "If we're good here, I'll head upstairs and help Matthew assemble the bed frame. The dressers are already up there, right?"

I nodded, rubbing my belly. "The movers took care of that."

He saluted me and left the room. Anna plopped down in the chair she'd just carried.

I sighed. "I feel overwhelmed. All those boxes in the dining room."

My mother waved away my concern. "One room at a time. You'll get there. We'll help. But first," she said, picking up her purse from the floor. "I'm going to nip back home and get the lasagnas. We'll break in your new kitchen."

"I don't know where my plates are…" I called after her. The door slid shut behind her.

"Eh, paper towels will work," Anna said, standing back up and walking out of the room. "But right now, there's some wine in the kitchen with my name on it."

"Again, not sure where my glasses are," I said. "Or corkscrew, for that matter."

She slipped back into the room, grinning, one arm behind her back. "I figured, so I came prepared." She held out her hand, displaying a four-pack of mini bottles of pink wine with twist off caps.

"Genius. That's why they pay you the big bucks," I noted.

She joined me on the sofa, nestling in next to my feet. As she twisted the cap off one of the bottles, I clocked that her left hand was bare. The glittering cushion cut diamond that Leo – forever in my mind as *Leo the Midwesterner* – had given her in June was gone.

"You saw Leo today," I said. It wasn't a question. "How did he take it?"

Anna shrugged and tipped her head back, taking a deep glug of her wine before answering. "He was…fine. Quiet. I think he's known for a few weeks that this was coming."

"How are *you*, then?" I prodded her with my foot.

She leaned forward, dropping the empty mini-bottle in its cardboard carrier and pulling out a fresh one. "Don't judge," she said, twisting off the cap.

"Judge?" I said. "I'm jealous. Let me smell it, at least."

She smiled, then returned to my question. "I feel better now that it's done. The *should I* or *shouldn't I* was killing me, you know?"

I nodded, thinking back to my year with Andrew. Right after he left, I'd flirted with the idea of joining him in Vegas before coming to the realization that it was, in fact, a terrible idea.

As far as Anna and Leo went, I didn't fully understand why she ended their engagement. Leo was smart – intimidatingly so, sometimes – and clearly adored her. But truth be told, I didn't think I needed to understand. He just wasn't The One.

"Maybe I'm just not cut out for marriage," she said softly.

"Stop," I said. "Why would you even think that?"

She shrugged. "I don't know. Should I be sadder right now? All I feel is relief, to be honest."

"Remember when Andrew left for Vegas?" I asked suddenly.

"Mmm," she murmured through a mouthful of wine. "A month of caramel corn and rom coms. Why?"

"Now, I don't want you to think that I'm comparing me and Andrew to you and Leo," I said, shifting my backside to sit up higher against the cushion. "But hear me out. You told me back then that Andrew was great, but not The One. That my time with him wasn't wasted, and that who I am now *because* of him will make it easier to recognize when I *do* meet The One. Do you remember?"

She nodded.

"Well, you were *right*," I said. "When I got together with

Matthew the second time, I was a different version of myself than when we'd first met. And so was he. Whatever experiences and relationships he had gone through had turned him into someone I could truly fall in love with. And I knew it. I *felt* it. You will, too."

Anna's gaze drifted to the mantel. Most of my framed photos were still carefully wrapped in tissue paper and nestled in boxes in my new dining room. The lone photo on display – a black and white candid shot from my wedding – I'd placed there the moment I walked through the door.

"You'll find your person, Sporty," I insisted. "You will."

She turned back to me and smiled.

"This is me changing the subject. So, are you ready?" Anna asked, gesturing to my stomach.

"Not in the slightest," I said, patting my protruding bump. "Which is apparently the right answer, since everyone tells me that I'll never be ready, no matter how much I prepare."

As if to prove the point, the baby delivered a swift kick to my ribs.

"Here, feel," I said, reaching for Anna's hand. I placed it gently on my stomach just in time for another two taps, followed by a long squirm.

Anna smiled at the touch. "Hi Baby's baby," she cooed. "I'm your auntie Sporty."

Tap. We both laughed.

"Was it the kid thing?" I asked her. "With Leo, I mean."

She shook her head. "We were on the same page with that."

"Which is still a no?"

She nodded and pointed at my stomach. "Better you than me, friend."

I smiled and rubbed my belly again. I just couldn't seem to

stop touching it lately. "Matthew's *so* excited to be a dad. He says he can't wait," I said. "You should see his face whenever someone goes by pushing a stroller."

"Mmmm. Better you than me," she repeated quietly.

We sat in silence for a few moments, then Anna gave my bump a final pat and stood up.

"You're staying for lasagna, right?" I asked.

She shook her head. "I'm meeting Shelley. She's taking me out to, quote, 'celebrate my empowering decision.'"

I wrinkled my nose. Anna sighed.

"Kay, don't."

"I didn't say anything," I insisted. "My parents will be bummed you're not sticking around."

"Your parents are in their pregnant daughter's fancy new house," Anna reminded me. "They'll be fine. They won't even notice."

"That's b.s., and you know it. Stay with me," I pleaded. *Pick me*, I thought. *Not her.*

Anna took a deep breath. "Kay. I just *ended my engagement.* Let me lick my wounds my way, just this once, OK?"

"But that's why I invited you here," I said, stung. "So you can be with people who love you."

Anna slung her purse over her shoulder. "I *will* be with someone who loves me," she said. "Someone who actually wants to make the night about *me*."

She strode out my new front door, not looking back.

Chapter 27

My gray and orange sneakers pounded New Castle Ave. The wind picked up as I crossed Shapleigh Island, where New Castle morphed into Portsmouth Ave.

"Why is it called New Castle Ave. in Portsmouth, but called Portsmouth Ave. on New Castle island?" Matthew once asked me as we left the beach, brushing sand from Holly's still tiny feet.

"The road tells you where you're going, not where you are," I told him. "So Puritan Joe wouldn't have to stop his horse drawn carriage to ask for directions."

"Ah," Matthew said. "So Puritan road-namers saved us men from having to ask for directions. Heroes, all of them."

The causeway connecting Shapleigh, Goat, and New Castle islands was quiet this early on a Sunday, the sky still pink from the recent sunrise. To my right, a lone figure glided over the Piscataqua River on a standup paddle board, leaving gentle ripples in its wake. I breathed in the sharp fall air, tangy with sea salt. My frame was still tight with anxiety. By the time I reached the lighthouse beyond New Castle beach I'd be red-faced and wind-tousled, sweating from the three-mile run. But the majority of adrenaline would have leached out of my system. Hopefully.

I jogged past the New Castle Post Office, housed in a twee Cape Cod house, then swung left towards the entrance to Fort Constitution. When I spotted the entrance to the marine research station, I slowed to a walk. I'd gotten here faster than I expected.

Adrenaline.

I slipped a small water bottle out of my hydration belt and drank. My mouth felt tacky and dry, like I'd rinsed it with glue. It wasn't just because of the run. I unzipped my neon yellow running jacket a few inches and let the wind dry my neck and chest.

I turned down the short street that dead ended at the ocean. I was alone, save for a woman sitting on one of the boulders of the jetty, her back to me. Her right hand shielded her eyes from the rising sun for a moment, then tucked her chestnut hair behind an ear. Beside her sat two cups of coffee, steaming slowly.

I drained my water, slid the bottle into its pouch, and unsnapped my belt. The sharp plastic *click* caused the woman to turn.

"Hi," I said.

Anna took me in, her eyes flickering to my running jacket and leggings before returning to my face. One side of her mouth turned up in a rueful smile.

"You ran here," she said, shaking her head. "I think I went through 15 outfits last night and this morning, and you ran here."

I shrugged and walked closer. She was wearing a cream sweater and dark wash jeans underneath her thigh-length shearling jacket. She'd found the coat at Macy's five years ago.

I was with her.

"Here," she said, offering me one of the cups next to her. "Cream and one sugar."

"Thanks."

I stepped onto the jetty and sat in a nook the ocean had carved out of the rock, facing Anna. I leaned my back against the rock and stretched my legs in front of me, blowing on the coffee before taking a tentative sip.

I waited.

"How's Holly?" Anna asked.

I shook my head. "You don't get to ask me about her. Not yet."

She nodded and watched the waves for a few moments. I waited some more.

Anna looked back at me. "Thanks for coming," she said. "I know it probably feels way too soon. I just wanted to explain things in person before I left."

"For New York," I said. It wasn't a question. "When's that?"

"In a week or so," she said. "It'll be easier to stage and sell the condo if I'm not living there."

"What about your job?"

She shrugged. "I quit. It wasn't what I really wanted to do, anyway."

I brushed away a piece of dried seaweed that had landed on my leg. "What did you really want?"

Besides my husband, I thought.

She exhaled, and took a deep sip of her coffee. *Black*, I thought automatically, *with way too much sugar*.

"What did I really want?" Anna said. "Let's see…I wanted my mother *not* to die when I was 17. I wanted my dad to be present for the next few years and not stuff his grief behind a double shift until I graduated from college. I wanted to go to Chicago."

She paused, staring down at the tops of her boots.

"But I couldn't have any of those things, Kay," she said, looking back at me. "So the only other thing I wanted, I *really* wanted, was to be part of your life. Your family."

"But you *were*," I cried, frustrated. "You always were."

I set my cup down and leaned forward. "I know you and Matthew were together at the end of college. I never asked you to break up with him back then," I said. "How could I when you didn't even give me the chance? You could have told me, you know."

She shot me a skeptical look. "Kay, I know you. You would have been pissed."

"For like a *minute*," I said. "You just assumed I wouldn't be able to handle it. You never took the chance to find out."

Anna exhaled again, and nodded. "That's right. I didn't," she said. "I simply picked you over him."

"And," I said, my anger waking up. "You *absolutely* should have told me when I started dating him in England. Or when we came home engaged. What the hell was that about?"

Anna was calm. "Again, I picked you."

"What's that supposed to mean?"

"Kay, there was no way in hell I was going to ruin your engagement over a short-lived relationship from nearly five years before," she said. "No way."

"Right," I snapped. "It was a much better plan to lay low and blow up my life after we were married with a kid."

Anna said nothing to this. I leaned back against the rock, seething.

"Have you been in love with him this whole time?" I asked.

Anna rolled her eyes and raised her coffee to her lips. "He's not *that* great," she muttered into the cup.

I sighed and moved to get up. "This is pointless," I said. "Good luck with the move."

Anna put out her hand to stop me. "Kay, don't. I'm sorry, OK? That was a shitty thing to say," she said. "I'm sorry."

I looked over to Portsmouth Harbor Light, avoiding eye contact. But I didn't leave.

She tucked a strand of hair behind her ear. "I just…I'm trying to get you to understand the context of it all. What it was like for me."

I waited, still not looking at her, scanning the bay instead.

"Look, it sucked when I ended things with Matt. It hurt like hell, because I *did* love him then. But I loved *you* more, and I wasn't going to risk hurting what we had. Not for anything," Anna said. "I'm not blaming you for the decision I made. I got over it, but it was hard."

I adjusted my back against the rock and kept my eyes on the water. I still couldn't look at her, and it shamed me.

"And then two-three years later, there you both are," she said, with a humorless laugh. "In England together."

I forced myself to look at her. She was leaning back, legs crossed, supporting herself with one hand while the other held her cup.

"And this time, I can't do anything. Not without losing you," she continued, her eyes fixed on a battered red fishing boat tilting lazily in the waves. "So I decided to keep my mouth shut, and told Matt to do the same. I think he was relieved."

I thought about this. Anna had been in my daily life since we were thirteen. Every day, she'd had to stuff down her secret history with Matthew. Every damn time she saw me. What did that do to a person?

It made her screw your husband. The answer slid into my head unbidden. But no, that wasn't the right answer. The right answer – the real answer – was coming. I zipped my jacket back up, protecting my dropping body temperature, and stayed silent.

"I was fine with it, you know. At sweeping my thing with Matt under the rug," she said. "As long as it meant *we* – you and I – were good. But it wasn't the same after you got married. You kept shifting me further and further down your list of priorities. Not on purpose, I know. But it happened. Slowly but surely."

"But that's just…life, Anna," I said, unsure where this was going. "I was a wife, a mother. I had a career. This is *life*. It didn't mean you weren't important to me. And you had other, you know, priorities that were higher than me."

She laughed again. The bitterness of it chilled me even more than the wind.

"Like you were going to let that happen," she said.

* * *

Then (Portsmouth, New Hampshire – April 2018)

I thumbed the gold locket Matthew had given me absently as Anna and I wandered the aisles of Babies R Us, a copy of Jenna's gift registry in hand. My daughter – *daughter!* – napped against my chest, snug in her sling.

"Let's get her the baby carrier," I suggested, planting a soft kiss on my sleeping daughter's head. "I love mine so much. I use it all the time. That, and a bunch of diapers. She's going to need *all* the diapers."

Anna looked at me, a bit strangely, I thought. "I'm getting her my own thing, remember? I'm just here for the pizza you promised me after."

I stared back at her, my mouth open in concentration. Did she tell me?

I shrugged. "Sorry. Mom brain," I said, tapping my temple. "What're you getting her again?"

She smiled. "A month of laundry service. Pick-up and delivery."

I put down the vintage teddy bear I'd been holding and turned to her. "That's *brilliant*," I said, impressed. "How did you come up with that?"

Anna picked up a plush banana rattle and poked me with it. "Because you wouldn't stop talking about how you needed a laundry elf when you brought Holly home."

I grabbed the rattle from her. "But *you* were my laundry elf," I said. "No, you were my laundry *goddess*. I wouldn't have survived that first month without you."

Anna flicked the tentacles of a magenta stuffed octopus. "Yes, but only because I love you deeply. No offense to Jenna, but I'm not handling *her* stinky nursing bras."

"Surely my bras were not stinky?" I asked in mock outrage.

"No comment," she said.

I glanced down at the banana rattle. "This is actually the cutest thing I've ever seen," I said. "I'm getting one for Holly. No, I'm getting two. I'll put the other in the baby carrier for Jenna."

I tossed the rattles in the cart Anna was pushing. "I'm so

happy our babies will be so close in age," I said with a sigh, rubbing Holly's back through the sling. "We'll be able to do all those 'mommy and me' classes together."

"Well, *I'm* certainly not going with you," Anna said. "But I cheer you both on from the stands."

My gifts purchased, we stashed the shopping bag in Anna's car, retrieved Holly's stroller from the back and walked next door to the restaurant. At the table, I eased my baby out of the sling and into the stroller, tucking a soft fleece blanket around her.

"Will she be OK through lunch?" Anna asked.

I nodded, confident. "I nursed her just before you picked me up. She'll be sacked out for at least another hour, so I'm splurging on a glass of red."

Anna grinned and signaled our server. "You read my mind, Baby."

Once we'd received our drinks and ordered lunch I leaned in, propping my elbows on the table.

"So, I was able to book the room for my parents' 40th anniversary," I announced, smiling.

"At the place on the wharf? Hey, that's great," Anna said, pleased. "Do you still want me to look into musicians?"

I nodded, relieved. "Yes. That would be such a huge help, thank you. And…I have another favor to ask."

"What is it?"

"So, Joy and I want to do a series of toasts-slash-speeches over the course of the dinner to kind of sum up ten-year chunks of their marriage. What was happening in the world and what was happening in their lives. Like cute stories and jokes, you know?"

"I love that," Anna cooed. "That's so sweet."

"I know, right?" I said. "So anyway, my uncle Bobby is doing the first decade, and Joy is doing the second. I'm going last, and we both want you to do the third decade. Would you?"

Anna smiled softly. "Of *course*," she said, reaching for my hand and giving it a brief squeeze. "I'd love to. Can I make fun of Aunt Mary crashing our prom?"

"You better."

Anna sat back and took a sip of her wine. "So, what's the date? Did the venue have a cancellation on their actual anniversary, or did you book it a week later like we talked about?"

"Neither," I said. "It's the week before. The 14th. Oh, thank God, I'm starving."

Our server set down the tray of pizza and I dug in, lifting two gooey slices onto my plate.

Anna was looking at me, crestfallen.

"What?" I said, blowing on my pizza.

"I can't go on the 14th," Anna said. "I won't be here, remember?"

I frowned. "Where will you be?"

"Mexico," Anna said. "Playa del Carmen. I won't get home till that Sunday. I told you this."

I bit into my slice and nodded as the memory came back. She *had* told me, but I'd tuned out as soon as I realized she was going with Shelley and other as-yet-unmarried members of their UMass Econ crew.

"I'm sorry, Anna," I said. "I really am."

Anna picked at an errant black olive that had found its way, unordered, onto our pizza. "I just really want to be there to celebrate with you," she said.

I swallowed. "So do I," I insisted. "Can you come home a

day early?"

She lifted her eyes to me. "It'd be more like two days," she said. "I'd have to fly back on Friday."

I sat back, a ripple of annoyance stirred in my gut. I'd just *had a baby*, for crying out loud. I was operating on little to no sleep. I couldn't be expected to remember everything. Besides, this was for my *parents*. They'd practically raised her.

"Well, I paid the deposit," I said. "So I can't change it. But look, it's fine if you can't make it. It won't be the same without you, but my parents will understand. They'll want you to have a good time. With Shelley. We'll find someone else to do the toast."

I turned to the stroller and fiddled – unnecessarily – with Holly's blanket. The *with Shelley* part was a cheap shot, but I knew it would work. My mom knew all about Shelley's side comments and subtle snubs, and Anna knew that she knew. Anna could live with *my* disapproval – more and more, lately, it seemed to me – but my parents'? Never.

Anna sighed. "I'll figure something out," she said.

I beamed at her. "I knew you would," I said, raising my glass. "Here's to planning the best anniversary bash ever. Together."

We clinked. The ripple of annoyance had been replaced with satisfaction. But was I happy that my best friend could be part of my parents' celebration, or was it because Anna would be cutting her time with my nemesis short?

Both, I decided. *It's fine for it to be both.*

Chapter 28

My legs were stiffening. I hadn't stretched them after the run and my muscles were starting to protest. I gingerly got to my feet and stepped towards the pavement behind the jetty.

"I'm just stretching," I said. "I'm not leaving."

I rested one heel on a rock and leaned forward, enjoying the pull of my hamstrings.

"I don't know what you want me to say here," I said, cautiously. "You want me to say sorry for keeping you away from Shelley as often as I could? I hate to break it to you, Anna, but Shelley's a first-class bitch. I was doing you a favor."

"No, you were doing *you* a favor," Anna said. "It was fine for you and Jenna to bond over motherhood – I totally supported you in that – but God forbid that *I* bond with someone else. You hated that we were friends."

"Well, yeah. Because she's awful," I said. "I never understood what you saw in her."

Anna drained her coffee and tucked the cup into her navy distressed leather bag. "Shelley's a good friend," Anna said. "She's loyal."

I switched legs, shaking my head. "Loyal? She's *horrible* to me. I would think that after all this time that would matter to you. She's been horrible to me from day one."

Anna stood up, brushing sand from the seat of her jeans. "And why do you think that is, Kay?"

"Because she wants you to herself," I said. "She's jealous of me. Of our friendship."

Anna threw up her hands. "No, that's *not* it. Kay, you just don't get it, do you?"

"Then explain it to me, Jesus!" I shouted, furious. "Tell me why Shelley hates me, when I've never done anything to her. And tell me how this all ends up with you *sleeping with my husband for months!*"

I spun around to face the ocean and screamed. A long, guttural scream that had been building inside me for weeks. It rose, met the wind, and was swallowed up by it. God, it felt good. It occurred to me that Anna may have chosen this spot for this exact reason. That I, or she, or both of us, would need to unleash a demon or two.

I sank onto my haunches. A few yards away, a seagull cocked its head and stared, as if gauging whether this outburst made me a threat. Seemingly satisfied that I wasn't, it hopped to a lump of seaweed and scavenged for bugs.

Anna sat back down, the soles of her boots planted on the jetty, her hands on her knees. There, sitting in the power stance she'd taught me when we were 16, Anna suddenly looked so much like her mother.

"Kay, Shelley was there when Matt and I were together," Anna said, calmly. "She was there for the aftermath when I broke it off. She saw what it did. To both me *and* him. And she knew that I did it for you. And then you married him."

I turned this perspective over in my mind, cautiously.

Examining it as if it were seaglass with hidden sharp edges.

"Shelley was the person I could talk to about this. The *only* person," Anna added. "She doesn't hate you, Kay. She just loves me and doesn't want to see me get hurt."

My eyes misted over. I stood up, walked over to the jetty, and sat down next to my friend.

I rubbed at my tears with the heel of my hand. "But I didn't know you were hurting over Matthew," I said.

"I know," Anna said gently. "That's why I needed her as a friend."

I drew in a watery breath. "It was so much easier when I thought she was just being a bitch and I could hate her," I said.

Anna chuckled softly.

I looked at her. "I still don't see how this leads to you sleeping with Matthew," I said. "Or why you pulled away from me before that."

Anna sighed. "You talked about this at your session, didn't you?"

"Matthew told me how it happened for him," I said. "The… PTSD, I guess I would call it. From when Holly got sick."

I glanced over at Anna. "He didn't tell me how bad it was," I said quickly, unsure as to why I felt the need to say it. "If he had, I could have helped him. But he didn't tell me."

Anna looked back at me, her face neutral. "And you didn't notice."

I turned back to the sea. "I'm not a mind reader, Anna."

"You didn't need to be a mind reader," she said. "Just observant. When I met up with you all at Sebago last summer? I saw it immediately. He was a shell, Kay. A completely different person. Keeping you safe from Holly's – and his – trauma wrecked him."

We sat in silence for a few moments.

"Shelley was a friend to me when I really needed one, and couldn't go to you," she said. "So I knew exactly how Matt was feeling, and that he really, *really* needed someone to talk to."

"But you did more than–" I began, but Anna held up a hand.

"Yeah, I know," she said. "It went too far. *Way* too far. But you know what, Kay? The fact that he was in that position really pissed me off."

I stared at her, incredulous.

"You have this guy," she continued. "This guy who adores you, who's an amazing dad. This guy that I gave up *for you*, and you left him hanging. You didn't see it. And there he was, confessing to me that he can't sleep, he can't focus. And then all of a sudden he's telling me that I broke his heart."

My gut roiled with a sour combination of jealousy, fury, and shame.

Anna stood up again and took a few steps further out on the rocks, arms folded in front of her. She turned to face me.

"I'm not justifying what we did, Kay. What *I* did. I *can't* justify it. Not to myself, not to my dad, and definitely not to you. All I can do is explain how it happened for me. And for what it's worth, I'm sorry. I truly am."

Anna stood before me, her hands deep into the pockets of her coat, looking at me with frank honesty. She wasn't hiding from it. She wasn't trying to convince me of anything. And now she stood, waiting for a response, be it my rage or my tears. I had neither. I was empty.

Still, she waited.

"When Matthew told me he was leaving me, my first instinct was to go to you," I said. "Not Joy. Not my parents. *You*. You were family to me."

She raised her eyebrows, skeptical.

"What?" I asked.

* * *

Then (Route 95 to New Hampshire – Last April)

The rain lashed down around us. It thundered onto the roof of Anna's car and spilled over onto her windshield, so quickly that the wipers could barely keep up. Her long fingers squeezed the steering wheel so tightly that the line of her bicep was visible below the cap sleeve of her dress. Her spine was ramrod straight, not touching the back of her heated seat.

On the passenger side, I rocked back and forth, willing the sea of angry red tail lights in front of us to dissolve.

It was rush hour on Interstate 95 North. *Strike one.*

It was Friday. *Strike two.*

And it was *pouring. Strike three, yer out.*

I checked my phone, even though I'd checked it less than a minute ago. Even though my notifications were at the loudest possible setting. There was nothing new from Matthew about Holly.

We slowed to a stop, again. I crumpled in frustration and agony, hunching over and covering my face with my hands.

Anna rested her right hand on my back, briefly.

"It's OK," she whispered. "She's going to be OK."

I lifted my head and stared through the windshield, focusing on nothing. I nodded robotically. "She is. She is," I mumbled.

"She's OK."

I glanced at the message thread between Matthew and me. The message that had *pinged* its way into the pit of my stomach as Anna and I were exiting the restaurant to head to the theater.

I just left you a message, Matthew had written. *Holly's fever is way too high. I called Dr. Sato and she said to bring her to the ER. She will meet us there.*

I'd stopped in the middle of the sidewalk on Stuart Street when I read it, causing a freckled boy in an Emerson sweatshirt to crash into my right shoulder. The fact that Holly's pediatrician – always a calm, steady influence – was rushing to meet Matthew at the hospital turned my bones into gelatin.

"What's wrong?" Anna asked, alarmed. "Is it Holly?"

I nodded, unable to speak, as thunder rolled over the Common.

I never should have left her, I thought in Anna's car. *I knew there was something wrong. I knew her fever wasn't normal.*

"Kay, you couldn't have known," Anna said from the driver's side.

"What?" I said, pausing in my self-flagellation to look at my friend.

"I just wanted to say that, if you're sitting there punishing yourself for being stuck in traffic with me instead of with her, stop," she said. "Ditch that talk *right now* and focus. Let's assume she's going to spend the night in the hospital. Make a list. Tell me what Holly's going to want from the house. I'll get it."

Anna had always excelled at getting me out of my own head. And if ever I needed to, it was now. I shook myself out of my stupor and thought.

"C'mon," she persisted. "What will she want?"

"Her purple pajamas," I began. "Her stuffed kitty and yellow fleece blanket. A hairbrush and some ponytail holders. Her toothbrush and bubble gum toothpaste."

"Good," Anna said, changing lanes. "What else?"

"Books. She likes *Angelina Ballerina* when she's sick. Her crayons and a drawing pad."

"Snacks?"

"Pudding cups and caramel corn."

Anna chuckled at *caramel corn*. "Apples never fall…"

Despite myself, I smiled.

A few minutes later, we finally glided down the off ramp just south of Portsmouth Hospital. My body crackled with adrenaline. The need to be with my daughter was staggering, eclipsing anything I'd felt in my past. Anna's car leaned into the curve that led to the hospital access road.

Déjà vu washed over me.

Anna and I, speeding down this same road following the frantic call from her father about her mother's accident, all thoughts of seeing the latest installment of Pirates of the Caribbean *forgotten, the car silent with dread.*

Anna swerved expertly up to the Emergency entrance to let me out just as I was texting *I'm here* to Matthew. I blanched.

"Can you grab that spot over there and come in with me?" I asked her, my hand shaking as I pointed out the empty space. "I…can't go in there by myself."

She pulled in swiftly, and we speed walked inside.

Anna, clutching my hand, pausing at the automatic doors even after they'd swished open. Me nudging her gently forward.

I scanned the room, desperate for Matthew. I spotted him in a bank of empty orange plastic seats, checking his phone.

His face was pinched and pale.

I held my breath.

He looked up at me, stood, and smiled.

Anna's father at the far side of the waiting room, hunched over, his forearms on his knees, his head low. We walk towards him slowly. We are just a few paces away when he lifts his head. His expression blank.

I ran to my husband and sank into his arms, sobbing with relief. Anna a few steps behind.

"She's OK?" I asked, gasping. "She's OK?"

"She's OK. It's OK," Matthew said, resting his chin on the top of my head as I cried. "Let's go see our girl."

Craig Becker stands up and envelopes his daughter in a brief, fierce embrace.

"Dad?" Anna asks, searching his face.

"Honey," he says, brushing a hair from her cheek. "Let's go see your mother. We need to say goodbye."

The fluorescent light above us buzzed and flickered. A beige door to our right swung open, held ajar by a smiling nurse in salmon-colored scrubs.

"For Holly?" she asked. "You're all family?"

The fluorescent light above us buzzes and flickers. A beige door to our right swings open, held ajar by a somber nurse in royal blue scrubs. Somewhere unseen, a clatter of metal pierces the white noise.

"Mr. Becker, sir? This way," she says, quietly. Respectfully. He starts through the door. "Is this your family?"

Anna clutches my hand and leans into me. I transfer her hand to my free one and loop my arm tightly around her waist, physically supporting her in her grief and shock. She nods to her dad, her eyes pleading.

"Yes," he says firmly. "They are my wife's family."

We support Anna, one on each side, and pass through the door.

"You're here for Holly?" the nurse asked again. "You're her family?

"Us two, yes," I said. I clutched at Matthew's hand and pulled him through the door, leaving Anna on the other side.

Chapter 29

Anna was still standing, but she'd gradually turned away from me and towards the ocean. The waves lapped further up the jetty than when I'd first arrived. Soon we'd have to retreat to the pavement, unless we wanted to get wet.

I huddled in my spot, getting more chilled by the second. This deep into the fall, the morning sun was no match for the wind, and I longed to swap my running jacket for a fleece. I got up, and picked my way over the uneven rocks to where Anna stood. My eyes searched for and latched onto the red fishing boat, now a half-mile further from shore.

"I can see how that must have hurt you," I said carefully. "I'm sorry."

Anna shook her head. "You don't have to be sorry," she said. "Your daughter was in the ICU, for Christ's sake."

I looked at Anna. "You started withdrawing from me after that," I said. "From all of us. If I had just brought you through that door with me–"

"No, Kay. You shouldn't have," Anna said, still watching the water. "It should have been just you and Matt."

"But when your mom–"

"That was different," she said. "We were kids. My dad was about to take me to see my dying mom and I wanted you with me. Of course he wasn't going to stop that. Look, was I hurt? Of course. Was it the reason I started pulling away? No. I put space between us because that was the day I realized that I needed to. Because it was time for me to. Long past time, actually. I did it because I needed to be someone beyond 'Kay's friend' or 'the Barrett's unofficial third daughter' and I had no idea who that was."

She looked at me. "I needed to finally stop glomming onto your family and fix my own. Or create a new one."

My breath caught. "You mean with Matthew?"

Anna turned back to the ocean, shifting her gaze southward toward Whaleback Light. She didn't respond.

"Anna," I said. "When I came to you that night, you said 'I'm sorry, Kay. He was supposed to tell you.' What, exactly, did you expect him to tell me?"

A gust of sea air blew her hair back, revealing the first tears I'd witnessed her shed in more than a decade. Still, she said nothing.

"Did you keep seeing him so that he would leave me for you?"

She shook her head and brushed at her face. "I think I always knew that ending up with Matt was never going to be an option," she said. "I thought about it for, like, a minute after Joy found us out. But before that? No. Not if I'm honest with myself."

"Then *why*?" I asked. "Why did you keep seeing him?"

"Honestly? Because I *wanted to*," she said, facing me. "Because once I'd decided to go my own way, I felt like choosing myself over you for once."

"You nearly destroyed a *family*," I said, my voice hard with quiet rage. "*My* family. It wasn't just me you were picking yourself over."

She turned back to the water. "I know. And that made it a hell of a lot easier to stay distant from you."

Her words tugged at a recent memory. My mind grappled for it for a few seconds before snagging it. Something Matthew had said during our session with Elena Garciá.

"You figured you'd blow up the bridge back to our friendship instead of trying to cross it later and failing?" I said.

She looked at me warily, her face closed. "Why do you say it like that?"

"Matthew said something similar to me recently."

She nodded, then turned away. "He said something like that to me, too. About blowing up the bridge," she said. "Right before he moved to a hotel."

We studied the ocean in silence. The knot in my gut grew more insistent, even though it was unsure as to its final destination.

"What did he say, exactly?" I asked.

Anna shrugged. "That even though he'd, you know, 'blown up the bridge,'" she said, using finger quotes. "You were giving him a second chance and he wasn't going to throw it away. So he threw me away instead."

The knot, despite my love for my friend, unloosened the littlest bit.

We were silent for a few moments, watching the sea push closer. When a surge nearly reached the toes of my sneakers, I turned and stepped over the jetty. Anna followed.

My empty coffee cup was still upright, sheltered from the wind by the rocks. Anna reached down and tucked it into her purse.

"I'm sorry I hurt you," she said. "I'm sorry I wasn't honest with you back then, and I'm sorry I was a shit friend to you this year."

She slung her bag over her shoulder and waited. Anna had clearly said her piece and, for her at least, the conversation was finished.

I didn't know how to respond. What *could* I say? Thank you? Yeah, you *were* a shit friend? I'm sorry, too?

I was exhausted, cold, and shredded from too many emotions. I wanted to say everything and nothing. I wanted to hug her and push her over the jetty into the advancing tide.

"So this is it, I guess," I said.

Anna nodded.

"Forever?" I said.

The idea that I would never see Anna again was surreal. After more than two decades, my mind couldn't process it. Yet I felt oddly at peace, my shoulders relaxed. Our lives had been densely intertwined for so long, that the tiny breaks in what held us together were hard to notice, until suddenly they had become impossible to avoid. This distance felt not only necessary but vital.

Anna took a deep breath. "I don't know, Kay," she said. "I honestly don't. Let's just say 'for now,' and leave it at that."

I nodded slowly. "For now," I echoed. "Goodbye, Anna." I couldn't bring myself to call her Sporty, but the song lyrics scrolled past my mind's eye. *Goodbye, my friend.*

"Goodbye, Kay."

We both turned away, she towards her car and I to the top of the street. The double *chirp* of her car unlocking reached me as I broke into a slow jog. Behind me, Anna's car idled. I knew she was waiting for me to be far enough away to avoid passing me. Only when I reached Main Street and turned right towards home would she move, turning left towards… wherever.

I kept running, my cheeks streaming with tears.

* * *

I looked up at the grape arbor spanning our back deck. The leaves – what was left of them, that is – were yellowed and musty. I sat on the bamboo chaise lounge, still in my running clothes, warming my hands on a mug of fresh coffee. A thick fleece blanket covered my legs. In just a few weeks, we'd be folding the chairs up and storing them in the basement for the winter.

Weeks. Time had become elastic, stretching and pulling to fit a stunning amount of upheaval into increasingly smaller windows.

I marveled that it was still morning. Despite running six miles, and stopping at the halfway mark to have a life-altering conversation with my oldest friend, it was still morning. Inside, Holly was relishing the rare treat of eating her blueberries and protein-fortified waffles on the floor of the family room while watching *SpongeBob*, a privilege I'd bestowed knowing it would give me some of the time and space I needed to process my meeting with Anna.

Outside on the chaise, my stomach gurgled, protesting the miles without any food. My skin itched with the salt of sea air and dried sweat. I needed a lot of things; a shower and a meal were just the beginning.

But first, warmth. And a moment of peace.

Behind me, the door from the kitchen to the deck creaked open.

"Can I sit with you?" Matthew asked.

I looked over my shoulder at him. "Of course."

He stepped out, clad in his faded UMass flannel pants and a gray long sleeve cotton shirt, his own mug of coffee steaming.

He eased onto the chaise lounge next to me, the navy and white striped cushion sliding a little as he moved.

We sat in silence for a few moments. I knew he would wait until I was ready to talk. I knew what I had to say, I just didn't know if I had the courage to say it.

If you don't, then you'll be that person who needs protecting, I thought. *Don't be that person. You're* not *that person.*

"So, I have to say a few things," I said. "And the first thing is that I'm sorry. I'm sorry I didn't see how much you were hurting after Holly got sick."

Matthew opened his mouth to protest, but I put up my hand.

"I know you tried to hide it from me, but I should have seen it. I didn't, and I'm sorry. I really am. I'm sorry you had to deal with that on your own for so long, and I'm glad you found a therapist that you like."

Matthew sat with my apology for a moment.

"I appreciate that, and at the same time I don't want you to apologize," he said. "*I'm* sorry. I'm sorry I wasn't honest with you about Holly, and I'm beyond sorry for betraying you."

He held his hand out, palm up, between our chaises. I placed mine on his, squeezed it briefly, and let go.

"Anna's leaving," I said. "She quit her job and she's moving to New York soon. With Shelley."

Matthew nodded carefully. "OK."

I closed my eyes and took a deep breath, counting to four before exhaling. It was now or never.

"I think you should see her before she leaves."

Matthew paused before responding. "Is that what she said to you? That she wants to see me?"

I shook my head. "No, that's what *I'm* saying to you."

"I don't need to see her, Kay," Matthew said. "I want to be here with you."

I sat up and swiveled in the chaise lounge, placing my sneakered feet on the deck.

"Matthew, you *do* need to see her," I said softly. "At least one more time."

"Why?"

"Because you can't really know that you want to be here with me until you see her again," I said. "And because after being the one who pulled you back from the worst of your depression, she deserves better than a hasty 'I'm going back to Kay,' after you told her you were leaving me for her."

Matthew stared into his cup, silent.

"You were making *plans* with her, Matthew," I added. "Active plans to start a life with Anna. So if I'm going to trust that *this*," I gestured to the two of us and our home, "is really the road you want to take, I need you to face that *other* road a final time, now that everything's out in the open."

He looked back at me, unconvinced.

"If there's going to be an 'us' again," I said. "I need you to do this."

"It's not going to change anything," he said. "I want to be here. With you."

I nodded. "Then there's no reason not to do it."

He took a sip from his mug. "She might not even want to see me again."

"That's true," I conceded. "She might not. But you'll have asked."

Matthew gazed across the backyard, taking in Holly's swing set, the now-dormant tulip garden, and the small copse of birch trees where he and our daughter had hung a birdhouse last summer.

"*If* there's going to be an 'us'?" he asked, bringing his eyes back to mine.

I lifted one hand, palm up, in an *I don't know* gesture, the other still holding my cup.

"We still have some work to do, don't we?" I said quietly. "Every Thursday, with Dr. Garciá. Until it's resolved."

"Whatever resolution looks like to you," Matthew mumbled, finishing the quote from our therapist. He sat up and turned so that our knees were nearly touching. "What *does* it look like to you?"

I paused, mulling over the last few weeks, and in particular the last few hours. My morning with Anna had rewritten history and knocked me from what I had thought was my bedrock. What she'd done – both *for* me and *to* me – had me reeling. What I'd done – both unwittingly and by design – was now shining under a spotlight of my own making. How I would wrestle this into some semblance of order while salvaging my marriage was, currently, beyond me.

"Resolution?" I said. "I...I can't tell you what that looks like yet, Matthew. To paraphrase the Supreme Court, I'll know it when I see it."

I leaned a little closer to my husband and placed a hand on his knee. "But it starts with you seeing Anna, and then giving me some space."

"Space," Matthew said. He didn't sound surprised.

Saying it out loud was painful. Scary, even. The part of me that initiated sex the night of our letter-reading session with Dr. Garciá was screaming *You've won! Stop complicating things!* And yet, it felt right. It felt necessary.

"Yes," I said quietly. "What's happened between us – you and me, you and Anna, Anna and me – can't be swept under the rug. We can't just pretend it – *all* of it – didn't happen. And right now, for me at least, it's not healthy for us to be living together while we sort it all out."

Matthew took my left hand in his right, sliding his thumb gently over my engagement ring and wedding band. We eased back in the lounge chairs, holding hands and facing the yard.

"I could go see my mom," Matthew said after a minute. "For Thanksgiving. I could go out early, work from Arizona for a week or two. Take a few days off."

He turned towards me. "Would that be too much for you? Parenting solo for a while?"

"I think that's a great idea," I said. "Your mom will love to have you. And no, it wouldn't be too much."

"You think Dr. Garciá would let us do a few virtual sessions while I'm there?"

"Yes," I said. "I think she will."

"My mom won't be very happy with me when I tell her… everything," he said softly, looking down.

I shook my head. "She'll be happy that you're getting help," I said. "And that *we're* getting help."

Matthew squeezed my hand. "I'll miss you. I'll miss you and Holly."

I squeezed back. "I'll miss you. We both will."

We sat in silence, still holding hands, taking in the crispness of the fall day, and the rustle of dried grape leaves on the arbor spanning the deck of the home we'd made together.

Chapter 30

I yawned, shifting in the black vinyl and steel chair bolted to the wall at Logan Airport's baggage claim area. On the screen to my left, the status of Flight 984 from Phoenix blinked from ON TIME to ARRIVED. A quick shiver of relief ran through me, and I relaxed – as best I could, anyway – into the back of the chair, guessing I had at least another half hour to wait for Matthew to deplane and walk to baggage claim. Still, everytime someone descended the escalator from the arrival gates to baggage, I glanced over, irrationally hopeful.

I texted Joy an update. She replied from her car in the airport's cell phone lot, where Holly was currently asleep in the backseat. There was no way I was leaving Holly at home today; her excitement at seeing her dad again was too great. But I had to greet him alone first.

Thirty minutes.

"You're doing it again," I had told Matthew weeks earlier, shortly before he left to meet with Anna. She'd surprised us both by agreeing to see him before she moved. Although I suspected he was hoping to avoid this particular meeting, there was simply no way I was letting him off the hook.

"What?" he asked, looking confused.

I mimicked running my hand through my hair. "You claw at your hair when you're nervous about something."

"I do?"

I nodded. "Twice each time," I said. "It's your tell."

"Huh," he said. "How long have you known this?"

"Years," I replied, blowing on my tea.

"So why are you telling me now?" he asked, bemused.

I thought about his question. "I don't know. Call it a good faith attempt to improve communication. When I see you doing it, I'll ask you about it."

A little more than an hour later, he was home again. He came into the den and plopped next to me on the sofa. I waited.

"It wasn't bad," he said after a few moments. "It was OK, actually."

"Good," I said. I'd decided not to pepper him with questions, but instead to let him share what he felt like sharing.

"I apologized to her," he said. "For using her when I was…in a bad place."

"That's good."

"And then she apologized to me," he added. "She said she took advantage of me and the situation."

I nodded slowly.

"Do you think she took advantage of me?" he asked.

I paused before answering. "I think you both did what you did for different reasons. Whether she took advantage or not is irrelevant to your part in it," I said. "I think she was telling you that she went into it with open eyes, and that if you were worried you used her, she was assuring you that you didn't."

Matthew sat for a minute longer, looking thoughtful, then stood and stretched.

"I should finish packing," he said. "My Uber comes pretty early tomorrow."

It ended up being more than a week or two in Arizona. In total, Matthew stayed with his mother and Max for almost a month. Half of the time, he worked remotely, sticking roughly to East Coast hours so he could meet virtually with his therapist – and with Dr. Garciá and me – in the evening.

The second two weeks he took some much-needed personal time. He, his mother, and Max spent the week of and after Thanksgiving touring Sedona and the Grand Canyon. The daily dump of photos he sent via our shared Google Drive were jaw droppingly beautiful. Holly's new bedtime ritual included time for "Daddy's slideshow," as well as marking a purple X on the kitchen's whiteboard calendar, marking one day closer to her father's return. Each evening she did it, I saw the rivers of Dos Equis that had turned the October calendar into a rorschach of blue ink.

I shifted again in my seat. Twenty-one minutes.

Aside from the photos, there'd been no contact during the last two weeks of his trip. No texts, no phone calls, no emails. From either of us. When he called to say goodnight to Holly, she answered my phone and I stepped out of her room.

The radio silence had been Dr. Garciá's suggestion.

"This is a unique opportunity for you both," she had said. "It's a chance to quiet the noise in your head, what we like to call the 'monkey mind.' We talked about the need for each of you to decide what resolution looked like. During this distance from each other, I feel confident that your individual resolutions will make themselves known."

Matthew and I – each in our own little box on the computer screen, yet more than 2,500 miles apart – were silent.

"Are you both comfortable with that?" she asked us.

I nodded, my voice trapped under the lump in my throat. From his box, I saw my husband do the same.

"I'm sensing your trepidation, and there's a thought I want to leave with you both," Dr. Garciá said. "Remember, love is a *decision*."

I waited for her to continue, mulling the words over.

"People like to imagine that love is a self-sustaining entity, and should be effortless. It can feel that way in the beginning, and perhaps even for a long time afterwards. But eventually, in a long-term relationship, you simply *choose* to love your partner. Flaws and all."

Eleven minutes.

"As for the self-sustaining effortless part, I think we can all agree that effort is necessary," she continued. "But when the decision to love has been made, the effort is a little lighter."

Seven minutes.

My glances to the escalator became more and more frequent. Slowly, the downward escalator and the adjacent stairs began to fill with slightly rumpled, tired-looking travelers.

Nerves began to dance in my stomach.

Then, suddenly, he was there. I clocked his faded Levis as soon as they appeared on the escalator.

The dance in my gut became full-on acrobatics. *Wait*, the cautious part of my brain whispered. *Don't push too far, too fast again.*

Thank you for trying to protect me, I thought in response. *But I've made my decision. Now get lost.*

I stood and ran lightly to my husband. He slipped out of his backpack and let it drop to the tiled floor. We hugged each other tightly for a long, long time.

We broke apart and kissed, and then pulled back.

"I've decided," Matthew said.

"I've decided, too," I said.

He stroked my cheek. "I won't shut you out again. I promise," he said.

I nodded. "I know."

Matthew retrieved his pack and we walked to the carousel, already churning out luggage.

"Joy drove with us," I said. "She's in the cell phone lot. With Holly."

"Thank you," he said, clearly delighted. "I can't wait to see her." He plucked his hunter green suitcase from the carousel and turned to me. "I missed you both. So much."

"Believe me, we missed you," I said.

He smiled softly, putting his arms around me again.

"You look tired," I said. "Red eye tired."

"I *am* tired," Matthew said, still smiling. "I can't wait to sleep in our bed again."

"I'm tired, too," I said. "We'll take a nap together."

"Are you 'red eye tired'?" he asked, a playful note in his voice.

I shook my head, fighting to stop a smile from bursting across my face. "No. I'm red *line* tired."

"Red line?"

"Red lines, actually," I clarified. "Two of them."

I waited, nervousness again dancing lightly in my still-flat-but-not-for-long -belly. I waited much like I did when I told Matthew I was expecting Holly. Back then, it felt like a long wait before his smile stretched across his face, even though it had only been a matter of moments.

This wait didn't feel nearly as long.

His eyes flew open. "Really?"

I nodded, letting my smile break out. "Really."

Matthew tightened his grip on my waist and lifted me up, whooping and spinning me around once. The heel of my shoe brushed the beige hem of an octogenarian's raincoat. Its wearer looked sharply at us.

"Sorry," I said, when Matthew set me back down.

"It's not her fault," Matthew said, grinning. "She just told me that we're having a baby."

The wearer of the raincoat sniffed. "Be more careful with the *next* announcement," she said, then winked and marched on, pulling her wheeled case – a fittingly bright yellow – behind her.

Matthew unclasped his hands from my back, cupped my face, and kissed me again. "You're happy, right?" he asked me. "*I'm* happy. I'm really happy."

"I'm happy," I confirmed. "I've wanted this for a long time."

"Your parents are going to think we're nuts, having another baby after...everything," he said.

I shook my head. "They won't. They're getting another grandchild; they'll be thrilled. Your mom and stepdad will be, too."

Matthew looked at me. "We're not nuts, right? We can do this. I *want* us to do this."

I smiled up at my husband. "Oh, it's definitely nuts," I conceded. "But that's OK. Love is a decision. And I've decided that I don't care if it's a little nuts."

"Love is a decision," Matthew repeated. "I love you, Kay."

"I love you, too," I said. "Let's go home."

Chapter 31

*C*hicago - *June, Two years later*

My low heels clacked on the airport tiles as I strode through O'Hare, pulling my compact carry on behind me. The straps of my shoes pinched, but I couldn't place all the blame on swelling during the flight. My feet hadn't been the same since carrying the twins.

Should've changed my shoes at the office before leaving, I thought. Ah, well.

I clacked on, my eyes searching for the hotel shuttle to the Rosemont Hilton.

It had started with a text, shortly after Matthew had left for Arizona.

I'm sorry. I'd written to Anna. *I'm sorry I hurt you. I'm sorry I was so awful about Shelley. And I'm sorry I took you for granted.*

She hadn't responded at first, but reacted to my text with a heart. When I checked my phone the following morning, she'd sent a two-word reply at one in the morning.

Thank you.

That had been it for a long while. I considered reaching back out after Declan and Henry were born, but quickly rejected the idea. Using the news of my sons with Matthew to rekindle contact would be tone deaf in the extreme.

Instead, I waited a few months.

Happy birthday, I wrote, more than a year since we'd last spoken.

The next day, she replied.

Thank you. Congratulations on the boys. My dad told me.

I was patient. Cautious. I waited another month and texted again.

I saw Ginger and Scary on a new reality show! I hope you are well.

It grew, slowly, from there. Once a month or so we'd have a conversation through texts, always initiated by me. It was how I learned she'd moved from New York to Illinois to begin working on her doctorate in math. At the University of Chicago. It was how I learned she was planning to teach there permanently, and how she'd met – and fallen hard for – a linguistics professor originally from Greece.

She didn't mention or ask after Matthew, and I didn't offer details. Like Holly's old classroom riddle, I kept the duck away from the grain, and the fox away from the duck.

When the twins turned one, she reached out to me.

I'd love to see a picture of the birthday boys, she wrote. *I'm not on Facebook anymore.*

With Declan and Henry's birthday came the end of my maternity leave. Life fell into a soothing rhythm of work and home, at times chaotic and stressful, at others joyful.

In other words, utterly and happily normal.

When I was plucked to lead the renovation of the 1920s Pickwick Theatre in Park Ridge, I hesitated. The project was a dream, but could we handle the travel the work would require?

"Do it," Matthew insisted. "This is an amazing opportunity."

I didn't share my plans with Anna until just a few days before the trip. *I'll be in Rosemont for work next week*, I'd written. *Maybe we can grab a drink? Or dinner?*

I finally spotted my shuttle stop and stopped just before the automatic doors leading outside, glancing around for a fountain to refill my water bottle.

"Hi, Baby."

The voice came from behind me. I smiled to myself, surprised by the fact that I wasn't surprised. Of course she'd come to meet me.

I turned around, taking in the beautiful sight of my friend.

"Hey, Sporty."

Love is a decision, I thought. *And there are many, many kinds of love.*

THE END

About the Author

Kerry Crisley is a communications professional with a focus on the nonprofit sector. Fiction, however, is her first love; she wrote and directed an original play performed by her second grade classmates, and has been writing ever since. She lives in Wakefield, Massachusetts with her husband, their children, and their (very spoiled) rescue dog. When not at work, Kerry can usually be found reading, hiking, or getting into a wide variety of shenanigans with her book club. Her self-published debut novel, *Summer of Georgie*, was hailed as "funny, flip, sassy, and definitely likeable!" by Boston's WBZ Radio. Kerry is a current member of the Women's Fiction Writing Association, and also muses about writing, pop culture and wellness on her website, kerrycrisley.com. *When the Rose Briar Blooms* is her second novel.

Also by Kerry Crisley

Summer of Georgie

Summer of Georgie is a fresh and likably snarky take on the "middle age do-over," with an authentic portrayal of friendship, marriage, motherhood, and that inner critic inside us all.